THE BRIGHTEST BLAZE

VECTOR CITY SUPERS

BOOK 3

KELLY FARMER

The Brightest Blaze

Copyright © 2026 by Kelly Farmer

This is a work of fiction created without the use of AI technology. Names, characters, places and incidents are either the product of the author's imagination or are used fictitiously. Any resemblance to actual persons, living or dead, businesses, companies, events or locales is entirely coincidental.

ISBN (trade paperback): 979-8-9917483-6-0

ISBN (eBook): 979-8-9917483-7-7

ISBN (Kindle): 979-8-9917483-8-4

First Edition: March 2026

Edited by Mackenzie Walton (www.mackenziewalton.com)

Copyedited by Julie Cassidy (www.juliecassidyauthor.com)

Cover illustration and design by Steve Buccellato (www.legendhaus.com)

For the beautiful trans community

CONTENT NOTES

Please note that this is Book 3 in the connected Vector City Supers trilogy. It would really benefit you to read *Secret Spark* (Book 1) and *Fanning the Flames* (Book 2) before this. There are lots of returning characters and the same main couple well into their relationship.

As with the other books, the tone is light. However, there are topics reflecting today's social and political climate that may be upsetting, especially regarding a group actively targeting and trying to suppress a specific population (in this case, superpowered people). I'm grossed out by them too, so they don't get a lot of page time.

There is also on-page sex, discussions of off-page therapy, and discussions of family estrangement.

Take care of yourself, dear reader.

CHAPTER 1

Joan lounged on the ledge of a three-story office building, arms crossed over her Spark suit, bearing witness to a crime down below. Not Supervillain-level crime, like she thought she'd be doing more of as a Superhero. No, this was how she spent her time as one of the guardians of Vector City.

Watching two teenagers spray-paint a penis on a bus stop advertisement.

To be fair, the perky blonde showing off her pearly white smile thanks to the toothpaste brand did have her mouth open a little too round. The artistic concept wasn't bad, but the execution…

The girl and boy were barely hiding their identities in the darkness, wearing only thin hoodies. It was pretty hot this August, so even wannabe criminals were adjusting their wardrobes. The girl said something that made the boy snort-laugh and spray anatomically impossible balls considering how narrow the shaft was.

"Now it looks like two cherries hanging on their stems," Joan called down.

The teens froze.

"What's the squiggly stuff under the bottom part?"

They stared up at her, eyes wide. "Uh, hair?" the boy ventured.

"Really?"

"Yeah."

She gestured at the tip. "Honestly, I'm getting fruit, or a mushroom growing out of a pot."

"What if I made this part wider?" The boy held the spray can up to the shaft. The girl chortled something about girth.

Joan chuckled to herself. "You're asking the wrong person."

She kicked her heels against the ledge and pushed off. Easy blasts of fire from both palms guided her safely to the sidewalk.

Walking over, she asked, "What are you doing out here in the middle of the night?"

The teens shuffled their feet. "Nothing," the girl mumbled.

"Is everything okay at home? You're not avoiding anything or escaping a bad situation?"

"We were just bored," the boy said.

The light from inside the little shelter gave Joan a better view of the perpetrators. Both were white kids, fresh-faced and sporting random piercings.

"Don't you have summer jobs or something to get up for in a few hours?" she said.

They grumbled about working at an ice cream shop.

She held out a gloved hand. "Give me the spray-paint." She pitched her voice lower to hide her true timbre. Sadie said it only made her sound sexier, but it was a necessary part of a very public secret identity.

The boy looked warily at her palm.

"I'm not going to explode the can and injure all three of us. Hand it over."

He did so, pulling his hand back before it got too close.

"Go home before I spray-paint your names on this anatomic travesty. If I catch you doing this again..."

She let the heavy silence finish the sentence.

"Now shoo. Maybe pay more attention in biology class."

The teens sauntered past her, defiant glints in their eyes. "She was cooler as a Villain," the boy said.

"Yeah," the girl agreed.

Joan rolled her eyes. Then she looked at the marred ad and suppressed a grin. Okay, it was funny.

She was tempted to spray *Teenaged Dumbasses* with an arrow drawn to the dick. She just blocked out the whole thing instead, making sure there was no discernable penile shape.

Former Supervillain Spark, who might have done something like this at their age, was now tasked with making Vector City a better, safer place to live.

In the six months since battling with Quake and the other Villains who'd rolled into town, it'd been all about restoring what had been damaged. That included her image, and Mark's as Ice. Her twin was doing an excellent job talking to the press, getting people to like him.

Joan was doing an excellent job doing her job. Helping people, using her firepower for good in ways she'd never thought possible. Or at least as a subtle deterrent when she caught the norms doing things like tagging toothpaste ads.

She checked the large clock on one of the office towers up Mansfield Avenue. Almost three a.m. About time to wind up tonight's patrol. Maybe she could get home to crawl into bed and snuggle with Sadie for a few hours before she had to get to her café.

She started heading toward headquarters, burying the spray-paint in a public garbage can. It *was* combustible, after all.

Swift motion sped up behind her. Zee joined her, cream-colored Race bodysuit contrasting Joan's black-and-red ensemble. "Hey," they said.

"Hey."

"Anything exciting happen tonight?"

"Taught some teenagers about anatomy."

"Interesting."

"You?" Joan asked.

"Called a cab for a very drunk couple from out of town."

"Wow."

Zee smirked and said, "It's not all photo ops and glory, Spark."

They walked in comfortable silence. Technically, Zee was supposed to be watching Joan. She and Mark were still on probation. The other Supers monitored her more closely, but Zee gave her space. Gave her trust. That alone made her want to make smart choices.

"We did help that guy find shelter," Joan said. Before they'd split up, she and Zee assisted an unhoused man to a place that offered healthy meals and air conditioning.

"That meant a lot to you, didn't it?"

"You don't know what it feels like to not know where you're gonna sleep. The fear that claws at you."

Zee nodded softly. Mark had probably told them about the early days of the Malone twins in Vector City. Blowing through what little money their parents had given them in less than two months, as sixteen-year-olds without financial common sense would do. Then resorting to park benches and...

Fuck, that was depressing. Joan shook the thoughts away. Thankfully, Perry had taken them in and introduced them to the lucrative career of Supervillain.

Now Joan was on a better path. And she had Sadie and their home together. And real friends who would support them if needed. Food truck friends in particular.

Hmm. Food truck friends.

"It's Tuesday," Joan said. "Powered by Plants parks in front of Sadie's Café on Tuesdays. They have that breakfast sandwich Mark loves. He'll probably stop by to get one."

Zee shot her a look, knowing exactly where this was headed.

"He's not working tonight," Joan said.

"Good for him."

"I bet if you texted him about meeting for brunch, he'd be up for it."

"I'll be exhausted," Zee said.

"You sleep less than any human being I have ever met." It was one of the side effects of their super speed—they just sped right through sleeping. Apparently, it was a blessing and a curse.

They made a vague shrug. "He'll be focused on the food truck."

"Are you two fighting again?"

"No."

"Mark's being cagey. Like how you're being cagey."

"I have no claim on him. What he does is his business."

Joan scratched at the sweat trapped in her facemask above her eyebrow. "You're usually happy to be up in one another's business."

"*We're not dating,*" Zee said, exasperation coating every word.

"Right, right. You're not dating."

"Everyone wants to put a label on things. Societal norms and outdated patriarchal ideals make people think they can impress their beliefs on others. It *is* possible not to feel the need to quantify something. I don't feel the need. Mark doesn't either."

"My my, so many words," Joan teased.

Zee scowled in an old, familiar way. "Don't make me send you to prison."

"Okay." Joan didn't bother concealing her smile. "You're not dating. Even though Mark's met your mom—"

"That happened by accident."

"And now has dinner with you and your mom every couple of weeks."

"She likes him for some reason."

"Mark's very charming. And he loves her cooking."

"We're not dating," Zee grumbled, turning the corner.

Her brother and Zee's "not dating" was Joan's favorite pastime, since the Vultures were on pace to have another losing baseball season. Two commitment-phobes doing everything possible to alert the world they were not a couple despite spending a whole lot of time together. Not being into labels was fine, but Mark was most definitely jutting one foot out the door.

Then again, so was Zee. They kept a lot of themselves private from the other Supers. Joan only knew bits and pieces from Zee hanging out with Mark and Sadie. She knew their dad died when they were ten, and they'd been raised by a very supportive mother who knew they were Race and kept it a secret. Zee spent most of their free time volunteering at an LGBTQIA+ youth center. Helping out in a different way.

Wailing sirens a few blocks away snapped them both to attention. *Fire trucks.*

Zee looked in that direction. "We should see what that's about."

Cringing slightly, Joan said, "I'm not the fire department's favorite person."

"Who knows more about fire than you?"

"The putting them out part is not my specialty."

"C'mon, I'll race you," Zee joked, and was gone.

"Damn it." She shot flames from both hands and propelled into the air.

She flew past the darkened office towers and apartment buildings. It was quiet at this time of night—her favorite time to fly. It'd been when she'd felt the most free in her Villain days. Honestly, she felt pretty free doing it these days, too. No agendas or appearances, no paperwork. Just Joan.

The wind whipped the long black wig attached to her mask. Ugh, so annoying. Maybe if she got a new suit, she'd get rid of it. Being more true to herself, less using her Spark persona to hide, it made sense.

Of course, she'd have to dig into her savings to pay for the bodysuit and accessories made of specialty materials by a niche tailor. Or else someone would have to find money in the city's budget. That was something she didn't feel right asking the norms to cover.

Besides, the guy who used to do her and Mark and Perry's suits was not on this side of the law.

She spied the flashing lights and swooped lower to follow the fire truck and department SUV. Lending a hand even if they didn't want it from someone who'd created problems for them a time or two.

Think about the greater good, she reminded herself for the umpteenth time. *Superheroes think about the greater good.*

A few hours later, Joan wearily approached the back entrance of Superhero HQ. Dawn had broken, streaking the sky with orange and pink.

Firefighters, as it turned out, had a lot in common with her. They spent their time obsessing over something most people ran away from. Their call had been a false alarm from an old building's system shorting out. So they'd spent some time chatting, then bringing Joan—well, Spark—back to their firehouse to meet the crew and discuss better ways to contain a blaze. Zee had left her a long time ago and was probably already home. Or at Mark's.

She pulled off a glove and set her hand on the biometric scanner to gain entry. Blissfully cool air conditioning slapped her in the face. As much as the night had turned into a pleasant surprise, she couldn't wait to shower, check in, and get home.

The second the door closed, she yanked her facemask off with a relieved, heavy breath. She rubbed at her cropped hair. She freaking loved this new short haircut with the fade. Possibly more than Sadie, though Sadie thought it was "the hottest thing on you, which is saying a lot."

Unzipping her Spark suit only brought marginal relief. She pulled her phone from an inside pocket and checked for anything important. A few bits of nothing from the SuperWatch app. An email from Padma with the subject *Rescheduling our meeting* that Joan would dodge until their liaison to the mayor showed up and cornered her.

She was a teensy bit behind on reporting to her mandatory quarterly check-in with the Super shrink. A month, to be exact.

The welcoming scent of fresh-baked muffins greeted her as she headed into the white-tiled kitchen. Figures, Darlene was already there. She had a home—at least, Joan was pretty sure. But she never seemed to go to it, always at HQ or out doing something for the people of the city. Even her recent interest in learning how to bake was mostly being carried out here.

"What did you make?" Joan asked as she snagged a glass mineral water bottle from the fridge.

Darlene chewed on a pale muffin studded with blueberries. Her long brown hair hung loose over workout attire. "Something is wrong," she stated. "I don't know what happened, but something is wrong."

Joan took a long drink, then peered at the muffins still inside the pan. They looked okay. Maybe a little dense.

She pulled one out and tugged on the paper. At first bite, it was overbaked in one part and almost raw in another.

Yeah, something was wrong. She forced herself to swallow. There was a weird aftertaste, too.

"I measured each ingredient," Darlene said. "I followed the recipe. I don't understand what went wrong."

Joan surveyed the ingredients strewn across the large breakfast bar. Milk, eggs, AP flour, baking soda... *Ah.* "Did you use any baking powder?"

Darlene waved at the box of baking soda. "Yes."

"Baking powder or baking soda?"

"They're the same thing."

Joan stifled a laugh at the rookie mistake. Darlene was really trying her hand at having a hobby. Not that she'd admit to it, least of all to her former nemesis. Since Gus—aka Amazing Woman—had come into their lives, she'd repeatedly warned Darlene there was more to life outside of being Catch. Joan wasn't a big enough asshole to squash the one thing she and Darlene could talk about.

"So, baking soda's a little different," she said. "They're both leavening agents, but—"

"They look exactly the same."

"The powder's a little bit finer. More powdery." *Hence baking powder.*

Frustration oozed off of Darlene. "Why do two different things that look the same have almost identical names?"

Joan set the muffin on the pale-gray granite top. "It was a solid effort. They would've been good otherwise."

"They're terrible." Darlene grabbed the pan and forcefully slammed it on the garbage can to get rid of them. She couldn't even have a hobby without being overly intense about it.

"Keep at it," Joan said. "Mark and I don't always make things that are edible."

The digital clock on the oven read 6:05. She really needed to get a move on if she had any hope of catching Sadie.

Ward came into the kitchen, smiling like the evil morning person he was. "I'm excited to try your latest creation, Ms. Catch." He spied Joan. "Good morning, Ms. Spark. Er, just Spark. I'm sorry. I know you said I didn't have to—"

"Call me Joan. The formality is ridiculous."

"Yes, ma'am." Pain flashed in his brown eyes behind his glasses. "I'm sorry. I'm just so afraid I might say it in public. The formality keeps me from slipping up."

"The muffins were a failure," Darlene said, dropping the pan in the stainless-steel sink with a loud clang.

"I'm sorry to hear that." Ward caught Joan backing out of the room. "Ms....Joan, I know you're busy and have a lot on your plate, but if you could please connect with Padma about the several items she's reached out to you about, then she'll stop bothering me about them."

"Yup. I'll email her today."

"Thank you. I'm also happy to pass along anything to her or set up any appointments you might require."

"No thanks, Ward." Joan sucked down her water and headed for the back stairs. She didn't need a sidekick. Ward was great, but—

"Can I get you something to eat?" he called.

"Nope," she called back. "I need a shower more than anything."

It still felt the tiniest bit naughty being in headquarters alone. The first few weeks, she couldn't take a piss without someone going with her. But now she could access pretty much everything, including the jail cells in the basement that scared the shit out of her. Superpower blocking was always on down there, and it sucked.

There was the whole third floor she hadn't known about with several changing rooms connected to nice, big bathrooms. The showers were glorious and conveniently had room for two. She and Sadie quite happily discovered that last month on their one-year anniversary. They'd both had to work, so Sadie brought her a late dinner from their favorite ramen place. Then gave her one hell of a dessert.

She walked by the very same bathroom, the memories bringing a smile to her face. She tucked her water bottle under one arm to text Sadie she'd be home soon when she passed the gym and her best friend in the whole world.

Kade spotted her through the open doorway, because of course he did. Because of course he was already up and working out. What was with all these morning people?

"Hi, Joan!" he roared. Then he pulled one earbud out. "Was that too loud? I have my music on."

His god-awful hard rock music. "Hey, bud. It's humid as hell outside. I need a—"

"Do you want to work out with me?" He jutted a thumb at the weight bench.

She did love the state-of-the-art equipment, but: "Not today."

"Too early for you, huh?"

"Way too early."

"Ward wants to talk to you."

"I already saw him," Joan said.

Kade looked around the room. "Where's Zee?"

"They got in before me."

"What were you doing? Otis doesn't like it when you and Mark patrol alone."

"I was with a bunch of firefighters. The safest people I could be around."

"That's funny." He grinned his wide, friendly smile. He was such an open book with zero internal monologue. One of his best qualities.

Joan gestured down the hall with the glass bottle. "I need to get home to see Sadie before she heads to the café. But tomorrow, okay? We'll do Pilates to work on balance."

"*My* balance," Kade said, which Joan couldn't really refute. He was so top-heavy with his huge muscles that his legs didn't stand a chance at holding him upright if he got off balance. Which happened a lot.

"Have a good one."

"You, too. Say hi to Sadie. Oh, hey." He trotted over to the doorway. "Say hi to everyone at Sadie's Café from me. But from Kade, not Lunk. They know me as your friend Kade, so say hi from Kade, okay?"

"Okay."

"Thanks." He chucked her shoulder, and it almost sent her into the wall on the opposite side of the hallway.

She hurried to the changing room that had her clothes and shit before someone else could stop her. It had a comfortable blue loveseat on the far wall (tested by her and Sadie on Joan's birthday back in April). The small cedar shelving unit held her plastic bin of toiletries and Mark's three bins of body washes and hair products and grooming gadgets.

She quickly showered and dressed in a lightweight, short-sleeved white button-down, red Bermuda shorts, and matching red-and-white sneakers. She checked the time on her phone. Just about 6:45.

Three new emails populated her lock screen regarding Super-Watch claims. Ugh, she'd handle those later.

Ah, dang it. One was from that florist she'd promised to help push their claim through. Okay, one last thing, and then she'd head home.

She went downstairs to the office just off the conference room. It reminded her a little of a newspaper office from the 1920s with the wooden desks side by side in three rows. Each Super had one, though she and Mark mostly shared one and used the other for snacks and a stash of fast-food napkins they still liked to doodle on.

She flipped the cover open on the laptop and dragged it away from the in-bin that was blessedly empty for the moment. Beside the bin, Mark had put a framed photo of him and Joan in front of Hot and Cold the day they'd opened their food truck. A reminder of his motivation to fight the bad guys, since Villains had literally destroyed his dream. She found it a bit depressing, but whatever. They had good memories from those few months.

It didn't take long to put in her personal request to move along the claim that still hadn't been resolved from when Squawk blew out the flower shop's windows. And also to give them a thousand dollars out of her pay for lost revenue.

She opted to handle the other two claims so she could have a full, actual day off.

Only…*shit*. Now it was after seven. Sadie usually left around 7:30.

Joan moved quickly and silently to the parking garage. She pulled her black sedan into early morning traffic. It'd be so much faster to fly, but the neighbors might wonder why Spark kept landing on the balcony at apartment 714.

Repairs along Leyton Avenue were just about completed. It'd been a laborious task—manpower and financially—to fix the decimated street and damage to buildings. The Supers had lent their help and support, but still, it'd been a rough few months. Donating the insurance payout from Hot and Cold's destruction to get it done faster had felt like the right thing to do.

She made it home by 7:22, trotting up the stairs on tired legs.

Sadie never expected her at any certain time, but a quick snuggle was a great way to start one day and end another.

The rainbow-colored crepe paper wreath on their door welcomed her home. She unlocked the door, glad for the warning beep from the alarm system. Sadie had been diligent about setting it when home alone. Now more than ever, their sanctuary needed to be kept safe. A Villain-turned-Hero was definitely on more than a few shit lists.

After toeing off her shoes, she followed the sound of Sadie's electric toothbrush toward the bathroom.

"Hi, babe," Joan called.

Sadie leaned back, long red hair dangling behind her as she glanced out the open doorway. "Hi, honey," she garbled around her toothbrush. She bent over the sink, spit, and added, "What a nice surprise."

Joan reclined against the doorjamb, admiring the lightweight beige pants molding to her girlfriend's lower half. Her pale pink Sadie's Café T-shirt had the simple logo on the back in black: a coffee cup and saucer with steam rising off the top to form an S and a C.

"How was work?" Sadie asked before starting to brush again.

"Not too bad." Joan regaled her with the night's highlights as Sadie finished her oral hygiene routine.

Sadie pulled liquid concealer from her makeup caddy. She dabbed a few dots on the purple smudges under her eyes.

"Did you sleep okay?" Joan asked.

"Sort of."

"Up late working again?"

"Just going over a few things." Sadie grinned over her shoulder. "And I always sleep better when my girl's there keeping my feet warm."

"Tonight," Joan assured her.

"Yay."

Stomach grumbling, she went in search of something easy to eat. She rummaged around one of the glass-front cabinets and discovered peanut butter puff cereal. Hell yeah. Cereal and then a long nap sounded amazing.

As she got a bowl from a different cabinet, she took note of how tidy the kitchen was. And the living room, sparkling in the early morning sunlight. They'd scarcely been home enough lately to mess it up. The office was probably a disaster, but that was Sadie's organizational chaos—er, method.

"There should be something good and quick to eat," Sadie said from the bathroom. "I picked up a few things on my way home last night."

"Aw, thank you. Sorry I couldn't join. I love grocery shopping together." It was one of Joan's favorite date nights.

"We'll go this weekend."

"Okay."

Sadie breezed into the office. "I should be home early tonight," she said loudly so as to be heard.

"Great. I'll make us something special for dinner. What would you like?"

"Anything's fine. Everything you make is good."

Laughing, Joan said, "Darlene tried baking muffins this morning."

"Oh no," Sadie laughed in return. "How bad were they?"

"*Bad.*"

Joan grabbed the milk from the fridge, snagging a banana from the fruit bowl on her way by. Sadie emerged with her pink commuter bag, looking like the badass business owner she was. She set it against the island, then moved into the open kitchen.

Joan abandoned her breakfast for Sadie's arms instead. They shared a quick kiss. "Mmm, minty fresh," she said.

"Mmm, hot night in a latex bodysuit," Sadie teased back.

"I showered."

She nestled into the crook of Joan's neck. "Yes you did, with that citrusy body wash I love."

Sadie's new-ish lilac-and-lily perfume tickled her senses. Joan breathed deep, letting the familiar comfort wash over her. They swayed slightly together.

"Perry's stopping by today for our weekly meeting."

Chuckling, Joan said, "Who's more excited, you or him?"

"Him, obviously, but not by much."

She shook her head with a grin. "I can't believe I'm living with Perry Junior."

"Paperwork," Sadie said with glee. Real glee.

Per was thrilled someone finally found spreadsheets as interesting as he did. Sadie had surprised herself—what she'd once feared was now one of her favorite parts of running her own business.

She slowly drew away from Joan. "I think Gus might be coming in this weekend for the Friendship Park ribbon-cutting thing. We should try to have a barbeque or something afterward."

"Sure. It'll be nice to see her."

It'd be hilarious to be there as Spark for the official reopening of the repaired park, then change and head back as just another person enjoying a summer afternoon with loved ones.

"Oh, Zee might stop by the café this morning," Joan said. "Since Mark will be around for his favorite breakfast sandwich. I told them to have brunch together."

"If they're talking to each other this week."

Making a mock nonchalant face, Joan said, "They're just hanging out, whatever, it's no big deal."

"Because they're not dating."

"They're *not* dating."

"Sure," Sadie drawled. "And I'm a natural redhead."

Joan winked at her, signaling she knew with in-depth authority that was not the case.

Her beautiful girlfriend smiled and ran her fingers up the shaved sides of Joan's head. "Oh my *god*, you are so sexy with this haircut." She planted a kiss on Joan's cheek. "Like ten times more confident with that little swagger you've acquired."

A warm flush crept up Joan's neck. She *was* more confident overall. Not having to hide twenty-four seven had opened her up.

Sadie kissed her other cheek. "Sorry, honey. I have to jet."

They kissed, and then Sadie moved to get her bag. Joan unpeeled the banana, her stomach louder in its demand to be filled. She smiled at Sadie as she slipped into her rainbow-striped sneakers at the door. A professional heading off to live her dream.

"Go get 'em, boss lady," Joan said.

Sadie straightened, one hand tucked under the thin strap of her bag. She grinned broadly and tilted her head. "I love you."

"Love you more."

"I love *you* more."

They went several rounds of "No, I love *you* more" before Sadie laughed and headed out.

Joan sliced the banana and poured milk over her cereal. She was so damn proud of how far Sadie had come in the year they'd known one another. Her confidence was also increasing every day. She was growing Sadie's Café slowly, intentionally. And she liked working out and was getting stronger and less afraid to smash her fists into the punching bag at the warehouse.

The couch beckoned her over. Joan paused to glance out the sliding glass doors to the potted vegetable garden that'd overtaken their little balcony. She had to harvest today, and definitely needed to water. It was her calming ritual.

She sank into the gray cushions with a tired groan. Food and sleep before anything else.

She managed to lean forward to grab the TV remote off the coffee table. A cooking show might give her inspiration for dinner. Her finger slipped trying to balance the remote and cereal bowl, and she punched in the wrong channel.

The Badger News Network roared onscreen with three white men arguing loudly about fuck all. Oh god, not this shit.

Big letters along the bottom of the screen asked *Should restrictions be placed on the superpowered?*

One particularly douchey-looking brunet was saying, "If this technology is available, why aren't we using it more? Superpowers have caused one point eight million dollars of damage this year in Destine alone. Vector City is still trying to dig its way out of multiple massive Villain attacks."

"Vector City," the newscaster said from behind the desk. "Who opted to solve their problems by adding two Supervillains who claim they're on the straight and narrow."

The douchebags huffed out laughter.

Joan's blood bubbled in irritation.

"Villains don't change," the brunet douche said. "Whatever side they're on this week, they're forcing good, taxpaying people to expend money for their missteps."

According to the graphics, this was Dale Terwilliger, political analyst. What did a political analyst even do?

Wait, she knew this guy. He was the mouthpiece for some group dedicated to being assholes and pitting the norms against the superpowered. Otis kept assuring the rest of the Supers there was no cause for concern—these things popped up from time to time. But then Superheroes saved the day, and the complaining died down.

Dale Terwilliger stared into the camera. "My group, the Citizens for Human Power, aims to restore the balance of power to the people. The real people. Not these genetic misfits running around in costumes pretending they don't do more harm than good."

The other political analyst—old and gray-haired—said, "We can't let these freaks continue to destroy our livelihoods."

"There would be no need for Superheroes if we didn't have Supervillains," Dale Terwilliger said. "It's that simple. We need to track and suppress anyone with powers. That will put a stop to this madness."

"It'll be a great day to see that happen," the newscaster agreed.

"Eh, eat a bag of poorly drawn dicks," Joan told them.

Superheroes did things like stop trains from ramming into school buses, and getting reimbursement claims to go through, and yes, preventing Villains from leveling their cities.

"You're welcome, bunch of assholes," she muttered, and changed the channel to literally anything else.

CHAPTER 2

Sadie walked from the bus stop, relaxing meditation playing through her earbuds. She pulled her hair into a ponytail and took a deep breath. Well, as deep a breath as she could with the increased tightening in her chest. Every step brought her closer to her café. Sadie's Café.

The coffeehouse with her name on it, and all the responsibility on her.

Knollwood Village was lovely in the morning. Despite being a night person, she had to admit she loved how the sun dappled through the trees and shimmered off the store windows. It was such a pretty neighborhood.

Traffic on Hampton Street had been lighter the past few weeks than when the coffeehouse opened almost four months ago. More locals on vacation or working reduced hours over the summer than in April. Which wasn't great for business, since fewer customers were stopping in and lingering over the specially crafted drinks her staff provided.

My staff.

Her heart skipped a beat, but she breathed that out. She'd gone over payroll last night and rechecked everything twice. All was good.

"Breathe long, and deep, and easy," the meditation guide soothed through her earbuds. "You've got this."

You've got this, Sadie. Everyone believes in you.

She pulled the earbuds out and shoved them inside her bag. Sure, she was in a constant state of low-grade anxiety. And sure, running her own business had been an up-and-down roller coaster of emotions. The moment she caught sight of the four small white metal tables outside the wide picture windows, it all melted away for a few moments of bliss.

Two middle-aged women were chatting at the table closest to the doggie station. A beautiful golden retriever wearing a blue-plaid bandana stared up longingly at his person.

Sadie smiled at them. The words painted near the bottom of the window said it all: *Where Friends Gather.*

"Good morning," she said brightly.

The women returned the greeting. The dog wagged his floofy tail.

Sadie bent down to give him some scratches. "Aren't you just the cutest?"

The golden licked her face, then hopped up on long legs. Then proceeded to point out the plastic jar filled with little dog treats on a small stand.

"No more treats," the owner sighed.

"Uh-oh," Sadie said. "I think you've been caught."

The dog sat politely.

"You're too adorable." Sadie rubbed between his ears as he looked past her at the forbidden treats. To the humans, she asked, "How are your drinks?"

"Good," the doggie's mom said, and her friend agreed.

"Great. I'm Sadie, the owner. Thanks so much for stopping in today."

She glanced at the logo adorning both windows—the same one on her T-shirt. And on the open/closed sign hanging inside the glass door. She bid the dog farewell, stepping around the plastic water bowl. She'd have to come out later and toss a few ice cubes into it.

Crisp coolness and the sharp scent of coffee grounds welcomed her inside. A few people were scattered at the dark walnut tables in front of portable devices. The vertical slat chairs all coordinated in shades of reds and deep pinks. An R&B track from when Sadie was in high school grooved quietly from one of the corner speakers. The patterned pillows on the emerald-green couch in the back needed to be fluffed.

One customer waited for his drink near the elm wood counter while another placed an order with Nyah. Estelle spotted Sadie from where she was finishing up a hot drink to go. "Morning, boss," she said.

"Good morning," Sadie said.

Estelle preferred to wear the black T-shirt with the little pink café logo on the chest. Her long black braid was held back with a headband as colorful as the tattoos up and down her toned golden arms.

"Hey, Sadie," Cam said over his shoulder.

"Hi, Cam. Ooh, I love your eyeliner."

"Thanks." He could absolutely rock that subtle hint of navy against his blue eyes. It matched his nails pretty well. He was as much a cuddly teddy bear outside as well as in.

Sadie scanned the fairly clean and organized back bar. "How's it going today?"

"So far, so good."

Estelle smiled at the young guy at the edge of the counter. "Medium house blend with whole milk. Here you go, my friend."

"Thanks for stopping in," Sadie said.

Nyah flipped the tablet for her customer to pay. Her cropped natural curls were a fun summery look.

The woman tapped the screen with her credit card. She was a semi-regular who was nice enough but had the annoying habit of taking work calls on speakerphone.

"Nice to see you again," Sadie said anyway.

Studying the back wall featuring local artists' work, she decided that yes, the layout finally had the right flow. A mix of paintings and photographs, a mosaic tile piece, a wire sculpture. Her plan to rotate them out every few months had stalled because coordinating with the artists was one more thing on her never-ending To-Do List.

Except Gus's piece. The bright acrylic on canvas of Hampton Street in the 1980s (when she'd lived in the Village) had a permanent home at Sadie's Café. The red *AA* in the lower right corner always made her smile. Gus was her landlord, after all.

Landlady? Landperson? What was the gender-neutral term?

Her heartbeat kicked up again. Wonderful. Even overly gendered real estate terms could set her off these days.

She pushed past the long Progress Pride flag that served as a separator from front of house to the back. The pantry that had previously been converted to an office had just enough space for the desk and two rolling chairs left by the prior tenant. At least it had a door so she could lock it and not have public freak-outs, or call Joanie to cry if she had to. Which she had only done once.

Not cry. That happened once a week. She just hoped no one ever watched the security camera footage 'cause Sadie was an ugly crier.

She touched the note Joanie had stuck to the bulletin board on the day the café soft opened.

You're doing it! Living your dream!
I believe in you and am so proud of you.

Joan had been around that day like she'd promised. She'd missed the official opening because of Superhero duties. But she stopped by all the time and was supportive with upbeat texts about Sadie's awesomeness and capableness.

She couldn't find out about the crying jags or she'd be so disappointed with the truth.

Nyah popped her head inside. "What time is Perry getting here?"

"Noon-ish," Sadie said, setting her bag on the cluttered desk. "Let's touch base when you're free."

"For sure." Ny glanced over her shoulder and the café logo hoodie she wore no matter how hot it was. "Just so you know, Estelle was twenty minutes late again this morning."

"Was she? Shoot."

"I told her this was the final verbal warning before I have to write her up."

"That sucks." Sadie drummed her fingers on the desktop. "Is everything okay with her? Something going on in her life?"

"She talks about her ADHD and bad time management. I think she's just young, and it's hard to get up and go."

"I get that. Do you want me to talk to her?"

Nyah shook her head. "You don't have to. She sincerely apologized and assured me she really likes working here. She said she just has to get her shit together."

"The customers love her. I love her. Darn it." Sadie crossed her arms. "Maybe I'll tell her how much we value her. That would've motivated me at her age."

"I did. I thanked her for always staying late to make up the time."

"She picks up shifts, too. Thank you for telling me. I value you the most-est."

Her trusted manager grinned. "Are you trying to butter me up for when we're open on Sundays?"

"We already agreed I'll work Sundays."

The plan was to be open seven days a week starting in September. Hopefully the cost of operations wouldn't outweigh how much they brought in. Maybe she could hire another part-time barista by then so she could better balance ownership duties with filling in behind the counter. Something she planned on discussing with Perry today.

She followed Nyah back out. Estelle chatted amiably with the speakerphone patron while prepping her iced coffee.

Oh yeah, the community bulletin board on the wall by the edge of the counter had to be purged of old items. *Later.*

"What's today's random fact?" Sadie asked, checking the little chalkboard on the counter. "Sloths only poop once a week? Huh. I didn't know that."

Cam snagged the almond milk from the small fridge. "Nature is magical."

During a monthly staff meeting, her two second shift employees had suggested they share daily random factoids for conversation starters. Leaning into the coffeehouse's culture of connection.

Sadie loved her team. They worked hard and had great attitudes. Other than the guy who'd stopped showing up after the first week because he "just couldn't deal," they were a great group. And she'd hired Estelle to replace that guy, and Estelle was a perfect fit. She just had to set more alarms or something.

The bold yellow exterior of Powered by Plants couldn't be missed outside. Beth-Ann had stepped out to check Wren's parking job.

Sadie knocked on the window to catch her friend's attention. Beth-Ann saw her, and they shared a wave.

They had to get together for another game night soon. Her former food truck friends were among the very few who knew the real reason Joan and Mark weren't always available, or why they had to leave suddenly.

Sadie stopped by an empty table against the brown brick wall to pick up the dishes. The square piece of parchment paper on the ceramic dessert plate held remnants of blueberry muffin. She had to place an order with the bakery this morning for more lemon poppyseed scones. Those were a big hit.

Her phone buzzed in her back pocket. It jarred her pulse, then soothed her since it was from Joanie.

Heading to bed. Chicken tikka masala for dinner?

Sounds good babe. Sleep tight 

Joan reacted with a heart. Poor Superhero needed sleep more than Sadie did.

She dropped the dirty dishes in the bin against the back wall, then noticed a familiar tall figure heading through the entrance. Zee had also recently decided to lop their straight ebony hair into a messy crop. Everyone seemed to be cutting their hair lately, but they all looked damn good. Sadie knew after that failed attempt in college that she couldn't properly pull off short hair.

"Well, well," she teased. "Fancy seeing you here on a Tuesday."

"Mm-hmm," Zee said, then turned to Nyah. "Hi, Nyah. How's it going?"

"Hey. Great." Ny never did a good job hiding the delight bursting from her at knowing Zee was one of the Supers. She'd figured out who Joan and Mark's coworkers were in no time.

Cam and Estelle offered fist-bumps and hellos. Zee was well known for being a really good tipper.

"Meeting anyone here?" Sadie said.

"I'm mostly here for your tea." Zee studied the drink menu written on the large chalkboard above the back bar. "I'll have a medium iced matcha latte with soy milk."

Soy milk. Right. She needed to go over yesterday's numbers to see if the slight upcharge in soy milk was offsetting its increased cost to purchase it. Another thing for her To-Do List.

Nyah punched in the order. "Do you want to get something for Mark?"

Zee raised one sculpted eyebrow. "He can buy his own."

Okay, apparently they hadn't made up for whatever they'd been arguing about last week. Taxes, maybe? Or the weather, or which action movie hero was the hottest? They could argue about why the sky was blue, but playful teasing was their love language.

"Anyone else joining you today?" Nyah asked.

"No. Oh, Kade wanted to make sure I say hi to everyone from him," Zee said as they pulled their phone from slim-cut white pants.

Nyah giggled.

"He's so sweet," Sadie said. "Say hi back."

As far as most people in her life were concerned, Zee and Kade were Joanie and Mark's friends and not in the restaurant investment group they were supposedly running. They got off the topic of jobs as quickly as possible.

Cam leaned on the counter to see out the nearest window. "Mark's here," he said excitedly.

Of course, Mark stood at Powered by Plants' side door chatting with Wren.

"You can take the boy out of the food truck…" Sadie said.

Zee scribbled their signature on the tablet. Then they glanced sideways at Sadie. "Are you okay? You look a little off."

I've been living by "Fake it 'til you make it" for the past four months. When am I going to stop faking it?

"I'm fine," she said with a smile. "Look at this place. It's a dream come true."

Don't forget that, Sadie. You are living your dream.

It was overwhelming, it was stressful, but it was wonderful, too. She had to remember her why, like one of her meditations suggested.

You made a place for friends to gather.

"Okay." Zee's dark eyes said they knew she wasn't being fully open, but they'd respect her privacy.

They chit-chatted with Cam as Sadie stepped behind the other tablet to take orders from a sudden influx of customers. The food truck being parked in front usually brought people in here to get a drink while Powered by Plants prepped to open. The mutually beneficial partnership was really paying off.

See, Sadie? You're making smart moves. You're doing well.

Plus, she was still crafting drinks and interacting with customers. Doing the things she loved.

As she shook a black tea and lemonade, the door opened. Cam held up a hand in greeting. "Hi, Mark. Zee's already here, in your usual spot."

Mark cast a pretend uninterested glance toward the couch, which visibly frustrated Cam. He was shipping those two hard.

Sadie grinned at Mark. "Did Beth-Ann kick you out again?"

"Wren wanted me to stay and do prep work with her." He was sporting a deep blue short-sleeved polo and jeans more relaxed than he usually wore.

She poured the drink into a Sadie's Café tumbler. Handing it to the early twenties girl with a cute pixie haircut, she said, "Here's your half and half. Thanks again for getting the reusable cup. You'll get fifty cents off every time you use it."

The girl's eyes brightened. Good marketing and good for the environment was worth losing a little profit. "Thanks," she said. "I like supporting this place. I feel really safe here."

That warmed Sadie's heart. "Thank you for saying so. Everyone is welcome at Sadie's Café."

"Except assholes," Mark chimed in.

Sadie shot him a look, though the customer laughed. "We do have a pretty strict no a-holes policy," Sadie said.

And no provisions in my lease agreement excluding the super-powered.

The customer thanked her again, then headed out.

Looking back and forth to the back corner, Mark said, "Did Zee not get me a drink?"

"Nope," Sadie said.

"Come on," he grumbled. Gesturing at the front door, Mark said to Zee, "I bought you breakfast."

"Thank you," Zee said, then returned to looking at their phone.

Mark muttered under his breath. A twinkle of enjoyment sparkled in his ice-blue eyes.

"I'm so glad your sister doesn't like unnecessary drama," Sadie said.

"I don't either."

She raised doubtful eyebrows at him.

"Okay, maybe a little necessary drama."

Mark walked over to Nyah, giving her a high-five over the countertop. Palpable energy from him and Zee trying not to notice one another tugged between them.

Cam turned to Sadie and said, "If they don't make it as a couple, I will literally die."

"Don't say that. Mostly because don't put that into the universe. I don't want you to be disappointed if they're not committed to commitment."

"They're committed," Cam insisted. "You can tell when they look at each other. This is a forever kind of love. I will die on that hill."

Sadie just laughed and shook her head. Cam also said that about her and Joan. At least that was hopefully true. She didn't doubt her or Joanie's feelings or commitment. If only she could find the self-assurance Joan saw inside of her.

Joan opened her mouth, but froze in shock. Then relief. Then… "How long has this been going on?"

"Off and on for a year or two."

"That's why you're not worried."

Otis shook his head. "Their base of operations is in Destine. The Supers there keep tabs on them."

Destine. Ah. "Aura told you about this."

"She did."

"Is that still a thing?" Joan asked. Otis's romance with Sherrelle (alias Aura) was even more mercurial than Mark and Zee's.

"That is not your concern."

"Tell her I said hi." She couldn't help—

Oh, shit. If the middleman was actually Nuance, was he the one who reached out to Greta? And why?

Was a Super in another city on to her? She was in more trouble than they thought if so.

"The reason I texted in the first place is because the Oceanview Supers want to talk to you," Otis said. "And Ice."

Old fear reared its ugly head. "Do they think we're involved with Iris?"

"It's not that. You have a unique perspective. And we are the city that's managed to rid ourselves of Villains. Twice." He puffed up proudly at that.

"So they want us to get rid of their Villains, too? What, Prowl and Ether weren't enough?"

Otis looked like he was about to say something, but changed course. "I do think that's what they'd like. They want to consult with all of us, but particularly Spark and Ice since you know how Villains think."

Joan snorted in disbelief. "I'm not sure if I should be flattered or insulted. We're only good for them when it's convenient."

She was getting tired of cleaning up other people's messes no matter what side of the law she was on.

"The optics will be good," Otis said, taking his usual wingback armchair. "Former Villains helping with the apprehension of a newly turned Supervillain."

"I don't think she's a Villain," Joan said, sitting on the couch nearest him.

"In all your time as a criminal, did you ever threaten to blow something up as leverage?"

"No, but that wasn't our style."

"Your judgment is being clouded by your past. The longer you're a Hero, the more you'll understand."

"I still don't think she's full Supervillain," Joan muttered. Why was everyone so quick to label Iris? In her mind, she was doing what was right.

Kind of like you did, Spark?

Shit.

And shit for the Supers possibly having Greta on their radar. Joan had spent the better part of her adult life making sure Greta stayed protected. And now her friend was a target. She could probably get her cohorts in Vector City to leave Grets alone, but she had no sway in Destine other than with Sherrelle.

She'd have to play this right. See how much they knew about Greta.

Ward rushed into the room, breathing hard like he'd been running. "Mr. Flight, I was able to get you an eight o'clock reservation tomorrow night. Hello, Ms. Sp—Joan."

"Excellent," Otis said.

"The table in the back corner, as you requested. Would you like me to pack your usual go bag?"

"That won't be necessary."

"Where are you going?" Joan asked.

"A bistro on the coast with excellent steak frites."

The coast. As in somewhere near Destine. "I see that *is* still a thing with Sherrelle."

Otis ignored her sly smirk and turned to Ward. "Go to Georgio's tomorrow and pick up my suit."

"Yes, sir." Ward typed on his tablet. "For Flight, correct?"

"Yes. They will take care of things."

Take care of the bill, you mean.

Her expression must've given away her thoughts because Otis raised an eyebrow at her. "I don't need to justify anything."

Joan reclined against the back of the couch. "If you're so concerned about our public image, stop taking free shit. That'd go a long way."

"There's not nearly as much as you think there is."

"Anything is one thing too many."

Otis sat back as well, crossing his legs for effect. "I have been patient with your quips and snide remarks. I thought Zee had gotten through to you and your brother. Our citizens often want to thank us. We've built relationships with many of them. If they want to give us things, we should accept those gifts."

"Yeah, but a lot of people don't want to. They feel obligated. Start turning shit down and that'll stop it."

He harumphed and asked Ward if there was anything to report on more official matters. For a dude concerned about bad optics, Otis couldn't see he was the lead perpetrator of said bad optics.

Mark poked his head in. "There you are."

He walked in sans mask, black-and-blue Ice suit unzipped. Darlene followed, pulling her navy-blue gloves off and shaking her hands.

"You're really this abominable temperature all the time?" she said.

"Not *all* the time," Mark said. He raised an eyebrow, letting her fill in the rest.

Her face wrinkled in disinterest. "No one wants to hear about your sex life."

It was so unexpected coming from her that Joan burst out laughing.

"What's going on here?" Mark asked.

"Fun and games," Joan said.

Otis sat up straighter. "News from Oceanview."

He briefed the duo, and then Ward found Iris's latest video. Joan got up to watch it.

Iris was earnestly angry and pretty damn serious, warning everyone that she'd use her X-ray vision to make sure all the animals were humanely removed from the facilities...or else.

Darlene shivered, visibly trying to warm up. Joan set a hand on her shoulder blade to send some heat into her. Darlene planted her hand atop Joan's and got a quicker hit.

Mark's eyebrows scrunched together. "Yikes. Iris is not playing around."

"Does Oceanview have a plan to stop her?" Darlene said.

"They don't exactly know where she is," said Otis. "And she has the advantage of knowing how they do things."

"Plus freaky-good eyesight, so, y'know..." Mark gestured with two fingers from his eyes to Joan. "Can see them coming from miles away."

A video call came in on the TV screen. Ward hastened over to accept it.

The caller's camera jostled and shot at the ceiling before a tan, maybe fortyish man with flowing blond hair came into view.

Mark instantly perked up. "Hello there," he said.

"Hey, what's up?" the guy said in a mildly raspy voice.

Otis stepped forward. "Ray."

"Flight, man, how's it goin'?"

"You know Catch. These are—Ward, get out of the way. This is Spark, and this—"

"I'm Ice, but you can call me Mark." He grinned.

"Hey." The Oceanview Super bobbed his head. "Everyone thinks my name is Ray, but it's actually Jay."

This guy's powers involved shooting bright, blinding rays of light. And also apparently being the living embodiment of a surfer boy. He looked like he spent more time catching waves than Villains, which, given Oceanview's track record, was accurate.

Ray Jay bobbed his head again. "It's wild how you used to be Villains, but now you're, like, Heroes."

"Yeah," Mark said. "Wild."

"And the rest of you guys trust them?"

"We do," Otis said.

Pride swelled in Joan's chest.

"That's wild," Ray Jay said again.

Darlene crossed her arms. "I understand you need our assistance with Iris."

"Yeah, man. You guys did a rad job with Prowl and Ether. We hated those guys. We don't hate Kelsey, though."

"Kelsey is Iris," Otis provided.

"She's got some issues to work through. Could you, like, do something about her? She's not in Oceanview anymore, so it's cool if you want to take over."

"She's not in Vector City either," Joan pointed out.

"She's, like, wherever." Ray Jay scratched at his ocean-blue T-shirt. "This research lab is in the middle of nowhere."

"Then why don't *you* go after her?" Ward said. Then his eyes widened, and he covered his mouth.

"We will if she shows up to detonate the place. But we don't want it to go that far. If you could talk to her... You guys who were Villains could reason with her that, like, that's not cool."

Joan shared a look with her brother. Yup, they were expected to clean up Super messes for the rest of their lives.

"We can talk to her if you know where she is," Joan said.

"We could reach out by DM or phone," Mark suggested.

Ray Jay shook his shaggy blond mane. "Nah, man, she's blocked all of that."

"Then...?" Joan shrugged her hands. "If you want us to help, you have to help us."

"Don't you, like, know how to find Villains?"

"Villains we knew. You know more about Iris than we do."

"Yeah, man, that's true, that's true."

"I swear, if he calls us *man* one more time…" Joan muttered to Darlene.

Darlene raised her chin. "Ray, I shouldn't have to point out two of us are women. We have a gender nonconforming Hero as well. Stop addressing us as *men*."

"Yeah, man, sorry about that. I'm cool with everyone."

Darlene frowned deeper. Her nails scraped against her spandex-clad arms.

Joan couldn't help the small smile tugging at her mouth. Sometimes Darlene was pretty okay.

"She won't fight you 'cause she doesn't believe in fighting," Ray Jay said. "But you can't overpower her. Her sight, man— sorry, ladies and men. She sees everything. She'll see your moves before you do them."

Joan's phone buzzed with a text. So did Mark's. She didn't answer for fear of it being Greta.

Another text buzzed. Mark chuckled, so it wasn't a bad thing.

Then a third text.

"It's Kade," Mark murmured.

Okay, not an urgent priority. Getting in touch with Greta, however…

Otis boasted to Ray Jay about how Vector City had a good track record of dealing with Villains. Hmm. They did have that reputation—the city that formed alliances with Villains, yes, but also got results.

Joan could use talking to Iris as a way to show Destine she was trustworthy. That making a deal with her was a deal for the right reasons.

Only she had to tell Greta the awful truth. And oh yeah, for Greta to not tell anyone she was still friendly with Spark and Ice because that would open a door none of them wanted to walk through.

The video call on Ray Jay's end got all wobbly before it abruptly cut out.

"Did his phone fall off his surfboard?" Mark said.

"I'm sure he'll call back," Otis said, but he didn't sound thrilled about it.

Mark shook his head. "Oceanview. We did like to party there back in the day."

"I don't need to speak with him anymore," Darlene said. "I'm going to change, do my reports, and make scones again. I know what I did wrong."

"Scones can be tricky," Joan said. "Don't give up."

Darlene nodded once before heading for the door. Her glazed cinnamon scones the other day had tasted pretty good but crumbled like sand.

Otis resumed his seat. "Answer it when Ray calls back," he instructed Ward.

Mark nudged Joan toward the loveseat against the wall. "Look at Kade's texts. Your heart will melt."

Joan pulled her phone from her skinny jeans pocket and checked the screen.

> I asked her out and she said yes!!! We have a satellite!
>
> Date. A date. That was autocorrect. Worry!
>
> That was autocorrect too! Sorry!

Her heart actually did melt a little. "Sadie said Nyah likes him, too."

Mark flopped on the couch. "I had a sneaking suspicion she did. She giggles a lot around him."

"We'll see what happens."

He stopped typing (presumably) his reply. "What's up?"

Sitting beside him, Joan said, "I feel like my head's about to explode."

"Headache?"

"Brain-too-full-ache. We have to do what we can with this Iris situation." She subtly glanced in Otis's direction, signaling a private conversation needed to happen.

"I see."

Once they finished talking to Ray Jay, she'd escape to a changing room or her car to call Greta. They were barely speaking as it was, and now Joan had to possibly drive an even bigger wedge between them.

It was not a phone call she was looking forward to making.

CHAPTER 7

Friday afternoons always had that buzzy excitement of the weekend about to begin. Sadie exited the café to clear off two tables, soak in the sunshine, and hopefully absorb some of the energy permeating North Hampton Street.

Powered by Plants had closed up for the day, and Cajun Soul had just parked to start theirs. It was a tight squeeze until Wren and Beth-Ann pulled out, but this ensured both trucks had access to the prime spot.

She tossed the plastic to-go cups in the recycle bin at the curb. Beth-Ann stepped out of her truck. "The meetup starts at seven. Are we going to see you there?"

"Probably not this time," Sadie said. "It's been a long week. Why would they have a women's entrepreneur meetup on a Friday, anyway? We're all exhausted."

"Because most of us are entrepreneur-ing the rest of the week."

Sadie cradled the two dessert plates against her stomach. "I was hoping to be home to see Joanie before she passes out."

"How's she doing?" Beth-Ann asked as Wren joined them on the sidewalk.

"Work keeps her busy."

"I'm sure it does," Wren said.

Joanie and Mark were on call should the Oceanview Supers locate or find a way to communicate with Iris. Apparently, that was high on Joan's To-Do List, along with protecting Greta and trying to find out what was going on with Nuance and secret infiltrations and…and…

Honestly, there was a lot. Sadie was probably missing a few things while swimming in her own lists.

"Your work keeps you busy, too," Beth-Ann said. "Talking to women who understand where you're at could be really helpful."

"I need to do a few things if I have any hope of not coming in tomorrow," Sadie said.

Wren untied the white apron covering her all-black ensemble. She hadn't shaved her dark hair in a while, and it was a cute little peach fuzz. "You know you can't put off coming with us forever," she said in her lilting Scottish brogue.

Sadie had only declined going to this networking thing twice. So what if this was number three?

"Anyway…" she began, taking a step back.

Beth-Ann shook her head so hard, her pale ponytail swished. "Nuh-uh. Come with us. It'll be really beneficial."

The semi-permanent rock in Sadie's stomach rolled around and poked at her gut. She fidgeted with the plates. "Those things are for CEOs and women who run investment firms and have fancy office jobs."

Wren huffed out a laugh. "Do I look like I have a fancy office job?"

"You two have big plans, though, with opening your own brick-and-mortar restaurant."

"I'm sorry," Beth-Ann said. She bent to the side to stare at the café. "I think that window says Sadie's Café. You own your own business."

"Yeah, but it's just a coffeehouse."

"So? We just want a quaint little restaurant. A lot of the women at these meetups run small, local businesses."

"I think most of them do," Wren said. "We've all got similar problems."

Sadie stared down at the cement. She wasn't as go-getter-y as her friends. They'd been able to scrape and save and buy what they had with their own money. Sadie'd had to rely on her girlfriend, her girlfriend's twin brother, an ex-Villain, and a retired Superhero. She would've never been able to do this without them.

The side door to Cajun Soul opened. Tenia smiled from the doorway and said, "Hey, ladies. Happy Friday. We've got our youngest son helping out tonight. Should be fun."

They greeted her in return. Beth-Ann waved her over. "Sadie needs one of your pep talks."

"A pep talk? What's shakin', bacon?"

"There's this women's entrepreneur meetup we've been trying to get her to attend for months. She doesn't think she's really a businessowner."

"I didn't say that," Sadie defended.

Tenia stepped down and headed over. "Miss Sadie, I have seen firsthand how much of your heart you've put into this place. Every businessowner should care as much as you do."

"I do care. I'm just..." She chugged in a shaky breath. "...intimidated by smart business-type people."

Wren crossed her thick arms. "Have you seen her spreadsheets?" she asked Tenia.

"They're so detailed, it's scary," Beth-Ann said.

"This girl loves paperwork," Tenia agreed.

Sadie opened her mouth—first to laugh that *she* of all people enjoyed paperwork, then to say it was really Perry's paperwork. But they were sort of right. She was very organized and could account for every penny. She was constantly tweaking her spreadsheets to better meet her needs.

"Sometimes I feel like I'm crushing it," she said, then admitted, "Other times, I feel like I'm being crushed. Which I know you've said is what it's like. We're all figuring things out day by day. Well, everyone except Joan. She knows exactly what she wants. It inspires me to see her focus and dedication."

Something dawned in Beth-Ann's blue eyes. "Come here," she said, walking back to Powered by Plants.

"Uh-oh. Am I in trouble?"

"I have something to tell you that I don't want to say in public."

Uh-oh. Sadie stepped cautiously aboard, taking in the fresh scents of kale and pineapple. Wren and Tenia followed, almost like they knew what this was about.

Beth-Ann settled her hands on her hips. "You are more than just a Superhero's girlfriend, Sadie. We love you and Joan together, but you're pretty great on your own. We wish you could see that."

Sadie darted glances between her friends. "I'm not tying my identity to her," she said. "Am I?"

"We hope not," Tenia said.

"I don't think I am. And Joanie's always pumping me up about being a badass boss lady."

But she wasn't giving herself that level of encouragement. It was all driven by fear—of failure, of letting everyone down, of being the flighty, non-office-job-holding barista...

Oh. Of course. She hadn't considered that until now, but it made total sense.

Her friends looked at her with concern and compassion.

"I..." Sadie switched the dessert plates to her other hand. "I have a college degree I've done nothing with, which my parents will gladly tell you about. I think that's maybe in the back of my head. They've always wanted me to get a *real* job. And now I think I'm doing something real, and..."

She scratched at her nose, holding back sudden tears.

Beth-Ann nodded. "But it's not what they perceive as real."

"They're supportive," Sadie was quick to add. "They really like the café. They *are* proud of me."

"Trauma runs deep, hon," Tenia said. "I was the first woman

in my family to go to college. All I heard for years was 'Oh, Tee-Tee thinks she's too good for us now.' That messed me up for a long time."

"That's terrible. I'm so sorry."

Tenia lightly shrugged. "I burned out in the corporate world trying to prove myself to them. So Morris and I retired early from our stressful finance jobs. We used that money to buy our food truck and do what we really wanted. We didn't give a fig what anyone thought, and we're loving it. Most of the time."

Wren leaned toward Sadie. "I'm intimidated by book-smart people, too," she murmured. "I've only worked in food service. What we're doing is real. What *you're* doing is real."

"Thank you," Sadie whispered, squeezing her friend's hand.

"Wren and I are lucky to have supportive families," said Beth-Ann. "But it took *years* before they stopped asking if we were sure we wanted to do the 'no meat thing' because it's too niche."

"We'd make more money if we served meat dishes," Wren added.

"Your food is phenomenal," Sadie said. "And you're both vegans. It's a part of you."

"My brother said we're like Iris, but less blowy-uppy," Beth-Ann said.

"He did?" Wren half-laughed.

"He texted that we could feed all the animal rescuers."

Sadie blinked at the moisture coating her eyes. "Rescuers? Did that lab agree to release the animals?"

"They did, if you can believe it," Beth-Ann said. "Maybe an hour ago?"

"Wow." That was great—er, maybe not the blowy-uppy threat that got the results. Those animals would have much better lives, and plus Joanie wouldn't have to get involved.

Sadie drew in a long, deep breath. She felt a little better. A little lighter. Her friends were doing exactly what they wanted. She was living her dream. Joan was too, and they were committed to supporting each other.

And she'd done so much since meeting Joan: helped start a food truck, opened her own coffeehouse, successfully kept a trio of former Villains on the straight and narrow…

She didn't have superpowers, but she was powerful in her own right.

Now she wanted to cry happy tears. She set the dessert plates on the stainless-steel counter and opened her arms. "My girls," she said, wrapping them all in a group hug. "What would I do without you?"

"I think this means you'll come with us tonight," Wren said.

"Yes. I want more of this energy."

After some giggling and extra-long squeezing, they pulled apart. Beth-Ann turned to Tenia. "We'd love for you come too, if you can step away from the truck."

Tenia's brown eyes widened. "I don't trust those two not to irreparably damage something without me watching them. But let me know in the future."

Sadie picked up the dishes, intent on letting her friends get back to things. "Can you…"

An embarrassed flush warmed her cheeks.

"What?" Beth-Ann said.

"It's really silly, but at this meetup? I want to state with pride that I'm a small business owner. If I start acting like it's not a big deal, will you two call me out? I need to be more confident about that."

"You got it."

"I'll yell at you like I'm in chef mode," Wren teased. Or possibly not teased.

Sadie thanked them again, then stepped into the warm summer sun.

She'd get home to Joan later than planned, but as a better version of herself. That would make both of them happier in the long run. It just sucked how little they were seeing one another right now.

Even though Iris's victory was a good one, it meant she'd only keep pushing for more. And the need for Spark would be more. The world needed her, so Sadie had to share her. Which was fine.

She loved Joan with all her heart, but her friends were right. She was more than Spark's other half.

I am a badass business owner.

CHAPTER 8

Working the heavy punching bag at the warehouse on Sunday was more important than ever. Sadie concentrated on her jabs with focused precision. She'd opted not to use her boxing gloves to get a better feel for the contact and impact. Though she'd wound a few too many layers of hand wrap to feel much of anything.

Joan held the bag from the other side. "That's it," she said. "Picture Melvin's face and go to town."

Sadie conjured up the image of Trick in his ugly mauve suit and struck with renewed energy. The support chains rattled, making the well-worn bag jostle from side to side.

"Oop. Hang on a sec." Joan steadied the wobbly bag.

Sadie stepped back to catch her breath and give her arms a break. "Are you sure you wouldn't prefer working out at head-quarters? With equipment made this century?"

Joan pressed on the duct tape holding the bag together. "There's a comfort here. It's not state-of-the-art, but it's like how Mark and I learned how to fight. Scrappy and with what we had to work with."

"Scrappy like me," Sadie joked, doing a one-two-three-air-punch-then-kick combo.

One of the takeaways from the wonderful meetup the other night was the importance of making time for a little self-care. While most of the businesswomen talked about scheduling massages and manicures, she'd realized this was a great way to get rid of excess stress and amp up feeling strong. Plus, it was something she and Joanie liked to do together. And it pretty much always led to some feisty sexytimes.

Joanie's short blue shorts and skintight black athletic tank and tousled cropped hair were definitely going to accelerate that part of the afternoon. Sadie pulled up on her sports bra through an old Halloween pub crawl T-shirt. She'd slacked off on shaving, so it was a leggings day.

Joan's phone dinged. Sadie shadow-boxed at where it sat on the floor beside the cushioned workout bench. "No phones at the gym, Malone," she growled.

"I don't get to do no phones anymore." As Joan headed over to it, she said, "And what if it's Kade reporting on the big date?"

"That's the only exception."

Nyah and Kade were having their first date today: playing some *Sea Voyage Five* followed by a nice Italian dinner. Ny was about to be either shocked or impressed at how much food Kade could pack away. He'd assured everyone he would pay for the meal.

Joan's eyebrows raised in surprise as she looked at the screen. "It's Greta. She wants to know if she can come in."

"How does she know we're here?" Sadie shook her head. "Never mind. She probably has a tracker on your car or something."

"She pinged my location." Joan gave her a slightly annoyed look.

"What?"

"Nothing."

"Well then, let her in."

Jeez. It wasn't like assuming something illegal was that far off the mark.

Joan went to the side entrance and undid the deadbolt. Then the door lock.

Greta stepped inside in her usual leather jacket and black jeans. Her hair was twisted up in a bun. "I am loudly announcing my presence," she stated.

Sadie waved in acknowledgment, ignoring the obviously snarky tone. "Hello and thank you."

"It's workout day? Why didn't you tell me? I would've come prepared."

"Because we're still mad at each other?" Joan said, closing the door.

"Right."

Sadie tucked her wrapped hands behind her back. No sense giving Greta any ideas.

"Don't let me stop you," she said. "Though can you feel anything through the two inches of wrap on those hands?"

"We were just finishing up," Sadie lied. "I'm sure you're here for a reason."

"Yes. To talk to Joan somewhere I know is safe."

Joanie planted her lightly wrapped hands on her hips. "Did you get in touch with him?"

Greta eyeballed the decaying punching bag. "It's too late. I can't retract my threat that Spark and Ice will mess him up."

"Great. Now Nuance has confirmation you're still connected to us."

"The bigger problem is that I unknowingly worked with a Super." She shivered. "I'd rather be wanted by an angry thug."

Apparently, Greta had wasted no time in reaching out to her contact. Before Joanie could tell her not to because it was a voice-mimicking Superhero.

Joan pulled another irritated face. "I was going to use the publicity from talking to Iris to show the Destine Supers I'm trustworthy. That hasn't happened yet, but I'm sure it will at some point."

"Because the Oceanview Supers are a joke."

"Yeah. It's not that I don't want to get involved. I just want Oceanview's Supers to get more involved."

"Good luck with that," Greta said.

Sadie took a tentative step toward her. "You didn't get what Nuance asked for. You're protecting that information. Maybe he'll see that as a good thing."

Joan raised her eyebrows like she hadn't considered that.

Greta just scowled. "He thinks I couldn't do it."

"But if anyone could, *the* Greta could. Think about it. You're friends with superpowered people, so you wouldn't want to hurt them."

"I still want to know why it was specifically you they hired," Joan said.

"Me, too." Greta crossed her arms and leaned against the cement-block wall. Her whole vibe was tired. She usually exuded a *Don't mess with me* confidence that seemed to be missing today.

What would be the harm in letting a few Superheroes think she was on their side? It wasn't like that would get back to the criminal element she was so worried about.

"You know what could really make a difference?" Sadie mused aloud. "If you did something to help the Supers."

If Greta had superpowers, the glare she shot at Sadie would've incinerated her.

"Not work with them. You could make it up. Just say that you helped Spark and Ice with something. Joanie could corroborate the story."

Greta grumbled under her breath.

Joan thought for a moment, then said, "You did help when we took down Trick and them."

"No, I helped *you*."

"You made sure everyone knew we weren't with them anymore. That was helpful."

"I can absolutely not afford to have connections to any Super. And in case you forgot, everyone turned against you for not siding with Trick."

Sadie shrugged. "Then just do something nice. A noble gesture."

"Like paying for Super damage?" Greta cast a glance at Joan. "The way you used to?"

"I still do," Joan said.

"Not taking handouts is not the same as—"

"Joanie still pays for stuff," Sadie said. "From her own pocket."

"So I should make a big donation to the National Museum of Superheroes?" Greta said, then paused. "Having a wing there named after me would be brilliant."

Joan chuckled like she couldn't help it. "That would be hilarious."

The old friends laughed, then seemed to remember they were supposed to be mad at each other and stopped.

Greta pushed off the wall. "Things like that only work if people know about them. Iris announced that she paid for all those rescues to take those lab rats. People are really warming up to her. She doesn't know she took a page out of the Spark Handbook for Altruistic Villainy."

"You could follow that example, too," Sadie suggested.

Greta's hands balled into fists. "Stop trying to turn me into something I'm not."

"I'm not—"

"I steal things, Sadie. It's who I am. Joan can tell you it's as much a part of me as shooting fireballs is for her."

Joan nodded slowly. "We need to find a way to get you off of Nuance and the Citizens for Asshattery's radar. Can you go to your place in France for a while?"

"I'm not running away," Greta said. "We're figuring this out."

Nice to hear both of them say *we*. There was still hope.

"At least lay low," Joan said. "Until I have a chance to clear the air with Nuance. I have an in with Aura, so it shouldn't be too hard."

"Can you do it soon? This is annoying."

Joan's reply was cut off by the garage door opening. Perry's slate-gray sedan pulled in next to Joanie's car. Gus sat in the passenger seat, squinting behind her glasses as the sunlight gave way to the dimmer warehouse lighting.

"Who's with him?" Greta said.

"That's Gus," Joan said. "I texted you about her when we were still talking. I thought Perry was just friends with her, but it goes a lot deeper than that."

"Wait, that's Amazing Woman?"

"What are they doing here?" Sadie wondered.

Quick movement swished behind her. Greta had disappeared.

"Grets…" Joan released a little huff of air. "It's okay."

Perry shut the engine off and climbed out. "What are you doing here?"

"No, please, come in," Joan said, dripping with sarcasm.

"To the warehouse I own?"

"You do?" She seemed genuinely surprised.

Sadie walked over to help Gus. "We were exercising."

"Why don't you work out at your new headquarters?" Perry asked.

She gestured at him. "Thank you."

He closed the garage door. "Gus has never seen what used to be our base of operations."

Gus eased her way out of the car in a breezy aquamarine sundress, waving off Sadie's offered hand. She took in all the drabness. "You couldn't afford something better?"

"It was inconspicuous," Perry said.

"That it is. Hello, Sadie."

"Hi, Gus." Knowing the older woman wasn't a fan of hugs, Sadie squeezed her hand. "Guess what? I went to a really great meetup for local businesswomen. Most of them own small businesses like mine." Her heart pulsed an excited burst of pride.

"That's nice."

"I think I really needed to be around that energy."

Gus arched an eyebrow at what to her was probably a hippy-dippy statement. "I'm glad to hear it, whatever that means. I'm going to come with Perry to your weekly meeting."

"That's great. I want to switch out some of the art this week. I'd love your help with that."

"Of course."

"And we're going to have our first of hopefully many open mic nights on Saturday," Sadie said.

Perry looked like he was about to ask about the cost, so Sadie added, "I'm working. If this goes well, I'll get some trivia nights on the calendar and hire additional help for those."

He considered that, then nodded his assent. Another thrill swizzled through her chest. Big things were coming to Sadie's Café. She could just feel it.

Joan had gone to the small changing room. She murmured something, then something else. "It's fine," she said.

A few moments later, the top of Greta's bun poked out from the doorway.

Perry glanced over from the kitchenette. "You can come out."

She took a tiny step into the doorway.

Gus craned her neck. "Who is that? Don't sneak around. It's rude."

Normally stoic Greta's mouth hung slightly open as she stared at Gus. "Holy shit," she whispered. "That's Amazing Woman."

"Yes, yes," Gus said. "And you are whom?"

"Greta, my…an old friend," Joan said.

"Ah. Are you the thief?"

"I am," Greta said, clearly unsure of what to do in Amazing Woman's presence.

"I've heard all about…" Gus gestured at her and Joan. "That situation over the years. Thank god you two finally ended things. Joan, could those shorts be any shorter? I can see for miles."

Joan glanced down at her shorts. "I mean, they *could* be shorter."

"We weren't anticipating so much company," Sadie said, then started to unwrap her left hand.

Perry set his laptop case on the worn table. "This is where the ideas for Hot and Cold first started."

"Yeah," Joan said. "Mark and I used to sketch things out while waiting for Perry to start his boring meetings."

Gus raised her eyebrows at him. "He does love his agendas."

The private look that passed between them was filled with affection. Aww, they could be really cute when trying not to be cute.

Gus wandered over to comment on the state of the crappy kitchenette. Joan went to show off the window that used to block out the sun. It made her happy to let in the light now.

Greta stayed back, her body language tense. Sadie peeked at her as she unraveled the wrap from between her fingers. "Gus is the least likely person to care about what you do," she said, keeping her voice low.

"She parted with the Supers under bad terms."

"There is that, but she, uh…" She chuckled to herself. "Gus very much enjoys her retirement."

They stood in silence, watching Gus get the not-so-grand tour. Joan looked over with a small smile.

"She really misses you," Sadie murmured.

"I miss our old hangouts," Greta said.

Risking a glower or death stare, Sadie turned to her. "I would love for you to be in her life and not keep running in and out of it. Joanie really craves stability. She likes having things safe and consistent."

"That's why you're good for her." Greta looked her up and down. "You're what she's always needed. I always knew I wasn't."

Sadie set the hand wrap on the workout bench before starting to unravel her right hand. It was nice to have validation that Joan's friend approved of her.

"I was serious about sparring with you. Anytime you want, let me know."

"Thanks," Sadie said. "I know I should practice that more, but

I don't really like hitting anyone. And it's frowned upon in my line of work as opposed to what you and Joan do."

The corners of Greta's lips twitched.

"You should come by the café when it's open. I think you'd like our summer menu. And you could see Nyah, who—oh my god, guess what? She's on a date right now with Kade."

"Kade? As in Lunk Kade?"

"Yes."

"Wow." Her stony face didn't give away how she felt about that.

Perry led Gus toward the changing room. "Where did you store your big scores?" she asked.

"Never here," said Perry. "We split things up and took them home."

Joan followed behind them wearing her curiously questioning face. Something didn't add up for her.

"I guess that makes sense," Greta said. "With Nyah. They were mooning over each other the other night."

Sadie tried to hold it back, but she couldn't help saying, "Are you gonna stop hanging out with her, too?"

"I still have Amit."

Oh man, she hadn't talked to Amit in a while. He'd been a good resource in the early days of Sadie's Café. Moreso for Nyah, manager-to-manager, but they'd always been closer. Still, she needed to text him to say hi and check in.

It was Greta's relationships that mattered right now. "You *are* allowed to have more than one friend," Sadie pointed out. "Nyah knows who you are and who Kade really is, like me. And I've managed to have both of you in my life."

"I'm not especially in your life," Greta said flatly.

"You could be." Sadie smiled at her. "I don't know what you and Joanie have been through, but we could build something new."

"You'll take in another troublemaker?"

"Why not?" If this was what it took to get Greta and Joan back together, she'd take one for the team. "We could do a little light boxing, maybe have lunch."

"With Joan? I see through your ploy."

"Joanie doesn't have to be there." *Though I'd love it if she was.*

Rocking back on her heels, Greta said, "I'm keeping a low profile these days."

"Sure. We can—"

"We can box here."

Damn it, she was not letting that part of the equation go.

"You should learn how to take a hit," Greta continued. "I don't mind if you hit me. You'll probably enjoy it."

"I will probably *not* enjoy it."

"You don't want to whale on the person who's caused Joan so much grief?"

"No, I really don't," Sadie answered honestly.

Greta studied her for a long moment.

Perry's voice carried out of the changing room as they exited. "The workout equipment should go. The twins have a much better alternative."

"We like this place," Joan said. "What are you up to? Why are you so interested in storage and getting rid of shit?"

"We should be repurposing this space."

Joanie looked worried. "Are you gonna sell it?"

"No," Perry said. "But it should be used for something worthwhile."

"Mark and I have sentimental attachment to this place." She moved next to Sadie, exuding nervous energy.

Sadie tossed her hand wrap and linked her pinky through Joan's to ground her.

Perry sighed. "I'm not getting rid of it. Just trying to better use it. If you and Mark want to hang on to this decrepit old equipment, fine. Jesus."

"Thank you." Joan laced her fingers through Sadie's. She really liked hanging on to the things that mattered to her.

Like friends.

"Greta and I need this place, too," Sadie said. "She said she doesn't mind if we hit each other."

"What?" Gus barked.

"Boxing," Sadie amended. "With proper protection. Sorry, that sounded bad."

"I thought it was some sort of jealous lovers thing."

"No." She shook her head, catching Joan holding in a laugh. "Nothing like that."

"We just…" Joan cleared her throat. "Sadie's shy about punching someone."

"I'm not shy about it. I just don't like doing it."

"It can be hard the first few times," Gus said. "Then you quickly realize that Villain trying to melt your face is not going to respond to stern words. Perry, where's my water?"

Their elders went to the kitchenette. Joan's mood had seemed to lighten. Maybe Greta's had, too.

Okay, fine. If boxing with Greta was one step toward getting them closer…

"You don't have to do that," Joan said to Sadie. "If you're not comfortable sparring."

With Greta. The words weren't spoken but hung in the air.

Greta withdrew back into her blank stare. "But that could be my good deed for the Superheroes. Surely, they'll let me ride off into the sunset if I'm nice to your girlfriend."

Ugh, she was so frustrating.

"Forget I said anything. Text me when it's done with Nuance."

With that, Greta hastened to the hidden door and slipped out.

Joan pulled free and vigorously started to unwrap her hand. "You don't have to try so hard to get us to make up. This is how it is with us."

Well, Greta was spot on about one thing. She never was right for Joan, and vice versa. Their feelings were too volatile.

"You're still gonna help her, right?" Sadie said.

"Eventually. I have to get to the bottom of this thing."

"She really needs more friends. True friends."

"Too bad she only reaches out when she wants something from them."

She released a slow, calming breath. "Look, I'm annoyed with her, too. But she came to you despite her aversion to Heroes. I think she'd like to—"

"You're too sweet to see that she'll get what she wants and disappear again. I should've known better than to think…" Joan shook her head and snapped off her hand wrap.

"She's still protecting you," Sadie said quietly. "Can't you see that?"

"I'll protect her as much as I can. Don't expect us to hug it out and go back to how things were."

Ugh, now Joan was being frustrating.

CHAPTER 9

Iris's victory at the research lab had encouraged her to move on to the next thing that needed saving. Which was how, on an overcast afternoon a few days later, Joan and Mark found themselves at the edge of a dense forest that had been slated to be cleared for logging.

Ray Jay had alerted them last night that Iris had been spotted atop a tall tree in protest. News cameras, curious onlookers, and a small group of supporters were in the parking lot to the north.

Joan was purposely staying away from all that, making this about a one-on-one with Iris rather than a *Look at Spark and Ice doing the thing* event.

Mark swatted at another buzzing mosquito. "Damn it! Bugs! I hate the outdoors."

He was bothered by nature, but Joan was bothered by everything else. PMS was partially to blame. Sadie had just gotten her period, and the familiar achy swelling and crabbiness meant Joan might actually this month, too. Her super-special DNA gave her firepower plus the joys of irregular menstrual cycles.

There was also whatever Perry and Gus were working on. Why the warehouse? And Greta…Greta-ing. And Sadie trying to force an old friendship that was maybe past its prime. And Sherrelle inconveniently being on vacation at the same time as Otis to the same island in the Caribbean. Joan didn't have her number, and couldn't very well have a private conversation even if she did.

All this in addition to doing her actual job and unexpectedly hopping on a red-eye flight that morning.

"This is the first time it's been just you and me in a long time," Mark noted.

"Since joining the Supers," Joan said.

"I hope that supervision shit ends soon."

"We do work best together."

His phone chimed from his chest pocket. "Forgot to put this bad boy on silent."

"Kade asking for more dating advice?" Joan guessed.

Mark checked the screen. "Yup."

"Kind of sad that he only has *you* to ask for dating advice."

"Hey now. I give excellent advice that I don't follow."

Nyah and Kade had really hit it off. They'd already planned a second date at some gamer tournament. He wanted to make sure he wasn't coming on too strong (not physically—he couldn't help that), but that she knew he liked her. Yesterday, Mark had suggested having lunch delivered to her at the café with a note. It had worked per Sadie reporting how Nyah smiled the whole rest of the day.

Mark swatted at a swarm of tiny gnats. "Can we talk about this later in a climate-controlled indoor space? What's our plan?"

Joan nodded with her chin at the lush, leafy canopy. "Fly up there, try to talk her down by relating to her."

"'Kay. Then what? Are we gonna turn her over to the Ocean-view Supers?"

"We're supposed to, but…"

They shared a look.

"That doesn't feel right," Joan said.

"No. She's done a few bad things, but hell, we did *a lot* of bad things. And she's doing them to make the world a better place. We liked shiny things."

"Yeah, I don't know. Let's play it by ear."

Joan adjusted her gloves, then took a few steps back. Flying into a thick grouping of trees was not ideal. They'd agreed with Ray Jay that having just the two of them was best. Iris would know if she was being ambushed from her keen eyesight.

She blasted up slowly, letting Mark go first to find the best landing spot. She'd have to cut out her flames before then. The fresh air held the slightest hint of impending rain, but nothing that could extinguish fire.

Mark pointed to a makeshift campsite nestled in one of the tallest trees. There was some kind of hammock tent hung between the thick branches and a small temporary platform beside it.

"I don't see her," he said.

"She probably saw us coming and hid."

"Let's land there. She couldn't have gone far."

There was just enough of a clearing between branches that Joan was able to ease up on her flames and drop awkwardly on the padded nylon platform. Mark grabbed her arm to steady her.

"Hey, Iris?" he said, glancing around. "It's Ice and Spark from Vector City."

"We're just here to talk," Joan said.

A slight rustle of leaves to the right, a flash of pale peach and pink.

She readjusted on her hands and knees, Mark wobbling and swearing beside her. Joan raised her voice toward the neighboring tree. "You know about our past. We've been let down by the Supers most of our lives, so we get it. We understand what you're going through."

"Our city's Supers didn't listen to us either," Mark said. "Even when we were trying to do something good, they treated us like shit."

More movement, and then Iris peered beneath some leaves at

them. Her blonde hair was back in a messy braid. "Did my city's Supers send you?" she said.

"We honestly just wanted to talk to you," Joan said somewhat honestly.

"It's so like them to have you take care of their problems." Iris sat on a branch, legs dangling. "What you did with Prowl and Ether was the last straw. Not being allowed to help because they voted against it was totally unforgivable."

Mark's upper lip curled. "They voted against it?"

"Yeah."

"Douchebags."

"They don't care about the world beyond their little bubble. We could've been doing so much to address *real* problems. That's what I'm dedicated to now. This forest is hundreds of years old and home to several semi-endangered species of birds and slugs."

"Ew," Mark murmured.

Joan sat back on her heels. "We're all for that. And for clean drinking water, and slugs to have nice, happy lives. Can you use your visibility and social media for change? I don't want to be all 'violence isn't the answer,' but…"

"I'm a pacifist," Iris stated. "I don't condone violence."

Mark tried to sit back, then decided against it. "Blowing stuff up is kind of violent."

"That's necessary to get results. Nobody will get hurt. I make sure of that. Only the greedy corporations profiting off their workers and the Earth."

Joan risked raising a hand to gesture at her. "We can relate. We only took from big companies and would pay back small businesses that got hit by Super destruction. And yeah, sometimes our destruction. We shelled out a lot of guilt money. We didn't want the little guy to be harmed. We still don't."

Iris tilted her head. "Then why did you join the Superheroes? It sounds like you did more good as Villains."

Hmm. A legit question.

"For the insurance," Mark joked. "No, really, because we like helping people."

"I used to want to help people."

"But threatening to blow up a research lab?" Joan said.

Iris looked into the near distance. "The advocacy group down there followed the rules. Got petitions signed, attended meetings, organized protests. None of it worked. Something drastic will get the attention of the industries decimating our forests."

"What are you gonna do?" Mark said. "Set it on fire?"

She nodded at Joan. "You want to help with that?"

"No," Joan said, taken aback at the suggestion.

"I'm kidding. The trees stay. The logging facility, though…"

A steady breeze blew past, making the pad wiggle. Joan dug her gloved fingers into the nylon while Mark swore some more. "I hate the outdoors," he hissed.

"There's a better way," Joan said to Iris.

Swinging her legs to straddle the branch, Iris said, "Tell me what that is, 'cause I swear I've tried everything. This is the only thing that's gotten results." She made a face. "I'm not a Villain. Villains do bad things for bad reasons. I'm doing the right things for the right reasons."

"I believe you," Joan said, readjusting on her heels. This was such a ridiculous spot to have a heart-to-heart. "Trust me, I can relate. You're trying to do the right thing, but you're going about it the wrong way."

"You don't get it. The Supers don't do the right thing. They don't care."

"The Supers have made a lot of mistakes. They've let people down. But some of us care. There are a lot of people who need us."

"Most people don't care." Iris flung a hand toward the parking lot. "There are norms who don't even think we're human. Fuck them."

"Totally fuck them," Mark said.

They needed a new approach. Iris wasn't buying into the idea that her actions were causing more harm than good.

"What if we help you raise awareness?" Joan suggested. "Rally people to these important causes?"

"Why?" Iris said. "You don't actually want to. You just want me to stop."

"No…"

"Everyone wants me to stop, but I'm just getting started."

Joan raised her eyebrows at Mark for an assist. She was sounding more and more like an old nag. He was relating on a better level.

"Kelsey," he said. "My real name is Mark. This is Joan. We're twins."

"Not like that," Joan said to him.

Iris broke into a smile. "Ha! I knew you were twins. My sidekick owes me twenty bucks." Her smile dimmed. "Er, my former sidekick."

Mark tried to sit, managing a weird squat with one leg extended. "Our parents kicked us out for messing up our small town. When did you leave home?"

"After high school. I could hide my powers pretty well."

"And you decided to become a Super."

"I thought it was the best way for me to do the most good."

Nodding, Mark said, "Makes total sense. We became Villains because we couldn't do anything right. We tried to get out a couple of times, but Joanie set her cubicle on fire at work. And I singlehandedly ruined the walk-in freezer at this culinary school I was attending."

Iris laughed. "How?"

"I was like, 'How cold can this freezer get?' Only I made it so cold that it blew out the power and flash froze everything in it. I think it shorted out the electricity in the whole kitchen."

She laughed harder. Mark was doing a pretty good job on the relating front.

"We had to keep going back to villainy because we couldn't hack it in the real world." He glanced down at the pad. "We opened a food truck last year. That was really cool, no pun intended. It got crushed into oblivion by Smash."

"*The* Smash?" Iris said.

"Hell no. That ass-wad took away my dream. I'd rather be doing that than sitting on this deathtrap trying not to get shit on by some damn bird."

Joan's heart squeezed. *What?*

Iris leaned forward, studying Mark. Her eyes flashed just enough to be noticeable. "Do you like being a Superhero?"

Joan looked at him, too.

Mark shrugged slightly and put on a smile. "Yeah, I like it. I mean, I love it. It's awesome."

Pointing at his hands, Iris said, "You're fidgeting, so you're not telling the truth. And that's a fake smile."

"What's she talking about?" Joan said.

Mark shrugged again and snorted, but yeah, that was not a genuine smile.

"It's not just X-ray vision," Iris said. "I'm really observant, too."

He planted his hands on the pad.

She turned her gaze to Joan. "Your sister's body language is very tense. She's ready to fight at the drop of a hat."

"I fight for what I believe in, like you," Joan said, trying to get this back on track. Though what was up with Mark? "We want the same thing. Can we work together? Find a compromise?"

"I'm done compromising. Especially with Supers." She sprang onto the branch. "You should go now. Unless you want me to livestream how awkward it's gonna be for you to fly out of here."

Mark wobbled to his feet. He looked between Joan and Iris. "So, do we fight, or…?"

"I wouldn't recommend it." Iris hopped onto another sturdy branch. "I know this forest well, and you'll only burn it, or freeze it, or else fall. I don't want you to get hurt. You're actually not that bad." She shook her head, then gestured at Mark. "*You're* not bad." She waved at Joan. "You're just like the others."

Joan stood and planted her feet. "I assure you, I'm not."

"You said what you thought I needed to hear."

"No, I'm serious. You remind me a lot of younger me. I was angry at the world. I did bad things because I felt like I had no other options. Let me help you the way I wish I'd been helped."

Iris bunched a handful of leaves. "I want to believe you."

Joan's phone buzzed against her chest from her inside pocket.

The wayward Super's eyes flashed again. "Is Sadie the redhead on your lock screen? She's texting to check in."

"Wha… How…" *Oh.* Joan rolled her eyes. *X-ray vision.* "Someone who helped me, a lot. Don't do this alone. We can be your allies."

"Maybe I'd trust you more if you were still Villains. But you're here to capture me and get me to submit." Iris pulled herself behind part of the tree trunk. "Go ahead and try. Watch out for the drone."

Joan looked at her palms. She couldn't fly over there, so jump?

She bent her knees and pushed off, almost missing the neighboring branch.

Mark flared shards of ice from his hands, getting whacked by leaves and sticks as he tried to round the tree. "Goddamn nature!"

Iris evaded him, going lower, further into the thick canopy. The buzz of a drone hummed overhead. Joan wanted to move, only Mark had iced everything over and made it a dangerously slick situation.

"I'm kinda stranded here," she told him.

"Where did she go?" Mark landed, then slid off and had to blast up.

A burst of snow covered Joan that she had to blink away.

"This is looking really bad for you," Iris called from afar.

Shit. Joan had to do something, so she shimmied down the trunk to—

"Fuck!" Her fingers slid off the bark and she fell swiftly. No choice but to right herself with fire blasts.

Which of course caught on all the leaves. Which meant she had to fly away from them and ignite more shit.

Mark yelled something that got lost in the crackling. A moment later, ice pellets rained down to douse everything.

Joan dropped into the V between two vertical trunk-branch things, breathing hard. Her heart pounded in frantic alarm. One of her biggest fears was setting off a horrible natural disaster, and she almost did just that.

She searched blindly for Mark. "I have to get out of here," she shouted.

He managed to coast over to her. "Hop on."

She jumped onto his back and held tight as he rushed up and out of the forest. Steamy smoke rose from her near catastrophe.

"Thanks," she said.

"This was not a good place for us," Mark said.

"Somehow I think she knew that."

He deliberately iced the drone following them, then headed for the forest edge.

When they landed on the dirt path, Joan gratefully found her balance. She sucked in a ragged gulp of air, shaking the nerves from her arms and legs.

Mark dusted little pollen balls off his super suit. "That is the last time I try to reason with an opponent instead of fight. It didn't work with Ether and Prowl, and that up there was just a mess."

"I hope we got through to her a little," Joan said. "Maybe she won't be so drastic."

"Or it'll make her more drastic." Mark started down the path.

She joined him, asking, "What was all that about not wanting to be a Super?"

"Nothing. I was trying to get her to trust me."

"But she caught you lying."

"I was trying not to fall off that pad. I thought I was gonna pitch down headfirst. Then who would Kade text about romantic gestures?"

"Me. I have a steady partner who's Nyah's good friend." She held out an arm to halt him. "Do you not want to be a Super?"

"Yeah, no, yeah, of course I want to. I just miss the food truck more than you do, that's all."

That was most definitely not all. "I thought you were happy," Joan said.

"I am. It's fine."

"No, really. What's up with you?"

"I've been…" He dug the toe of his boot into the dirt. "Ah, damn it. It had to come up sooner or later."

"What?"

"I've been talking to our therapist."

"The Super shrink?"

"Yeah." Mark scratched at his nose. "I've had a few sessions or whatever with her. It's been kind of good? Helpful? I have some things to get off my chest."

"Like what? You can always talk to me." Her heart lurched. "Unless it's about me."

"It's mostly past family stuff. Unpacking my rampant abandonment issues. Like, there's no way I can have a stable relationship unless I work through them."

Oh. Oh, wait. He was actually bettering himself. For Zee?

"Okay," Joan said. "It's okay. Why did you think you couldn't tell me? I support everything you do."

Mark rolled his eyes. "You think it's pointless to talk to her."

"It's not pointless. I just get more out of talking to you and Sadie. And Perry to a lesser extent."

And Greta—er, formerly Greta.

"You've always been stronger than me," he said. "You deal with shit. I don't. It's time I start dealing with shit."

"Does Zee have anything to do with this?"

"No." He glanced up, then back to his boots. "Sort of. Indirectly. It started because they're so close to their mom. It brought up a lot of stuff about how I wish I could be close to our parents, but I can't unless I forgive them. I hold a lot of resentment."

Joan hesitated, wanting an answer but also dreading it. "When was the last time you spoke to Mom and Dad?"

"A really long time ago. Around our thirtieth birthday. I was feeling some kind of way, like a tri-life crisis. I called them. It just felt shitty. I may have been very, very stoned, which didn't help."

"It read like their loser son called them while unemployed and high."

"Something like that."

Joan crossed her arms, gripping them to ward off an onslaught of anger. Mark didn't need that right now. He had to work through this without her influence.

"Have you talked to the Super shrink about our parents?" The tentative way he asked meant he wasn't sure how she'd react.

"Not really. She knows how we ended up the way we did. I said I don't want a relationship with them, and we left it at that."

Mark nodded slowly, then nodded again.

"I've always said if you want a relationship with them, that's your choice, and it's fine."

It wasn't altogether fine, but she understood why Mark would want that connection. Or at least closure.

"I get why they felt like they had no other choice," he said. "We kept messing up, and we never told them why."

Joan gave him the stink eye. "'We have superpowers, Mom and Dad. Isn't that great? Everyone will be terrified of us, and you'll be social outcasts in our tiny town.' The anti-Super sentiment must be a thousand times worse there now."

Mark dug his boot into the dirt again. Growing up in a place where people disliked big cities and individualism was not a breeding ground for acceptance. They'd never wanted to come out thanks to all the homophobic slurs the kids at school threw at them.

"They had to know we had powers," he said.

"I'm sure they did. I'm sure they still do. If they all of a sudden want us in their lives because we're the good guys now, I'd…" She bit back what exactly she'd do for Mark's sake, but it involved nasty words and slamming doors in faces.

He didn't resent Joan for getting them kicked out. But did he ever wonder what his life would've been like if she'd had a better grasp on her anger? Maybe he could have made it through culinary school if he hadn't had villainy to fall back on. Maybe he'd be…

Maybe, maybe not. Meeting Perry was what they'd needed. Having him teach them how to focus their powers.

She elbowed his side. "I'm always proud of you."

"Thanks." He elbowed her back. "Can we go indoors? I'm pretty sure I'm allergic to pollen and endangered slugs."

"Yeah."

They started walking. She knew Mark missed Hot and Cold, but hadn't thought it could be rooted in something deeper. Like it'd been another thing taken away from him. Good thing he'd never be rid of her.

"So what does Zee think about your therapizing?" she teased to lighten the mood.

Mark fought a smile. "They think it's…" He scowled. "Whatever. It doesn't matter."

"Yes, it does."

"No, it doesn't. I don't care."

"Right." Joan shoved him toward the grass.

Mark regained his footing. "Enough gross feelings. What are we gonna do about Iris? We're obviously letting her get away."

"Not intentionally."

"Oh, I'm doing it intentionally. That girl just needs someone to listen. I'll keep at it from afar. I think we were bonding."

"I should be the one," Joan said. "It's like looking in the mirror at my twenty-year-old self."

Her brother laughed. "That's exactly why it should be me."

"Fine. But you have to tell Ray Jay."

"Yeah, man, that'd be radical, dude," he said in a fair impression of the laidback Super.

Joan still had to do something. She couldn't stand by and let Iris go down a dark path she couldn't escape. Even if that meant capturing her to protect her from herself.

"Can she still talk to the Super shrink?" Joan said.

"I think that privilege has been revoked."

"Too bad."

CHAPTER 10

Sadie savored the last bite of her turkey sandwich. Joan wiped her mouth with one of the napkins from the holder on the breakfast bar at Super headquarters.

"That was great, sweetheart," Joanie said. "You make a mean sandwich."

"I learned from the best," Sadie said with a smile.

While it wasn't on par with the Harvest Moon they used to serve at Hot and Cold, it was still pretty good. Hopefully a little comfort food for her love after a frustrating attempt at reasoning with Iris yesterday. Joanie had seemed off when she got home late last night, and again this morning.

"I appreciate you bringing me lunch." She gave a small but gorgeous grin. "I'd thank you appropriately later if I could."

"If either of us could." Sadie rolled her eyes. They were both in the throes of their periods, which meant utilizing Joan's warmth as a soothing heating pad rather than anything fun.

Her phone buzzed from her back pocket with an incoming text. Nyah had been instructed to call if there were any problems at work. Texts were being avoided, especially the family group chat about what Carrie could and couldn't eat for Dad's birthday dinner even though it was a week away because of pregnancy tummy troubles. Because—excited as Sadie was to be a cool aunt —her sister was being very extra about everything. At least it was giving Mom new things to worry about instead of all of Sadie's life choices.

Joanie was also avoiding her phone. And TV. And anything that could smack her with the bad press from both failing to capture Iris and from narrowly starting a forest fire.

Mark had destroyed a Badger News Network drone, so he was in the doghouse for that. He'd released a statement saying it was an accident but refused to apologize. It had really been more of a public service than anything else.

Sadie rested her hand on Joan's thigh. "Feeling better, honey?"

"Yeah. I'm just drained and a little sore."

"I can give you a massage tonight. Or right now."

That made her moan. "Oh my god, I would love that. But at home so there are fewer clothes."

"Consider it done."

Joanie took her hand and squeezed it. Then she let go to grab her green-glass bottle of fancy mineral water. When did she turn into a fancy bottled water sort of gal? It was what they stocked here, though Ward would get her whatever she wanted, so…

"Do you ever worry about making that sparkling water bubble over?" Sadie half joked, half genuinely wondered.

"No." Joan's brows scrunched together.

"The minerals don't react to your hot palm?"

"I try not to have hot palms when I handle beverages."

"I know. Just curious."

Sadie snagged a white cheddar puff from the reusable plastic baggie. Joan took a sip, considered the glass bottle, then set it down.

"What do you think the Oceanview Supers are gonna do now?" Sadie said.

"Probably bug the other cities. They were 'totally bummed we didn't get the job done, man.'"

"They know her better than anyone. Why aren't they dealing with it?"

"She knows all their tricks. They need a plan she won't see coming."

"Literally," Sadie laughed.

Joan didn't laugh. She was definitely grumpier than usual today, which was understandable.

Sadie ate another puffy snack. She was pretty grumpy, too—Joan had unintentionally woken her up when she got home—but for everything on her mind, it was way worse for Joanie. A little extra patience was needed on days like this.

"Do you think the forest will be saved?" Sadie asked.

"They'll probably pass on it for now, then go back and clear it when she's occupied with something else."

"That's kind of sad," she said. "But you're probably right."

Joan took a handful of puffs. What would cheer her up?

"Do you think you might stop by open mic night?"

"When is that?"

"Tomorrow night." Sadie gave her a look. "I've been talking about it all week. A few of my friends from college are coming."

"Right, yeah. I think so? I have to work most of the day."

She shimmied her shoulders. "Maybe Spark can make a special guest appearance."

"We keep Spark separate so no one connects her to me." Joan popped a puff into her mouth.

"*I know*," Sadie said, annoyance leaking into her voice. "I would just love it if you could be there."

Joanie's eyebrows knit together like she was sorry for being in a mood. "I promise I'll try," she said, then offered a puff as a peace offering.

Sadie leaned over and took it with her lips, making sure to lick Joanie's fingers long and slow.

A tiny spark flickered in her amber eyes, which made both of them smile.

Mark strolled in wearing an athletic tee and joggers and a

backwards baseball cap. He never wore a hat unless he hadn't spent the night at home, nor had the time to style his hair properly.

"Then you give him dating advice," he said to his phone. "You're the one with the girlfriend."

"I will," an unfamiliar voice said through the speaker.

The hat was from an upscale athleisurewear brand Zee liked to work out in. Oh, yeah. Definitely borrowed.

Mark stepped between the high-backed barstools so Sadie and Joan could see his screen. A brunet white guy about their age sat against a pale gray wall. He had on a T-shirt for the women's professional hockey team in Yanton.

Joan's smile widened. "Trav, hey."

"Hey, Joan. Is that Sadie? Do I finally get to meet her?"

"Hi, yes, who…?" Sadie looked to Joan for introductions.

"This is Blip," she said. "Our buddy Travis. The nicest former Villain you'll ever meet."

"Insert joke about him being Canadian here," Mark said.

Travis chuckled good-naturedly. "I did a lot of work to get to this point. Great to meet you, Sadie. Joan hasn't told me nearly enough about you."

Sadie smiled back. "Nice to meet *you*. You've given these two a lot of support."

"I try, I try." He looked like he could be related to Joan with the wavy dark hair and bright golden-brown eyes.

Mark glanced at the breakfast bar. "You didn't bring me lunch, too?"

Sadie shook her head. "You have a significant other who could bring you lunch."

"Ooh, is it official now?" Travis said.

"No," Mark stated. "Zee never buys me things. It's an area of contention with us."

"Everything is an area of contention with you two."

Joan looked at the screen. "It stems from Mark giving Zee crap for years about how Supers get everything for free. Now Zee doesn't want to... What did they say, Mark? Make you complicit?"

"That makes sense," said Travis.

"*Anyway.*" Mark faced his phone. "You called for a reason that did not involve my personal life."

The Super wrinkled his nose. "Did I though?"

"I don't know. You called me."

"I called both of you," Travis said.

"Sorry," Joan said. "I don't have my phone nearby."

"Well anyway, you've probably seen the news about Dale Terwilliger."

Mark groaned. "That fuckin' guy. He's saying I deliberately wrecked that drone to censor free speech. How was I to know whose drone that was?"

"An assault against Badger News is an assault on America." Travis rolled his eyes and readjusted in his chair. A jagged white scar cut across the top of his forearm. "So, I figured I'd tell you two first. You can tell the others, of course, but I thought I'd start with you."

Joan and Mark leaned forward in tandem.

"Dale Terwilliger used to be my stepbrother."

"Whaaat?" Joan said as Mark went, "Gross."

"Yeah," Travis sighed. "Unfortunately. My mom married his dad when we were kids. His dad had been transferred to Yanton for his job. That's how they ended up here."

"So Mr. America hasn't always been Mr. America?" Joan said.

"No, he was never happy to be here. And he definitely didn't want me in his life, or my mom. He learned about my powers, which was my own doing. I'd blip in and out of his bedroom to scare the crap out of him."

Mark snorted.

"Hey, I was a Villain for a reason. I liked torturing him." Travis shrugged. "He despised me. I'm positive that's where his hatred of the superpowered comes from. Our parents got divorced when I was in high school, which was a good thing for everyone. He moved back to the States. It became his personal crusade to put a stop to people using their abilities."

"That makes sense," Joan said.

"I don't blame him for being angry with me. I was a total bastard. I've tried to make peace with him several times, but he wants no part of it. He says I'm a freak of nature who shouldn't be allowed to roam free." Travis looked down. "I'm so sorry I caused this."

"You can't take responsibility for his actions," Sadie said. "A lot of people don't trust the superpowered. Or are afraid because you're different."

"Yeah," Mark agreed. "He's one of many voices."

Travis shook his head. "But he's the loudest one. And listen, I didn't call to give you a sob story. I'm making amends every day, like you."

"Are you worried he'll expose your true identity?" Joan said.

"I was, but then it dawned on me that he's scared people will find out about our connection. Even though we're not related, it would reflect badly on him. His dad's got some political clout, and it would be a stain on him, too. That's a big part of this. To get back at me, sure, but also political connections. He's using his platform to grow his career."

"Of course he is." Mark shifted his weight onto one foot. "Serious question. What does a political pundit actually do?"

"Talk a lot but not actually do anything."

"No, he wants to do something," Joan said. "He's got plans."

Sadie met her gaze. *Like stealing sensitive information.*

"Wait a minute." Mark's eyes grew wide. "Your name is Travis Terwilliger?"

Travis made a face. "No. I have my dad's last name."

"Thank god."

"I've gotten word that the Citizens for Human Power are trying to access the technology that suppresses our powers," Joan said. "I don't think they've been successful, but…"

"That doesn't surprise me." Travis's mouth set in a grim line. "They would love to get their hands on that."

"Can we stop them? Do you have any ideas on how?"

"For starters, don't publicly involve me. That'll only make it worse with Dale."

"Sure."

"Like I said, this is largely about his political aspirations," Travis said. "The more power he gets, the more it fuels him. Take away his influence, and—"

"Ruin his reputation," Mark said.

Nodding, Travis said, "That's what would stop him."

"But it won't stop the movement." The words left Sadie's mouth before she could soften them. "They're louder every day. Dale Terwilliger may not care if he hurts people born with powers, but a lot of jerks out there do."

Joan gestured at Mark. "We could get the word out that the Citizens are doing shady shit. Make the public distrust them. I think we could get Destine on board with that."

She quickly briefed Travis on what Nuance was doing with the Citizens, which he tried very hard not to laugh at.

"Have you talked to Nuance yet?" Mark said.

"I haven't had the chance. I still need to connect with Aura." Joan did a visual sweep of the kitchen, then leaned closer to Mark's phone. "There's a sensitive matter connected to this. An old associate."

Travis nodded and didn't say anything. It went silent for several beats. The former Villains had secrets best left in the past.

"Once I have that matter resolved, we can make a plan."

"I'm on board," Travis said. He did his own visual sweep. "To be honest, I've had a hard time getting my coworkers involved. If I tell them the Citizens are actively trying to suppress our powers, that could be a game changer."

Sadie tilted her head to better see Joan. "You could just talk to Nuance."

"Aura knows us. She can vouch for me and Mark."

"But this is pretty important to you and…" She rolled her hands. "That old associate."

"I'll get it done." Joan shot her an irritated look.

"But if you can't reach Aura—"

"When did you become my ex's number one fan?" she snapped. "I will do this the way I want to do it."

Sadie blinked and sat back. Joan had never spoken to her like that.

"I'm worried about *you*," Sadie stated. "And how this situation affects you. It's been weighing on you, and I know you're concerned. It's obviously put you in a bad mood."

Joan huffed and closed her eyes. "I've got a handle on it," she said slowly, measured.

"Sorry for trying to contribute," Sadie grumbled. "The thing you say I can always do."

Mark cringed and darted a glance between them. "This is getting awkward."

She crossed her arms and slouched deeper on the barstool. Joan tensed up like she was about to burst into flame, which was a real possibility.

Travis started talking to someone off camera. "Really? Color me unsurprised. I'll be there in a minute." Back to his phone, he said, "Ray from Oceanview wants to talk to me."

"Shocking," Mark drawled.

"I guess I'll see what they want me to do. I don't blip in and out of treetops very well."

"You do you, but take it easy on Iris. She's an angry kid."

Sobering, Travis said, "I'd feel bad for her if she wasn't going about things like this."

"She responded to me listening to her," Mark said. "She wants validation without Superhero clichés."

He took the conversation out of the kitchen and toward the lobby.

The sudden quiet hung thick in the air. Stressed or not, they shouldn't be taking it out on each other. But Joan was telling Sadie to butt out. Joan, who'd made her a part of the team, who'd said Sadie was welcome to voice her opinion and point of view, to be listened to and respected.

Was being a Superhero changing her?

Joan exhaled a long breath. "If I go to Nuance, I run the risk of exposing Greta. And exposing the extent of her connection to me and Mark. It could go south fast."

"So you *are* protecting her."

"Of course I am. And me and you and everyone I care about. I'm still not trusted. Who's to say this isn't some conspiracy to make Mark and I examples of why people with powers are the worst?"

"That's a lot of pressure to put on yourself." Sadie rotated her stool to face Joan. "And kind of a wild theory."

"Look what the norms are doing to Mark about the drone. And me for that small fire, which yeah, that was actually bad. But they'll find any other excuse to make us look bad."

"Okay." Her heart lurched. Now it was becoming clearer. "I understand. I was just hoping you could resolve it, but it's more complicated than that."

"It's a lot," Joan said.

Sadie grabbed the mostly empty bag of puffs and re-sealed it. "I'll let you get back to it."

"You don't have to go."

"I have a lot to do, too." And she was a little miffed at being snapped at. It stung.

"Okay." Joan slid off her seat.

The energy was weird between them. Sadie usually felt more comfortable around Joanie than anyone, so it was doubly…just… off.

"I *will* talk to Sherrelle," Joan said, tucking her hands in her back pockets. "Otis is due back tomorrow, so she should be home by then. Maybe even tonight. I'll get it done, I swear."

Sadie nodded and managed an "Mm-hmm." She couldn't

imagine the stress Joanie was under, so saying less was less chance of saying the wrong thing.

She gathered the containers into her insulated bag, pulse thudding erratically. Her cheeks were probably as red as her nails, but a brisk walk to Sadie's Café would burn off her excess tension. If she booked it, it'd take twenty minutes. If she strolled, closer to a half-hour.

Zee stepped in from the back stairs dressed for a workout. They glanced around. "I don't suppose you've seen your brother?"

"He's talking to Trav." Joan feebly gestured in the opposite direction.

They smirked. "We're supposed to be going to the youth center in a half an hour. I can get there fast, but it'll take him that long just to find his gloves."

Sadie zipped her lunch bag, grateful to have left her heavy commuter bag at work.

"Is everything okay?" Zee asked.

"I need to get to the café," she said. "Have fun at the youth center."

Joan took a tentative step toward her as Sadie headed across the room. "See you later?"

We do live together. "I'll be home after closing."

That seemed to bother her based on the way Joan's eyes narrowed.

"You deal with your important matters, and I'll deal with mine."

That bothered her more based on how her mouth twisted.

Sadie clomped out of the kitchen. Definitely a twenty-minute walk today.

CHAPTER 11

Joan was fairly miserable. A stomach churning, heart aching, in need of a hug level of miserable. She sat in the backseat of one of the SUVs as Ward drove her and Kade around downtown, waiting for any Saturday afternoon distress calls to come in.

Kade prattled animatedly, a beaming ray of sunshine next to her. He had zero focus today unless it had to do with Nyah and how fascinated he was by her and her passion for video games.

"Now, you'd think *Sea Voyage Five* is the fifth game in the series, but the five refers to the crew of five beings sent on the voyage. The game is actually the eighth in the *Sea Voyage* series. That's special because of OchoStrike. Octopuses have eight arms, and…"

Joan refreshed SuperWatch on her phone. Not that she was staring at the device in the vain hope of getting a text from Sadie. She *hated* that they'd had that little tiff yesterday. She respected Sadie more than any person on the planet, and it sucked that she was feeling so put out.

Of course Sadie was entitled to her feelings, but so was Joan. And Joan didn't do feelings as well as action. She'd called the Destine headquarters last night only to be told by Sherrelle's new sidekick that she wouldn't be back until after Joan had to report to patrol.

Climbing into bed and not getting an automatic Sadie snuggle had been *the worst*. The mattress between them had felt like a cavern. Joan had to scooch in and gently wrap around Sadie, kiss her cheek, tell her she loved her and she was sorry. Sadie'd said the same, tugged Joan closer, and they'd drifted off, connected physically but not in that deeply emotional way Joan craved.

Maybe she should ask the Super shrink for some tips on how to better deal with stress. Or she could ask Mark to ask her.

No, that was a cop-out. And she owed it to Sadie to work on her issues with feelings and junk.

There were so many moving parts to her life these days. So many people and things to take care of. Villainy had prepared her for high stress with low stakes. What to do when the outcome was much more than *Oh well, the Supers thwarted us from borrowing the Vultures' championship trophy from 1987.*

Showing up at open mic night would be a good olive branch. Hopefully, it was a quiet day in Vector City and she could get over to the Village to show her support.

"...but when OchoStrike discovers he can tolerate being on dry land with the special helmet created by Doctor—"

"I know, buddy," Joan said. "I've played it."

"Oh. Okay." Kade went quiet, drumming his gloved fingertips on his thick black spandex thighs, a private smile playing about his lips. "We decided for our next date, we'd do something I like. I like going to the movies, so we're gonna do that." He considered something. "I think that's why I like video games. They're little movies."

"We're getting something on SuperWatch," Joan said, and sat up straight. "No, wait. It's an update on Iris. She left the forest to avoid being captured, but the activists..." She scrolled down to a picture of what had to be hundreds of protestors surrounding the parking lot and road. "Man, they showed up."

Kade leaned over to check it out. "Wow. That's a lot of people."

Hopefully, her peaceful protest had rallied the treehugging troops and not her threats. The Citizens for Assholism had been raging about Iris's interference with necessary industry. Yet another way a Super was creating mess.

Ward slowed down, then whipped into a parking space. "I think there's something going on over there."

A discount furniture store had what looked like a small truckload of plastic-wrapped sectional couch pieces sitting on the sidewalk. Four people in matching black knit short-sleeved polos argued and gestured at them and the double doors.

"Nyah was just saying she wants a new couch," Kade said, then sighed dreamily.

"Don't think you'll get a freebie," Joan warned him.

"I won't." He cleared his throat, then put on a roguish grin. "Let's go save the day, Spark," he thundered in his Lunk voice.

They exited the SUV to angry bickering. A middle-aged white woman with stringy hair pointed at the two-wheeled dolly a young white guy was holding on to. "Do you expect that to fit any of these? Use your head."

"Excuse me, madam," Kade-as-Lunk said. "Do you need assistance?"

The two other store employees did double-takes.

The young guy said, "Dude, you're…"

"That's right, citizen. We are Lunk and Spark, and we're here to help." Kade set his fists on his hips in a classic Superhero pose.

The woman narrowed her eyes. "We don't need help from *you*," she stated, acid in her tone.

He blinked, unsure how to react.

Joan nodded at the young guy staring at her. His plastic gold nametag read *Kevin*. "What seems to be the trouble?"

"Uh…" Kevin jutted his chin at the furniture. "We got a delivery, but there was an, um, disagreement about the delivery fee."

"Those men were trying to rip me off," the woman snarled.

"Then they just dropped these here and left. Can't get good help anywhere these days."

Behind her, the other two employees' faces said *You're the problem, lady.*

"I can get that." Kade went over to one of the wrapped couch sections and picked it up.

The woman waved her arms like signaling to an airplane. "Put that down! You have no right to touch my property!"

"Whoa, hang on." Joan held up a hand. "He can carry these for you no problem."

Angry Waving Woman turned on her. "Don't point your dangerous hands at me. You're trespassing. We have rights under the No Superpowered Activity clause."

"The what?" Kade said from behind the couch.

"The rider prohibiting superpowers from being used on the premises."

That fuckin' thing.

"Okay." Joan made a show out of lowering both hands. "We're literally just trying to help."

Kevin made a pained expression as if to telegraph *I'm not down with my employer.* "Lunk is really strong."

Kade took a few steps toward the entrance. "I can have these inside in a jiffy."

"*Put that down,*" the woman seethed.

"Are you sure?"

One of the employees—a brown-skinned man with a short ponytail—said, "Yeah, you should probably not go inside."

"I'll have you arrested," Angry Waving Woman said.

Kade squatted to set it down.

"Not there! You're blocking the sidewalk!"

Joan looked up and down the sidewalk. The pile of furniture was actually blocking it.

Kade started to straighten, but lost his balance.

She watched in slow motion as he tottered back and forth, bumped into one of the other couch pieces, bounced off it…

…and slammed through a large picture window.

"Noooo!" the woman screamed.

Fuck. Fuck fuck fuck.

Joan scrambled to do something. Kade had shattered a display of lamps and crushed a coffee table. The wrapped sectional piece rolled on top of a similar couch inside.

He sat up, shaking his head. "Sorry."

The woman raged at him with insults about his size outweighing his intellect. Her employees moved back, Kevin gripping the dolly in front of him like a shield.

Ward ran up beside Joan. "Oh no," he breathed.

Kade stood from the debris. Feathers from a ripped throw pillow fluttered around him. "I'm very sorry," he said.

Angry Waving Woman gesticulated wildly. "You destroyed my property! This is exactly why we shouldn't let you people roam free!"

The commotion had attracted a crowd. Cellphone cameras captured the scene. This was some very bad optics they did not need right now.

Joan approached the woman as gently as she could. "Ma'am, if you can give him some space to step out—"

"Get out now, you oaf!" She waved at the crowd. "Don't just stand there. Call the police!"

"We're usually who people call," Kade said.

Joan made a subtle slashing motion across her chest 'cause that was not the right thing to say. Then she focused on the irate woman. "We can help you clean up. I'll make sure you get full reimbursement and then some for your losses."

She glared at Joan, disgust curling her upper lip. "I wouldn't trust a word that comes out of your mouth." She pointed an accusatory finger. "You may have fooled everyone else with your Hero act, but a leopard can't change its spots."

Her own anger was mounting rapidly, but Joan had to keep from sparking. She blew out a frustrated rush of air. "Fine, you don't have to believe me. But file a claim on SuperWatch. Ward can help you."

She gestured for their sidekick.

He approached with a somber expression and his tablet. "On behalf of Vector City and its dedicated Superheroes, I want to first express my sincerest apologies."

Ward went through his spiel as Kade stepped out of the gaping hole in the building. Joan brushed a few feathers off his shoulder.

"She told me to put it down," he said.

"You shouldn't have grabbed it without permission," Joan said.

"Why wouldn't someone want our help?"

She looked back and forth at the shattered window.

"Oh."

The crowd around them felt too close. What she wouldn't give to blast into the air and escape. But she had to keep her nose clean and salvage the situation as best as they could.

Angry Waving Woman had taken to angrily waving at Ward, so Joan stepped beside him. "I promise you'll have the money by this evening. I'll personally deliver a check if you want."

"That's the last thing I want," the woman spat.

"Then Ward will bring it by, or do a direct deposit. Just give us the dollar amount."

Ward raised his tablet, poised to type.

"You think you can throw money at the problems you create, and that makes it all better." Angry Waving Woman indicated the broken window. "You're a scourge on decent society. I'm ashamed to live in this city. *You* are what make it a dangerous place to live."

"Daaaaamn," someone in the crowd said.

The words were meant to hurt, and yeah, they weren't entirely wrong, but they hit too close for comfort. Joan forced her hands to unclench.

Don't spark. Do not spark right now.

Ward took a step forward. "I can get you the payment, ma'am."

Tiny sparks flickered from Joan's fingertips. She turned away from the scene and shook her hands to get rid of them. If she were alone, or still a Villain, she'd one hundred percent fly out of there.

Shrugging at the employees, Kade said, "I was trying to help."

An elderly Black couple exited the store, looking rather vexed. "That was very rude, young man," the mister said.

"Very rude," the missus agreed.

"I was just trying to help," Kade murmured, more upset this time.

The mister shook his head as he passed. The missus bopped Kade with her boxy handbag.

"Ouch." He rubbed his arm, even though he couldn't have felt the impact. At least physically.

"Come on." Joan headed toward the SUV. At this point, the only thing they could do was—

"Look at Spark's eyes," a singsong-y voice said.

"Do you think she'll shoot fire out of them?" a similar voice added.

"That would be freaky," a third voice chimed in.

Muttered statements rippled through the crowd as it parted. A red haze was starting to cover everything Joan looked at. Her fire was definitely backing up, but better that than the alternative.

Kade shuffled behind her, saying "Sorry" every time he bumped someone.

Through the heated fog, her gaze crossed paths with a dark-haired woman's. "Just apologize sincerely," she said to Joan. "That's all we really want."

Joan paused, giving the woman her full attention. "I am truly sorry for all the damage I've created."

The woman nodded in acknowledgment. "Thank you."

Joan and Kade climbed into the backseat, locking their respective doors. The tinted windows gave them needed protection from prying eyes and a chance for her to quite literally chill out.

Yes, she threw money at problems, but at least she was doing something. And getting the other Supers to do it more.

She shook her head, suppressing the blaze roiling inside. *No good deed goes unpunished.*

"Women usually like me," Kade said. "Why was she being so mean?"

"You busted up her property. And she already didn't like people with powers."

"This looks bad, doesn't it?"

"Pretty bad, yeah."

Kade bounced his fists off his thighs. "Shoot. What's Nyah gonna think?"

"She's pretty understanding. If you explain what happened, it'll be okay."

"But I've been working on my balance so stuff like this doesn't happen." Frustration creased the skin between his eyebrows. "I'm trying, dang it. No, *damn it*. I did it again."

He punched the seat in front of him, making it shudder and popping the headrest up.

"Damn it!"

He banged his fists together. He was really mad. Like, mad in a way Joan rarely saw.

"Just a big, dumb Lunk," he muttered to himself.

"It's okay," Joan soothed.

"No, it's not. I'm Lunk. That's what I do. I lunk around." He crossed his arms. "I hate that name. I hate it." His eyes squeezed shut. "I hate my Superhero name!"

Joan tried to form words, but didn't really know what to say.

"I didn't even pick it. That's what everyone's always called me. The big lunk who breaks stuff, who knocks into everything. I wanted to pick a better name. I wanted to be the Strong Man. Wouldn't that have been cool?" He flexed his biceps. "The Strong Man."

"That would have been cool," Joan said for his benefit.

"But noooo, I'm *Lunk*. Ugh."

"Could, um... You could change it if you really want."

He shook his head vigorously. "Nobody gets names right when you change them. *The* Smash. Big Quake going by just Quake. People treat me like I'm not smart, but I always get someone's name right."

He was such a big softy, it hurt Joan's heart. "You know what? If you want to be the Strong Man, I'll call you the Strong Man. And you know Mark will. All our Supers will."

"It's not worth it," Kade said.

"Then you'll keep being the finest Lunk I've ever known."

He gave her a tiny smile. "Thanks, Joan."

"And you are smart. And kind. You're really kind." She shifted on the bench seat. "If the public knew how damn nice you are, they'd probably like you even more than they already do."

They quieted, watching the crowd dissipate and go back to their afternoon activities. Poor Ward was still getting an earful from Angry Waving Woman. Padma was not going to be happy about this bad press. What could they do to soften the blow?

She considered Kade staring morosely out his window. He was by no means a super genius, and she'd taken advantage of that more times than could be counted. That was generally Lunk's reputation, both with the norms and the superpowered. But that was from looking at his actions, not the kind of guy he really was.

Her breath caught.

That was what everyone did with her. Spark, who had the frightening fire ability.

Supers were looked at for what they did, not for who they were. No one knew about the code Spark, Ice and Breeze had to not rip off the little guy and help out where they could.

That had to change.

"Maybe it's time for people to get to know me," she thought aloud.

Kade turned to her. "Huh?"

"We should let the norms in a little more. Talk about things we *really* like, not carefully orchestrated photo ops. Be sincere."

"Like how Zee goes to the LGBTQIA+ youth center?" Kade said. "And Darlene reads to kids in schools?"

"Exactly stuff like that." For some reason, the idea didn't scare her as much as she thought it would. "I know a lot about art, and security systems. And fire, obviously."

"I like music and movies. Oh, Nyah and I should go to a concert. I like concerts, but I don't go to many because I'm so big, I block people's views."

They huddled closer in excitement. Today had been a total fuck-up, but something good was gonna come out of it.

Joan smiled and said, "Let's show the norms how human we really are."

CHAPTER 12

Sadie was still riding an emotional roller coaster by the time Monday's meeting with Perry rolled around. Stinging from a rare squabble with Joan, then feeling terrible for her and Kade, then to understanding and support for Joanie having to deal with that situation, then total elation at how well open mic night had gone.

It was hard to celebrate personal success when Joanie was struggling, but Joan had insisted she had a handle on things and was happy for Sadie. She'd been at Superhero HQ all weekend, which hadn't stopped her from texting Sadie funny GIFs and little love notes that Sadie sent in return.

Joanie really was trying, and that meant a lot.

As she poured Perry's Brazilian blend into a ceramic mug, Sadie caught him staring at the new pieces of art arranged by her and Gus along the back wall. "No Gus this week?" she said.

Perry glanced over his shoulder. "She had her fill of the city and wanted to get home."

"One of these days, I'd love to visit her there. It sounds so peaceful and nature-y."

The smirk toying at his lips said it was that way because Gus never had visitors. Especially not the whirlwind that came with the Malone twins and Sadie.

"Point taken," she laughed.

Cam sidled up beside her in a yellow knit hat. He'd picked the music today—some very deep cuts of seventies glam rock. "Can I carry that over for you?" he murmured.

"I've got it, thanks." She shook her head at him.

He harrumphed out a sad sigh. The power of Perry's handsome, grumpy nature was like catnip.

Estelle hurried through the door with a bag from the burger place a few blocks away. "It took *forever* to get served, oh my god. And my cousin was a few minutes late, and the whole thing was a poop show. I got back as fast as I could."

Sadie bit back *Remember when you promised to be back from lunch on time because I told Nyah to take the afternoon off?*

"I'm just dropping this in the back and I'll be right there."

"Did you get a chance to eat?" Sadie asked.

"A little, yeah, I'm fine!" Estelle called as she trotted by.

Sadie closed her eyes. Nyah'd had to write Estelle up last week for being an hour late without notice. She really didn't want to lose an otherwise good employee, but this was becoming a problem.

Perry approached the counter, making Cam whimper. "Should we start our meeting?"

"Yes, daddy," Cam whispered.

Sadie gently pushed past him to prevent Cam from drooling all over the counter. "Sure thing. I can't wait to give you all the good news from open mic night."

Estelle brushed the Progress Pride flag to the side just as they reached it. "Ready to go, boss," she said with a smile.

"Estelle." Sadie used her sternest tone.

"I know I know I knooowww. I'll bring my lunch the rest of the week."

"I want you to go out for lunch and take a break from here. Just be mindful of the time."

"I will, I swear, I promise." She sailed behind the counter. "I'll do better. I'm sorry."

Sadie heaved a heavy breath and headed for her office. "It's so weird being the one who has to discipline a young employee for things I used to do. I was not always punctual."

"Now you see how it was for management," Perry said. He moved to set his laptop bag on the desk, realized there was no space due to the security camera monitor and piles of paper, and set it on the floor.

"Funny how your perspective shifts with age and responsibility." She handed Perry the coffee mug and dropped into the desk chair. "On the flip side, I can see the results of how awesome it went on Saturday."

"Before we get to that…" Perry closed the office door, making the space even more confined. "What is this campaign Joan started with telling people how we reimbursed the norms?"

"Oh. That." Sadie's fingers stilled on the reports she'd happily printed for his perusal. "Padma—y'know, their handler—demanded two separate emergency damage control meetings. One for Joanie and Kade on Saturday, and then one for all the Supers yesterday. Joan convinced her that she's willing to embrace the spotlight as long as she can relate on a more genuine level."

"By dragging me into it?" Perry said as he sat in the other chair.

"She wants people to know Mark did a lot of good things, too. You're included by default, I guess."

"We never did those things for the attention. We did them because the Supers didn't."

"She's a Super now," Sadie pointed out. "She wants to actually do the things they always should have done. I think it's great. She's finally taking credit. It'll help the norms see her in a less scary light. That means a lot to her."

She handed Perry his stapled bunch of papers. "So anyway, open mic night went better than I could've dreamed. It was packed. At first I thought it was just my friends and Rosalind's theater friends, but there were a lot of people who showed up to support local talent *and* a local business. Isn't that great?"

Perry looked like he wanted to keep talking about Joan and the Supers, but he focused on the dollars and cents. Which prickled Sadie's skin. This was their time to discuss the café. She'd be happy to chat all about Joanie and the Supers after they were done, but business before pleasure during business hours at their place of business.

"One of the folks who showed up is interested in picking up a few hours for part-time evening help. We vibed right away. I could bring them on Friday nights and for trivia and open mic and other special nights where we'll need extra hands."

Perry flipped between two pages. "Friday evenings have been the least profitable."

"Yeah, but I don't like working them. I'm always really tired, and it might actually give me and Joanie a date night before I have to work every Sunday for the foreseeable future. Oh, they were open to working Sundays, or every other Sunday, or something like that. I totally forgot they said that." She touched the row of important sticky notes beside her laptop.

"Bringing on another paid employee when you're not sure what Sundays are going to be like..."

Now her prickles were growing into full-on irritation. "I don't want to overtax my current staff. I promised Ny she doesn't have to work them because she's committed to Saturdays. This is the right next step."

She paused, letting her words speak for themselves.

Whoa, she never did that. She hadn't even said it like "I think" or "Maybe." Just a statement. What she wanted for *her* business.

"I always value your advice, Per," she said. "You've said several times that this is my business. This is my decision."

Tiny movement bobbed at one corner of his mouth. "You're right. It's ultimately your decision. You have to deal with the consequences if it doesn't work."

"I will." She couldn't help smiling and adding, "But it's going to work."

A knock sounded through the door. She resisted the urge to

whip it open and declare to whoever was on the other side *I am a badass business owner making badass business decisions!*

It took her a second to register Amit standing there—her old boss in her new workplace. His black curls had been cropped in the Summer of Short Haircuts.

"Your employees sent me back here," he said. "That's not very safe."

"They've met you a few times." She gave him a quick hug. "Did you read my mind? I was just thinking it's been forever since I saw you."

"I sent you a text."

Sadie touched the back pocket of her lavender pants. (They went well with her black café T-shirt.) "I was charging my..." She glanced at her phone sitting on the far corner of the desk, charger sitting next to it. "Shoot, I got distracted, and my phone was *dead* dead."

As she went about plugging it in, Amit and Perry shared a chin nod. Had they met before? Probably at some point, but she made quick reintroductions.

There was barely room for the three of them comfortably, but Amit scooted in like he wanted privacy. "Nyah's not here?"

"She's got the afternoon off. We have a mutual friend who didn't have a great weekend, and..." Sadie glanced at both men. "Wait, I'm in the right company. She and Lunk have been spending time together."

Amit perked up. "Time together? Like..."

He was so nosy.

"Like dates, yes," Sadie said. "He's feeling kind of blue with that window situation, so Nyah's letting him meet her aunt to cheer him up. I think they're having a picnic."

Perry glared at Amit in his suspicious way. "Another norm who knows?"

"Yeah, but he figured it out a long time ago."

He muttered in Portuguese.

"Meeting the aunt, huh?" Amit said like secret identities were no big deal.

"I know," Sadie said. "They really like each other."

"Can we…" Amit leaned away from the door as he swung it closed. "I was interviewed this morning by a reporter from the *Chronicle* about Spark, Ice and Breeze paying for damage to Vector City Coffee."

"Really? Why now?"

"Spark mentioned it in a piece they're doing about reformed Supervillains. Which is her and Ice."

Perry grumbled into his coffee.

Sadie glanced at where he'd backed his chair into the corner. "I'm sure they'd want to interview you too, but you'd turn them down."

"I'm not reformed, just retired," he said.

She let that go. If that was how he chose to look at it, so be it.

"I told them the basics," Amit said. "The anonymous deposit, then finding out it had been from them. Being grateful because the Supers never did squat."

"No names?" Sadie said. "As in, not mentioning me?"

"I kept it vague."

"Thanks."

"I threw in the suggestion that they'd done the same for other businesses."

"That's great. Thank you." Sadie scooted the desk chair in to give herself more room. "Joan will appreciate that, too. She's trying to be more authentic in her public interactions."

"I thought you'd like to know." Amit glanced at his watch. "I was hoping to check in with Nyah."

"About zombies or whatever dystopian game you're playing together?"

"It's high fantasy. The dark elves are casting nasty spells."

Perry made a *What the hell are you talking about?* face.

"I could use your expertise." Sadie reached for her copy of last week's numbers. "Perry and I were just discussing—"

Another knock sounded on the door.

"Now what?" She danced in a circle with Amit to get to it.

Joanie's lovely face greeted her. "Hey, am I interrupting your— Oh hey, Amit. It's been a while."

"Joan," Amit said.

"How are you? How's Vector City Coffee?"

"Good, good."

"Nice." Joan caught sight of Perry in the corner, then smiled at Sadie. "I texted about an hour ago. I've got leftover bagels from our weekly meeting for you two."

Sadie accepted the brown paper bag. "Oh, thanks, babe. My phone died."

"There's an asiago cheese bagel that's really good with the chive shmear."

Joan tried to get in, but there definitely wasn't room for all of them now. She'd dressed in a hurry that morning but still managed to be delectable in her skinny olive-green pants and white short-sleeved button-down. Her sunglasses were nestled on top of her head.

Perry groused under his breath about people stopping by whenever they felt like it.

Sadie laughed and said, "Welcome to my world. I expect Mark to pop in next."

Joan gave a little cringe. "What if I told you he's parking the car?"

"I wouldn't be surprised."

She chuckled. "No, it's just me. I can't stay. Just wanted to drop off the bagels and say hi."

Sadie smoothed her fingers across Joanie's hip. "Hi."

"I came by to tell Sadie I got interviewed," Amit said. "Some feature the *Chronicle* is doing about…"

He muttered in Joan's ear. She nodded and said, "Thanks, man. Appreciate it."

Amit gave her a conspiratorial look like he was a part of Team Super. "Is this to combat the backlash from…" He mouthed *Iris?*

"Maybe a little."

There had been no Iris sightings for a few days. Her popularity with grassroots organizations was growing, so it was only a matter of time before she made her next socially conscious stand.

Joan focused on Sadie. "I've got something else that'll make you happy."

"Ooh, what?" *Secret pastries in the bag?*

Her eyes darted to Amit. "I finally spoke to Sherrelle."

"Finally," Sadie said. Information from Aura at last. "What did she say?"

"I guess she never got my message from the other night. New assistant in training."

Which meant new sidekick.

"But she was aware of the situation and didn't think there was cause for concern."

"That's good news," Sadie said.

Joan clearly wanted to say more, but not in Amit's presence.

Wiggling the bagel bag, Sadie said, "I need a plate and stuff for this. Joanie, can you help me?"

"Of course."

"And then all four of us can go over last week's numbers and talk about my exciting plans. Amit, take a look at those reports." She gestured with her chin at the desk. "Tell me your thoughts about how we're poised to be open on Sundays."

Her old boss raised his thick eyebrows and snagged the papers. He was curious enough to be interested and could also give good feedback as a longtime coffeehouse manager.

Once they were alone by the shelves of dessert plates and mugs, Sadie set the bag down. "What did Sherrelle really say?" she murmured.

Joanie stood close to her side. "As far as she knows, Nuance got asked to reach out to Greta because she's the best."

"Wait, people outside of Vector City know her?"

"In my old social circles, everyone knows about her. Sherrelle and I agreed they wanted the best, so they sought out the best.

The Citizens couldn't go directly to her, to cover their asses. So they went through who they thought was a good intermediary."

"Who's actually a Superhero," Sadie said.

"Yeah. So all in all, good news. I texted Grets. She gave it a thumbs-up, which means message received."

She turned to face Joanie. "Did your friendship with Greta come up?"

"It did," Joan said with a smirk. "You can't lie to Sherrelle. But she understood. I said I'd help in any way to keep the Citizens from gaining access to things."

Sadie nodded.

"She said she'd let me know if she hears anything different."

"I'm so glad." She touched Joanie's chest. "You must be so relieved."

"It's definitely a load off my back."

"You look like it."

Her whole body seemed lighter and brighter.

"Aren't you glad you *finally* talked to her?" Sadie couldn't help teasing.

"Yeah, yeah." Joan rested her forearms across Sadie's shoulders. "I'm happier than I've been in a while."

"I love that." Sadie tugged on Joan's shirt, bringing her closer. They didn't canoodle during business hours, but shameless flirting was okay.

"I have to finish up a few reports and claim requests, but then I'm done for the day." She slid her palm over Sadie's ponytail. "I want to make us a special dinner. Well, I want to nap, but then make an awesome dinner. We have a bunch of ripe tomatoes and peppers on the balcony."

"That sounds perfect. I can be out of here pretty early."

Joan drew her into a tight hug, enveloping her in warmth and the faint hint of citrus body wash.

Sadie smiled against her. Ah, there it was. The connection that seemed to be missing lately. She squeezed extra tight, telling Joanie that their love was strong. That they were strong.

"Would you like me to make you a little off-the-menu Kick Me Up before you go?" Sadie said.

"I mean, if you insist..."

"Just don't tell Amit. It's a proprietary beverage at VCC, even though I created it for them."

"It's not on your menu. You just happen to have the ingredients to make it for your needy but very grateful girlfriend."

Sadie glanced around to make sure they were alone, then gave Joan a quick kiss. "Love you," she murmured.

"Love you too, sweetheart."

They parted to head back to the office. Lord knew what Perry and Amit were discussing.

Her heart thrummed merrily, and Joanie gave that sexy-as-hell grin of hers, and Sadie's Café was rocking, and she was positively bursting from how well everything was going for both of them.

Joan's phone buzzed in her front pants pocket. She pulled it out, her smile evaporating as she halted her steps.

"What is it?" Sadie said.

"It's Sherrelle. I gave her my number in case... She texted me and Otis that we need to talk ASAP."

"Oh, no."

Another text buzzed onto her screen. Joan swore under her breath. "I have to go. I'm sorry."

Sadie shook her head before Joan even finished saying the words. "Go. Of course."

Perry had made his way to the office doorway. He'd also shifted into Super Mode. "Do you need me to go with you?"

"No, stay for your meeting," Joan said. "That's important."

A look passed between them. Sadie somehow felt it was also directed at her, like Joanie was asking him to stay just in case.

"Is everything okay?" Sadie said, starting to get worried now.

"It's fine. I like to know you..." Joan's mouth twisted. "Old habit. I just like knowing you're safe."

Seriously, what was going on?

Joan strode into the front, Sadie following close behind.

Cam spotted her and said, "Hey Joan, did you see today's random fact? Did you know there were that many cars in the river?"

"That's wild," Joan said, though her focus was straight ahead. At the door, she shoved her sunglasses on. "I still want to make us dinner." Her voice gave away how unlikely that would be.

Sadie smiled in understanding. "Dinner can wait, babe."

Joan squeezed her hand and headed out.

Her heart tapped in an unsteady rhythm—concern for her love, concern for the bigger picture issues.

Estelle rested a hip against the counter. "Restaurant emergency?"

"Yeah," Sadie said.

"Those'll happen."

She held in a sigh. "They certainly do."

"Anything we can do to help?"

Sadie turned and started to say no. Then she spied the community bulletin board. Flyers for local events, meetups, a fundraiser for a cat and dog rescue group. One was about getting involved with a communal garden.

Getting involved. Showing support.

Maybe there was something she could do for Joanie. For all the Supers.

CHAPTER 13

Joan stood with her arms crossed in the conference room, waiting for Sherrelle to appear on one of the large TV screens. The Destine Super had called for her cohorts in Vector City to gather together.

Otis was in the process of video calling her. Darlene had come up from the kitchen with flour dusting her half-zip athletic top. Ward fussed around the room, scrambling to get preferred beverages while keeping an eye on his laptop for imminent notetaking.

Kade was off doing something with Nyah—she forgot what he'd been rambling about after their weekly meeting.

Where was Mark? This wasn't an emergency per se, but he and Zee were just out on patrol. SuperWatch was being glitchy, which happened from time to time like any app, so she couldn't check there. Hopefully it was just a usual and customary hiccup and not something on par with Villains fucking with it.

The video call began to ring, followed shortly by an imposing image.

Four of the five Destine Superheroes were sitting on one side of a large circular table, decked out in their full gear. Sherrelle didn't have her facemask on, but everyone else did.

"Hey there, Sparky," she said.

"Hey, Sherrelle," Joan said, then swallowed the nervous lump in her throat.

Nuance—their leader, she supposed by his tall chair in the middle—nodded briskly at Otis. "Flight."

"Benoit," Otis stated without emotion.

Nuance grimaced. "No real names. This is a formal meeting."

It felt like the Destine Supers looked right at Joan: Nuance, Leap (a dude who jumped really high and far), and Flux (a woman who could go boneless and squeeze into or between anything). All staring at the former Villain they didn't trust.

Her fingers curled into fists.

Sherrelle scratched at her nose and said, "Forgive the formality. It, uh, turns out I was wrong."

"I didn't realize there was a connection between you and the thief known as Greta," Nuance said.

"Who?" Otis said.

"Greta?" Darlene seemed surprised. She turned to Joan. "Your longtime accomplice."

"Technically, I was more her accomplice," Joan said.

Otis's face screwed up in confusion. "What are you talking about?"

"A criminal frequently seen with Spark and Ice," Darlene said. "She didn't come up on our radar much considering she is not a Supervillain, but I noticed."

Of course she did. Nothing un-justice-y got past her, no matter what Joan did to shield Grets.

Onscreen, Nuance crossed his teal-clad arms. "Your former Villain didn't tell you she's friends with the most well-known thief in the country?"

Greta would rather you say the whole damn world, but...

"I imagine she was friends with many thieves," Otis said.

Shaking his head, Nuance said, "If you'd been paying attention, you'd have noticed they still talk."

"I do pay attention," Otis snapped, crossing his own arms. "Spark and Ice continue to be on monitored probation. We take thoughtful actions and weigh the pros and cons before making rash decisions."

The Destine Supers harrumphed and grumbled.

Darlene looked like she was about to smile. What the hell was going on?

Flux pressed her purple-gloved fingertips into the table. "The android assistants had an extensive test period."

"They still did less damage than Quake has to Vector City," Leap said in harsh Destine tonality.

Ah, that was the root of the animosity. The robotic sidekick disaster.

Ward stepped up, flipping his laptop screen so it became a tablet. Nuance waved to his left. Four presumable sidekicks with digital devices scurried to their respective Supers. The sidekick showdown would've been funny any other day.

"What's the problem?" Joan said. "Greta's an old friend. She came to me to tell me what the Citizens were doing." To Darlene and Otis, she added, "Greta was who they hired to get information on the power-blocking tech."

"She was instructed to give it to me, which she failed to do," Nuance said.

"She did us all a favor."

"What she actually did was confirm a belief the Citizens have."

Sherrelle pointed at Joan. "Those guys think Greta is Spark. It makes sense if you did a lot of jobs together back in the day. Things could be traced to you."

"More important to them," said Leap, "it's confirmation that Spark's taking these jobs. That you're still a menace to society."

"Greta saying she couldn't hack into the system means she's protecting everyone with superpowers," Nuance said.

"Because they think she has them," Flux added.

A loud buzz steadily filled Joan's ears. They thought that Spark...

They were trying to frame her. Find any scapegoat to further their cause.

"I missed this on vacation," Sherrelle said. "Otis kept us, uh, busy."

Otis cleared his throat loudly.

"Sorry, Sparky. I would've told you otherwise."

Joan glared at Nuance. "Why didn't *you* say anything? Why not ask me?"

He glared back. "I don't know you and can hardly trust someone with your history."

"Sherrelle can vouch for me." She gestured at her ally. "She can literally feel it."

"Had I known the Citizens were trying to connect all these dots, I would have." Sherrelle gave Nuance a look like *This dude doesn't tell me shit.*

Leap crossed sinewy arms over his green-and-blue bodysuit. "Helping other Supers isn't something Vector City is known for. Why would we do it for you?"

"We got rid of all our Villains," Otis stated. "Twice. What have you done other than unleash robot sidekicks on your city?"

Ward gave a sharp nod, like a *Hell yeah.*

Flux snorted. "Maybe if you'd helped with our problem, you wouldn't have had to recruit Villains to fight your battles for you."

"Are you serious?" Joan choked out a dry laugh. Un-fucking-believable. "You're bickering about nothing when there's a real threat right now. These assholes want to frame me. A heads up would've been great."

"I couldn't confirm whether it was true or not," Nuance said.

"Here's your confirmation." She slapped a hand to her chest. "I'm not Greta. She's a norm who's pissed as hell to have worked with a Superhero."

A flurry of emotion raced through her, speeding past her personal fears and roaring straight into the more pressing issue.

"I don't care what you think about me. Can't you see what that group is doing? It impacts *all* the superpowered. They want to stop us by any means. Whether that's framing a former Villain, or using Iris to show how we can turn bad. It's not going to stop until they get what they want."

Darlene took a step forward. "Spark is right. If the Citizens could prove she was still active in villainy, it would poke holes in the security of Superheroes."

"That's a good point," Sherrelle said.

Joan waved at her coworkers. "This is just one thing. What else are they planning? Who else are they trying to frame?"

Nobody had an answer to that, but the likelihood was high.

I picked a great time to clean up my public image.

Nuance shifted in his high-backed chair. "This is a good situation to monitor. It would be wise to share any information that could potentially impact more than just our cities."

"Agreed," Otis said.

Ward dutifully typed as the four Destine sidekicks did the same.

"In the meantime…" Nuance began.

"In the meantime," Joan said, "tell them they're wrong. Do whatever it takes to get them off my tail. And Greta's. Do not involve her any more in this."

Leap sneered. "Or what?"

"Or I'll show you what made me such a nasty Supervillain." Her eyes filled with an angry red haze.

"That'll do, Spark." Otis shot her a look. "What I want to know is how the Citizens found out about this Greta person's connection to Spark and Ice."

Joan shrugged. "Any number of former associates would've gladly thrown me and Ice to the wolves. They all ghosted us when we turned on Trick, Volt and Hide."

Flux leaned her cheek in one hand, bendy elbow propped on the table. "What are you going to do about Greta?"

She was probably asking Nuance, but Joan answered, "Leave her to me. I'll take care of her."

"You mean have her dealt with by the proper authorities," Leap said.

"Suuurrre," she said, drawing it out 'cause, um, no fucking way.

Mark needed to be here to give his wink and smile and *no worries* attitude because Joan was very worried.

"I suppose that's everything," Nuance said. He nodded at Otis. "Flight."

"Benoit," Otis said.

"Perhaps we'll have a call with the other major city leaders about this matter."

"Perhaps."

Things went quiet on the other end of the call.

Nuance made subtle head gestures at his sidekick, a skinny young Black guy.

"Hmm?" the sidekick said.

"End the call," Nuance muttered.

"Oh! Yes, sir."

The sidekick fumbled with his tablet, and the feed ended.

Equal swells of dread and wanting to throw up churned in Joan's stomach. This was just one giant flashing neon sign that the norms didn't trust Spark, other Supers didn't trust Spark, and any of them were more than willing to throw her ass behind bars.

That evergreen threat hovered over her like a relentless dark cloud.

"You should have told us," Darlene said.

"I was protecting an old friend," Joan said. "The same as how she was protecting me."

"We must pay attention to anything that seems odd," Otis said. "It's best not to fuel the fire of suspicion, either between Supers or with the norms."

Joan flicked irritated sparks from her fingers.

"We trust you, Joan," he added. "But you have to tell us the whole story from now on."

She nodded, thankful he'd made a point of showing some

support. If it came down to protecting her loved ones, though, they would always come first.

Darlene had walked to one of the conference chairs. She sat stiffly, a faraway look on her face.

Joan joined her. "What's up?"

"Gus warned me this would happen," she said quietly. "She said to be ready for the backlash against Heroes. We think we're doing a public service, but..."

"Not all of the public wants it," Joan said.

Darlene's head bobbed in sad assent. She cast a glance at Joan. "Amazing Woman was blamed when things went wrong. I can't help but feel a correlation between that and what's going on now. People always want someone to blame."

"Yup." *And this time, it's me.*

She waited for Darlene to swing back to one of her usual platitudes about how the fight for justice was worth it, but none came.

Joan's phone vibrated with an incoming text.

> Sorry Sparky. My coworkers can be dicks. I might have to get truthy with them. Regards to the Iceman.

A tiny smile tugged at her lips. Sherrelle was a good egg.

Zee stormed into the room, Mark hot on their heels.

"It's okay," Mark said.

"No, it's not okay," Zee seethed in an unusual display of raw anger.

"What fresh hell is this?" Joan muttered.

Mark tossed his gloves and mask on the conference table. "It's going to be fine. I'll take care of it."

Zee dropped into a chair and whipped their facemask off.

"What's going on?" Joan said.

Zee tossed their hands helplessly. "We got barred from the youth center because of that fucking no superpowers rider."

"You what?"

"It's just a speedbump," Mark soothed. "The city owns the building. Thorpie will clear this up."

Otis joined them at the table. "Tell us what happened."

"The board members want to protect the kids by limiting exposure to Supers," Zee said. "They think having us there invites trouble, so they're trying to add that provision to whatever documents they can. I understand wanting to do what's best for the kids, but this is not the way. It gives them the message that people who are different should be excluded. That's why most of them are there—to have a place to belong."

Shit. This was awful.

"They scheduled an emergency vote because of what happened with Lunk on Saturday."

Double shit.

Mark rested a hand on the back of Zee's chair. "But it won't pass because the kids are rallying behind us. And the director thinks it's bullshit. The mayor—"

"Mayor Thorpe's backing us causes friction with a lot of people," Zee said. "Especially now that we're considered domestic terrorists."

Joan's heart started thumping again. "Whoa, where's that coming from?"

"Dale Terwilliger's out there calling the superpowered our biggest threat to national security."

Quadruple shit.

Joan got up and went over to Zee. "Let's table that shit nugget for a minute. Can you just go there as yourself until this gets resolved?"

Zee shook their head. "I've been going as Race for years. There's no way I could show up and not have everyone make the connection."

"I have to pretend like I can't cook so no one connects Ice to our old food truck," Mark said.

"That place means everything to me." Zee's dark eyes shone

glassy and miserable. "I can't lose it. All the young queer folks, the staff and volunteers, they're all just…"

They swore and dropped their head in their hands.

"I'm sorry," Darlene said. "This is very sad news."

Mark knelt in front of Zee. "Think about everything you've done. The donations, all the sponsorships you've gotten them. There's no way this thing will pass."

"They're looking out for the kids," they said.

"They're going about it the wrong way."

Ward approached and said, "I could work with Padma on a statement and a social media campaign."

Zee shook their head again. "I don't want to draw negative attention to the center. They do a lot of good for queer youth."

Mark scooted closer, setting a hand on their knee. "I'll fix this for you."

They huffed out a humorless laugh. "All by yourself?"

"If I have to. With one arm tied behind my back. Backwards, standing on one leg."

Warmth pulsed through Joan. Her brother was trying to make Zee smile. The way the two of them were talking—sincerely, intimately, like they were the only people in the room—was really sweet.

"We can get Gus to buy the building," Joan suggested. "Then fire the entire board."

"Totally." Mark put on a grin. "Perry would gladly do the firing. He'd blow all of them straight out the front door."

Zee placed their hand against Mark's. "I appreciate the thought, but no."

Joan crouched beside her brother. "We've got your back. You've had our backs for a long time."

"We'd probably still be Villains if it weren't for you," Mark said.

"Yeah. Let us repay the favor."

A tear escaped the corner of Zee's eye before they brushed it away. Mark lowered the hand that had reached to do so.

"Do you know..." Zee cleared their throat. "Of course you don't. I never told you. I started volunteering at the youth center because of you two."

"Really?" Joan said.

"Something Mark said to me once in the heat of a battle. That you didn't have a place to go when you were struggling as teens. That really resonated with me. I thought I could be a better Hero by offering to help young people with nowhere to go."

"Like you could prevent the next wave of Supervillains?" Otis said.

"No," Zee said. "It was to do something nice. But I've gotten so much in return."

"You found a place to belong, too," Mark murmured. His expression said he understood completely.

Zee gave him a look in return that said Mark was right on the money. This was the thing they did for themself, not photo ops. Joan had no idea before working together that they spent so much time there because of the lack of press around it.

Squeezing their hand, Mark said, "Perry loves a good revenge. I'm just saying."

"You'd seriously make his day," Joan added.

Zee finally cracked a smile. "I'll keep that in my back pocket."

"I'm still gonna fix this." Mark swiveled his head. "Ward, my man."

"Yes, Mr. Ice?" Ward appeared beside him.

"I want to release a video. Joanie, we'll both do it and talk about oh, woe is us that we were homeless teenagers. Then we'll praise the youth center and how it offers a future that's better than turning to villainy. We'll sneak in some references to how the Superheroes have long been supporters of queer people."

"Will we be confirming that we're twins?" Joan asked.

"Yeah. Or siblings at the very least."

She had to work the "Okay" from her mouth. That felt like too much exposure.

But it was for Zee, and the kids, and wouldn't hurt her image right about now since she was about to be framed for untold crimes of thievery.

"Thanks, you two," Zee said.

"Anytime, rain or shine." Mark got up slowly, using Zee's thighs as leverage. "Preferably shine, and like, after noon."

Zee smirked and gave him a slight push, their fingers lingering down Mark's chest.

Joan stood as well and chucked their shoulder. "Let me know what I can do to help."

"Keep your brother from dropping an f-bomb in the video?"

"That's something he should be doing with *me*. How about dinner tonight? I was gonna make something special."

"Which I will obviously have to oversee," Mark chimed in.

"If you insist," Zee half-heartedly agreed.

She and Mark would fix this, even if it meant consulting Perry. Who would probably put together a half-hour presentation on his top revenge tactics.

"Tell us about this Terwilliger thing," Joan said, going back to another of the day's crap bombs. "We're threatening national security?"

"That." Zee pursed their lips. "He was on TV last night calling for action because we're the equivalent of domestic terrorists. Destroying good American people's livelihoods."

Ward held his tablet face out. "I found the clip I believe you're referring to."

"Ugh." Joan waved it away. "I don't have the energy for that."

"I don't want to give him any of my energy," Mark said. "Unless it's a great big icicle up his—"

"It's fueling the fear and anger around superpowered individuals," Darlene said. "I wish they would stop giving platforms to such things."

"It makes for good TV," Mark grumbled.

The paused video on Ward's tablet showed Terwilliger with his fist raised, looking like he was literally spitting mad, the logo for Badger News Network in the bottom corner. Yeah, Joan couldn't stomach that right now.

"He's a bigger threat to common decency than we'll ever be," she said.

An alert appeared onscreen.

SMOKE ALARM—KITCHEN

Darlene leapt from her chair. "The oven!"

She raced out of the room, Ward in hot pursuit. Mark and Zee chuckled, and Joan joined in. A nice way to lighten the mood a little.

Otis did want to see the clip, so he walked to the nearby touchscreen TV. Mark whispered something in Zee's ear, and Zee responded in kind. Pretty great watching her brother step up for someone he was *not dating*. He wasn't running away from a problem but rather trying to make it better. Like someone who genuinely cared about a partner.

Mark turned to her. "What was it you needed earlier? Did we miss anything important?"

Crap. This was about to bring the mood down again.

"You might want to sit," Joan said.

CHAPTER 14

Sadie held her poster in line with the ones made by her employees and smiled for pics. They stood in front of the counter, exhilarated by a Wednesday evening of artistic activism.

Justin—aka Dr. Devers—nodded over Sadie's phone. "Looks good," he said, and handed it back.

She thanked him, taking a quick glance at the photos. These, along with the ones she'd taken during the somewhat impromptu gathering, would be great for the café's social media and SuperWatch.

The tables were mostly cleared out. She still couldn't believe the turnout. Dozens of people with a little extra time and art supplies who wanted to make posters to hang in business or home windows saying they supported Superheroes.

Some were Super fans, like she'd been. Others didn't like to see a population singled out for their differences. A few were queer activists who were pro Race, Ice and Spark. One gal admitted she just thought Spark was really hot (which, yes).

Wren and Beth-Ann had ducked out earlier with *Superheroes saved this truck!* signs for Powered by Plants. Tenia had just stepped out to help Morris and their son close up Cajun Soul for the night.

"Let's hang these works of art," Rosalind said, snagging the tape dispenser from behind the counter.

The four café staffers staggered themselves across both large windows and the front door. "Put them wherever you want," Sadie said.

She smiled down at her poster—a fairly simple but colorful design on letter-sized cardstock.

All Are Welcome Here
#SuperSupporter

She'd used the colors for the Vector City Superheroes with little symbols like a flame and a snowflake. Spark and Ice were her favorites, after all.

Alexis stuck her bold *We Luv U Superheroes!* directly under the Sadie's Café logo on the far window. Her thick black curls had largely escaped her half-ponytail. "This is going to look so good," she said, her Colombian accent more pronounced from fatigue and the late hour.

"Thanks for staying a little past closing," Sadie told her employees.

"Are you kidding?" Rosalind pressed on the corners of her poster below the open/closed sign. "This was a total blast."

"Happy to help our Heroes where we can," Nyah said, then giggled.

Sadie raised her eyebrows, making Ny cover her face with overjoyed embarrassment. Her aunt had approved of Kade, and he was most likely going to stop by her place once he was done tonight.

Justin handed the tape dispenser to Sadie. They were putting their signs in the window closest to the counter. "They've had a few wins this week," he murmured for her ears only. "That's helped a lot."

"It really has," Sadie murmured back.

Yesterday, the Vector City crew had some real-deal Superhero action by preventing a disaster on one of the highway inter-changes. A semi filled with electronics had lost control and careened into a guardrail, blocking the flow of traffic. A gas tanker had nearly driven straight into a row of stopped vehicles but was caught in time by Ice and Lunk, while the dangling semi cab was pushed back by Flight and Catch before it fell onto traffic below.

A team effort, a big win. Joanie had mostly been crowd control and then welding the metal guardrail back together, but she hadn't minded playing her part.

The situation with the youth center—which was awful for Zee—hadn't yet been resolved. The board meeting had been moved to the end of the week, which Sadie took to be a good sign. The outpouring of support from the queer kids for an elder would hopefully put a stop to that awful No Superpowered Activity provision being enacted.

Joan and Mark had really gone to bat for their friend, sharing a deeply personal video about how important it was to have safe spaces for expression. They'd talked about being unhoused for a time, casually dropping that they were brother and sister. Sadie was so proud of them for being that publicly vulnerable.

Speaking of her Joanie… Sadie spied her talking to Tenia and Morris on the sidewalk.

"Joanie's here," she said, quickly pressing the corners of her sign next to *Where Friends Gather* so she could show Joan what they'd been up to.

She hurried outside, grinning at her gorgeous girlfriend in long navy-blue shorts and a thin white tee to beat the heat.

Joan looked at the window signs. "What's going on?"

"It's the little surprise I told you to come check out," Sadie said. She squeezed Joan's hand.

"You guys made signs?"

"That's nothing. You have to see inside."

Joan glanced at Cajun Soul. Tenia's sign, similar to the ones Wren and Beth-Ann had made, hung in the side door window.

"I got crafty," Tenia said.

"Thanks again for coming, my friend," Sadie said.

"Sure thing."

Morris nodded at Joan. "We're Spark and Ice stans."

"I'm a Cajun Soul stan," she said.

"Oh, we know," Tenia said with a smile. "And we use that whenever we can."

Joan laughed, her eyes darting to where Spark and Ice had signed the truck praising their food.

"Let me show you what we did." Sadie tugged Joan toward the coffeehouse.

Her staff greeted Joan, which she returned. Sadie watched with giddy joy as Joan saw the markers and pens, the small posterboard and cardstock, the people packing up to leave.

"I put the word out that we were hosting a night to make signs letting our Heroes know we're thinking about them. Almost forty people showed up. Which wasn't bad, considering we kind of threw this together. Everyone created very cool things and are taking them home or to work to hang in their windows. A few neighboring storeowners dropped in, so they'll have signs, too."

"You did all this?" It wasn't spoken, but Joan looked like she wanted to add *for me?*

"Nyah was a big help, and the dynamic duo." Sadie smiled at Alexis and Rosalind, who both curtseyed.

Joan seemed to be at a loss for words—at least ones she could say in mixed company. She noticed Justin, blinked, and said, "You came to this?"

Holding up two signs, he said, "I'm gonna hang these at home."

"Wow, that's..." She barked out a loud laugh, then gestured at the one that read:

Are they perfect? No.
Have they saved countless lives? Yes.
I am a #SuperSupporter

"That's pretty good," Joan chuckled.

"I thought you'd like it." Justin turned to Sadie. "This was a great idea. You should do it again."

Sadie nodded in agreement. "I think we will. Or something like it. Or host a gathering for people who want to be involved in some way."

Alexis snagged one of Sadie's plastic containers filled with markers. "We could leave a table with this and paper. People who come in could make something."

"Oh my god, yesss," Rosalind said. "It could be a special crafts table. Use this one." She selected an end table against the wall of art pieces. "The funky painting here will inspire them."

Sadie stifled a laugh. The funky painting was Gus's. *Amazing inspiration, indeed.*

"Great idea," she said. "Let's put the remaining supplies there, and then you two get out of here. I'll finish cleaning since you stayed late."

"I'll do the books," Nyah said, heading behind the counter.

Sadie gathered and moved her art supplies and the thick paper. She thanked the remaining attendees as they exited. Joan looked mildly dazed at the outpouring of support as she and Justin talked quietly by the couch.

This little passion project was already lifting the spirits of one Vector City Superhero. Mission accomplished.

Alexis decided to make a note for the table explaining what it was for while Rosalind wiped down the counter and tabletops. Joan had walked with Justin to the exit, so Sadie went over to them.

"Thank you so much for coming," she said, giving Justin a hug.

"My pleasure." He squeezed tight. Justin was a really good hugger.

Alexis waved goodbye with a red marker. "See you."

"See you later," Justin said.

"Thanks for the advice."

"Shoot me a text if you're still not getting the hang of it."

"I will."

Sadie smiled, her heart warming. Alexis was struggling with giving herself hormone injections, so Justin had given her some tips he'd used to make it easier.

He shared a goodbye with Nyah before heading out. Ny gave Sadie a thumbs-up as she stepped from behind the counter. "Books look good. You'll be happy with the numbers."

"Yay," Sadie said. That was a nice benefit of the gathering. It'd cost her money with some of the supplies, but that had come from her personal funds. Even if it'd cost the café, it would've been worth it.

"Need anything else?"

She almost laughed at how Nyah obviously had both feet facing away from her. Kade had gotten a boost from yesterday's highway victory, and Ny wanted to experience his "renewed vitality."

"No," Sadie said. "I appreciate you coming back in."

"Happy to help with this." Ny snagged her sign off a table.

"*Super Strong*," Joan read. "Where'd you get the idea for that?"

Nyah giggled, making Sadie giggle.

"Don't wrinkle it when you *lug* it home." Joanie suspiciously said *lug* like *Lunk*.

Ny burned with a deep blush and hastened to the Progress Pride flag.

Her other two employees were finishing up their tasks, so Sadie said, "I'll get the garbage and recycling and will mop. Go home. Enjoy what's left of the evening."

They didn't argue and called out goodnights en route to joining Nyah. Sadie locked the front door, then smoothed out the tape on one corner of Rosalind's sign.

"You really brought people together," Joan said.

"That's what this place is for," Sadie said. "But really, I wanted to do something for you and…" *The other Supers.* "This is a small thing I can do to help, especially with jerks out there trying to frame Spark."

"It means a lot."

"We're trying to get a hashtag going for Super Supporters. Maybe it'll take off in other cities. It's a way to let our voices be louder than the ones trying to suppress you—er..." She glanced back to make sure Alexis and Rosalind weren't there.

"I love that."

"I just want to *do* something."

Joan rubbed Sadie's hip. "You do a ridiculous amount of things for me, babe."

"Well, I love you a ridiculous amount."

"And I love you ridiculous plus one."

Sadie stared at the spray bottle and cloth sitting on a nearby table. Ugh, why was she such a nice boss and had offered to finish cleaning? "Any chance we could get Race to zip in and wipe down the chairs and mop?"

"Not sure if that constitutes an emergency, but maybe."

"Do you want to make a sign while you wait? I didn't make one for our place because I don't want to draw attention to it."

"That's smart, yeah. But I can..." Joanie walked over to the crafts table. "If you want, Spark can find out about your efforts and stop in to sign an autograph for Sadie's Café."

"If Spark wants to do that. She hasn't wanted to before."

"She only just learned about this place thanks to that hashtag."

Joanie picked up a smaller cut piece of posterboard. She took a black permanent marker and scribbled her praises for Sadie's Café, signing it with a jagged *Spark*.

Sadie noted the way the *S* and a few other letters had been written. "You have different handwriting for Spark."

"I always have," Joan said.

"That makes sense."

"It's another way to conceal myself, like the Spark voice." Her tone deepened. "You know the Spark voice, fair citizen of Vector City."

The timbre sent a shiver up Sadie's spine. "Damn, that's so hot." She touched a finger to Joan's arm. "Do you think the Spark voice could make an appearance when we're naked and doing fun things to each other?"

Joanie gave a slight smile, but it didn't reach her eyes. "I had to be Spark during a lot of those times before. The mask, the disguise. That's who I had to be for…" She looked at Sadie earnestly, the way that broke her heart. "I like being me with you."

"You're who I want, Joanie," she promised. "Always."

"I hope for always."

Her heart skipped a beat. They didn't talk about like, the *future* future, but she hoped for always, too.

She slid her gaze down to the outline of Joan's bra through her thin shirt. Regular bras were so much easier to remove than the athletic ones Joanie usually wore. "I am definitely getting the best of both worlds," she said.

The Pride flag swished as Alexis said, "I can't find my phone."

Sadie shoved several cardstock papers over the Spark autograph. Joan slipped the marker into its carton. Shoot, they needed to be more careful unless they were a hundred percent alone.

Alexis ducked behind the counter, then popped up. "Here it is."

"I told you!" Rosalind crowed from behind the flag.

When Alexis returned to the back, her chatter mingled with Nyah and Rosalind's.

Sadie carefully tucked the autograph between two blank pieces of paper. "I think I'll hide this in my office for a day or two to give Spark time to come and sign it. Less obvious."

"Good idea." Joan positioned herself to block Sadie's actions. "Actually, we should get rid of it. I don't want to make any connections between us. Especially not with these assholes trying to dig up dirt on me."

"If you want to. I'd hate if they have you looking over your shoulder at everything."

"We don't know what lengths they may go to. Let's play it safe."

"Okay." Sadie took the autograph over to the garbage can by the couch and tore it into teeny tiny pieces.

Joan followed, doing her visual sweep of the room. It was probably subconscious at this point, since she always had one eye toward potential disaster.

Poor Joanie. Forever having to hide.

"That must've sucked," Sadie said. "Not being able to truly be yourself with a woman for all those years."

"It kinda did." Joan paused, then said, "Greta was the first who knew me as both when we…"

"Mm-hmm."

"But she wanted me anyway. That meant a lot. I think it's why I so fell hard for her."

"Aww."

Joan ducked her head. "Is it weird to talk about her like that? It was a long time ago."

"It's not weird," Sadie assured her. "I like knowing you had someone to love who loved you back."

"Even if it wasn't the healthiest relationship."

She laughed hard at that. "I've been in love plenty of times in unhealthy relationships."

"We were broken in similar ways. She also had to make her own way at a young age. We barely had any real friends."

"You had each other."

"We did."

"I have a lot of friends, but I can't say I have a best friend. I've never connected that way with anyone. Or I guess I saved it for whoever I was dating." Sadie rolled her eyes. That was totally what she'd done. "I'm jealous of people with ride-or-die besties."

Joan regarded her, then smiled. "That's why you won't give up on me and Greta."

"Yes. And why you shouldn't give up on each other."

The chatter had died down in the back, so everyone else must've gone.

Sadie eased onto the velvety green couch. Ah, did that feel good. "Have you talked to Greta about the latest developments?"

"We texted a little," Joanie said, sitting beside her. "I'm taking the heat for her, which I think she feels bad about. As bad as Greta feels about anything."

"I'm sure she appreciates it."

"She doesn't love that Spark might get credit for some of her more daring exploits. And that she'll have to stay low profile until this blows over. But yeah, even she can see that from the outside, we could be the same person."

"But you can account for where you've been these past however many months as a Super."

"If that's enough."

Sadie slouched into the cushions and tucked her feet up. Ahhh, that felt even better. "You're surrounded by support, Sparky."

Joan chuckled at Sherrelle's nickname for her (which was very cute, and why hadn't Sadie thought of it?). "Quite literally," she said, gesturing with both hands at the window signs.

"Ugh, I should not have sat down," Sadie groaned. "I might just sleep here and finish cleaning in the morning."

Joan cooed and brushed Sadie's bangs back (which were getting too long, but when was there time for a salon visit?). "No. I'm taking you home and giving you a massage."

Sadie moaned louder.

"Was that a good moan or a bad moan?"

"It's an *I want that so bad but would have to get off this couch* moan. I don't even want to commute all the way home. It feels too far."

"My hardworking boss lady," Joan murmured.

That made her heart twinge. All that unwavering encouragement was so appreciated, but had been giving her anxiety. Self-induced for sure, but real.

Joan looked around, pleasure playing about her lips. "I really do love being here. Such good vibes. It makes me forget my troubles for a while."

"Thanks, babe," Sadie said.

She needed to tell her the truth. Joanie deserved that level of honesty.

Sitting up, Sadie said, "I was struggling for a while. I was overwhelmed and had very little confidence in what I was doing. I locked my office door and cried a lot."

"What?" Joan moved closer. "Why didn't you tell me?"

She waved a hand. "I didn't want to bother you when there's been so much going on."

"You're supposed to tell me. That's what we do."

"I just… I didn't want to let you down. You've been so proud of me. I didn't want you thinking I couldn't do it after everything you and Perry and Gus and—"

"Sadie." Joan set her hands on Sadie's shoulders. "You never let me down. You're a rockstar. I'm in awe of your love and dedication to this place."

"But you're an investor," Sadie said. "I want you to get a return on investment, and I want my employees to have good benefits and job security."

Joan started to speak, but Sadie hastened to tell her, "But I'm doing so much better now. I've gotten a ton of good advice from Wren and Beth-Ann, and Tenia, and the women from that entrepreneur group. I can say I'm really proud of what I created. This place brings people together, and I'm going to do more to facilitate that."

"Good." Joan smoothed her hands down. "I'm really glad to hear that. Just please, if you're struggling with anything, come to me. I can't help you if you don't tell me."

"I know, and I will." Sadie took hold of Joan's hands. "I'm still working on my people-pleasery tendencies. Owning my power, as they say."

Joan went quiet for a moment. When she met Sadie's eyes,

hers were filled with concern. "Did I make you feel like you couldn't talk to me? I'm still kicking myself for what happened last week."

"No," Sadie was quick to say, like she always did. Never wanting the other person to feel bad. But that wasn't entirely true. "Well, maybe a little. Getting snapped at for trying to help kind of hurt."

"I'm so sorry about that."

"It's been a lot of little things, too." She took a deep breath, finding the courage to continue. "Like with Greta. You're both being stubborn mules when you should be working together. When I've made suggestions on what you could do, you both shut them down."

"That's got nothing to do with you," Joan said. "That's a me and Greta thing."

"I want to help you. That's my nature, and you're the most important person in the world to me. When I can't do that, I guess I get a little defensive."

"That's understandable."

"But it doesn't make it right. I'm patient to a point, but when I get there, watch out."

"When you get to that point, tell me."

Sadie swung Joan's hands slightly. "You mean talk about my feelings and junk?" she joked.

"All that junk." Joan's mouth tilted in a half-smile.

"So it's enough to be like 'Joanie, I'm annoyed with you'?"

"As long as you're okay with 'Sadie, sweetheart, I love you but for the love of god, why do you put your socks right next to the hamper instead of in it?'"

That pulled a giggle out of Sadie. "That's an oddly specific example, Ms. Malone."

"Just spitballing," Joan laughed.

"I set my socks there if I'm not done wearing them. If they're all the way dirty, I put them in the hamper."

"Half-dirty socks," she muttered, shaking her head.

"So? You change your clothes way too much."

"I run hot. You know that. I've got to get out of my clothes as often as possible."

A swizzle of delightful possibilities twirled up her chest. "As often as possible, you say?"

"Several times a day."

Sadie tilted her head. "And night."

"Particularly night."

"Hmm."

Joan tilted her head in the opposite direction, lining their mouths up perfectly. "It's night right now."

"Is it?" Sadie shifted on the couch to nuzzle Joanie's nose.

"It is."

"I thought you didn't want to draw attention." She glanced up at the lights blazing overhead. "I think this would draw a wee bit of attention."

"Lights can be turned off so I can turn you on."

A chuckle rumbled in Sadie's throat. "What about all the really good security cameras you insisted on?"

Joanie just looked at her. "You think I don't know my way around a security camera?"

CHAPTER 15

Sadie dried her hands with a paper towel, the weight of her day's work dissipating. After rousing herself and Joanie off the couch (not in the way Joanie would've preferred), they'd split the tasks to clean and close up. The sooner done, the sooner home.

Joan tossed her balled-up paper towels into the narrow garbage can near the sinks. "All done?"

"All done," Sadie said, throwing hers away as well. "Thanks for the assist, babe."

"I guess I'm your sidekick, huh?"

"You do like calling me *ma'am* in certain situations."

"Yes ma'am, I do."

She tossed a flirty grin over her shoulder and headed for the office. It felt so much better being honest about her struggles. She really needed to get better at that.

Her laptop was open on the desk. Before packing it up, she wanted to check the day's tally. "Can you get the lights?" she called to Joan.

"Why do you turn the lights off before you need to?"

"So I don't forget to do it on my way out. I'm usually distracted setting the alarm while texting you or trying to find my earbuds."

Joanie didn't argue—she'd lived with Sadie long enough to know the distraction was very real.

The kitchen area went dark other than by the back door. Sadie clicked into the POS system and checked the daily reports.

"Oh my gosh," she said. "We killed it today."

"All those extra bodies?" Joan said as she joined her.

"Those bodies really added up. A lot of generous tips, which is terrific. My staff deserves them."

"That's great, sweetheart." Joan ran a hand up Sadie's back.

"Well, I *am* a badass business owner."

"Yes, you are. And I love hearing you say that."

She took another proud glance at the numbers before closing out of the program. "Better yet, I believe it when I say that now."

A grin spread across Joanie's face. "I can hear it in your voice."

"Get used to it. I'm going to become insufferably confident."

Joan laughed, then dropped a quick kiss on Sadie's temple.

Sadie looped her arms around Joan's midsection. "And how about you, my sweet Superhero? How are you really doing?"

"Yesterday helped." Joan slid her arms around Sadie. "We needed a win. I needed something to shove in Dale Terwilliger's face."

"He's so gross."

"Have Supers and Villains created a lot of mess? Absolutely. But you know who's created even more?"

"Fragile white men with an inflated sense of self?" Sadie drawled.

"Exactly," Joan stated. "But you don't see groups demanding they all be stripped of their power."

"I *am* looking to host more activities here," Sadie only half-joked.

"It's so annoying. Especially knowing he's got a personal beef with his old stepbrother. He's probably jealous Trav has super-powers and gets to do some cool shit with them."

"I'm sure that's a part of it." She held back that Travis had also harassed his stepbrother, so another part of her understood the animosity. But Dale Terwilliger was still gross and could've gone to therapy or something to better deal with it.

"Anyway." Joan smiled at her. "Helping you close up felt nice. It was very normal, and I needed a slice of normal."

"Any time you want to stop by and clean the washrooms, be my guest."

"Like I do at home?" She made an *oh* face, knowing darn well she'd just pushed a button.

Sadie pinched her butt. "You like cleaning the bathroom! And the kitchen! I love laundry and vacuuming and making the bed and tidying up my little piles."

"I know. I'm kidding."

"You'd better be. Confident Sadie will not put up with such smack talk."

"And you're the boss. The boss shouldn't have to scrub toilets."

A good boss would scrub any and every toilet as needed, but Joanie was just playing. So Sadie returned, "Since I'm the boss at home as well."

"Yes, ma'am," Joan purred.

A warm curl eased its way through Sadie's belly. "Very good, loyal sidekick," she said, taking a step closer and pressing Joan into her.

Orange and yellow flickered in her eyes. "I'm a big fan of this side of you. It's really sexy."

"Now you know how I feel whenever I look at you," Sadie said.

"In amazed awe that I get to be with you? That every day, you make me a better person? Like that?"

It was so sincere, Sadie could've melted straight to the floor. "Just like that."

They kissed, a mutual agreement that confidence was the aphrodisiac that had drawn them together at first sight.

"Mmm," Sadie mumbled against Joan's lips. "Let's get home."

She started packing her laptop and things into her bag.

Joan stood close, a little behind, a little to her side. "I love watching you put things in your work bag. You have those folders with your paperwork, so organized. You keep an eye on everything."

"I do," Sadie said, taking the plastic folders and setting them inside.

Gentle fingers touched her lower back. "There's a method to your madness. I joke about all your piles, but you know what's in every one of them."

"That's mostly true."

Joanie adjusted her stance, her palm sliding just above the waistband on Sadie's electric-blue pants. "I love the way you smile when you're here. The way you couldn't stop smiling during all the renovations to get this place open. You have the most beautiful smile. It lights up the entire city."

Pleasure wound its way through Sadie's bloodstream. "Thank you. Your smile liquifies my bones. Not to mention half the women in Vector City."

Warm breath tickled her left ear, causing a shiver to skitter down her neck. Her bag was packed, but she was suddenly not in a hurry to leave.

Joan nestled her mouth against Sadie's ear. "I could go on for hours about all the things I love about you."

"Okay," Sadie teased, reaching behind them to press Joanie's front to her back.

Joan's arms didn't wrap around her as expected. Her hands barely rested on Sadie's hips, her lips still grazing the shell of Sadie's ear. "I love when your hair's in a ponytail because I have easy access to your neck. It also reminds me that you'll take it out, letting those glorious waves free. I wait for you to do it at bedtime and think about bunching it in my hands while you're going down on me."

"Mmm, same." Sadie exhaled, her breath hitching at the end.

"Which part?"

"All of it. And thinking about grabbing your hair when you're doing things to me."

Warm lips brushed just behind Sadie's ear. "I love the way you respond to my touch. How you tell me exactly what you want. It's so freaking hot, sweetheart. You have no idea."

Her knees went wobbly. *This* was pretty freaking hot. "Uh-huh," she managed.

"I love our communication in the bedroom. You make me feel so safe and loved. It's a connection I can't even describe."

"It is. I look into your expressive eyes and know I'm so loved."

"You're worshipped, Sadie Eagan," Joan said. Her fingers tightened. "And you should be. Always."

Always.

Sadie dragged in some air. "This is kind of doing it for me."

"Is it?" Joan nibbled on her ear. "Me telling you all the ways you're wonderful?"

"Mm-hmm."

Her hands skimmed across Sadie's waistband, resting on her bellybutton. "You should see you the way I do. Brilliant and beautiful and damn near perfect."

"That's exactly how I see you," Sadie said.

"I'm so proud of how you refused to let go of your dream. Even when you didn't think it was possible, or other people made you feel that way. You stuck to what you believed in and made it happen."

Sadie smiled, then bit her lower lip. She wrapped her other hand around Joan's side, reflexively arching into her body.

"You learned everything you didn't know, but you already knew so much from starting up Hot and Cold. You're a genius with marketing ideas and design and colors and everything. The way you can sketch something that perfectly captures what—"

"I love that babe, but can we get back to the sexy stuff?"

Joanie's husky laugh rumbled against her. "I was trying to veer away from that, unless you want to…" Her thumb smoothed over the snap on Sadie's pants.

"Do what?" Sadie asked, her heart thrumming in anticipation of the answer.

"Well, I've been wanting to bend you over this desk since the first day you had possession." Joan tucked her thumb into Sadie's waistband. "Can I sweet talk my way into that?"

"Keep talking and find out."

She sensed Joanie's grin against her neck. No doubt it matched the one stretching across her own face.

"The security camera!" Sadie jerked her head to look at the plastic orb in the corner, placed to capture the desk and small safe beside it.

Joan swore and pulled back so she could wake up the desktop computer. "Part of the reason I made you get this system is because I know my way around it."

"For...?"

She glanced over her shoulder with a wicked smile. "For exactly this situation."

A thrill of desire burst through Sadie. She opted to play it extra safe and closed and locked the door. Then turned off the lights, just in case. Ooh, the glow from the monitor cast an oddly warm glow.

The office camera feed went black.

Joan stood up straight. "Lights off?"

"It makes this feel naughty, like we might get caught at any moment."

She stepped over slowly, her gaze focused and intent. "I am rather good at doing clandestine things in the dark."

"Oh, do you want them on?" Sadie reached for the light switch. "I don't want this to be like what you had to do before."

"No, it's okay," Joanie said. "You should be a little bad."

She moved behind Sadie to resume her position. Her fingers danced over Sadie's lower belly.

"Now then. Where were we?"

Sadie rested her hands on Joan's toned arms. "Can I tell you everything I love about you and want to do to you?"

"When I'm done." Joan breathed deeply against the side of Sadie's head. "You always smell amazing. Even after a day around coffee grounds, your natural scent is right here. I love finding it on my shirts after you borrow them, and on my pillow if you've hugged it when I'm not there."

Her touch moved deliberately down the center of Sadie's fly.

"I bet you can guess what my favorite scent on you is."

Sadie bit her lip again. "Is it your favorite taste, too?"

"It's my favorite taste in the world."

Her nipples tightened and her thigh popped to squeeze her legs together. This was *really* doing it for her.

Joan achingly dragged her fingers up Sadie's fly. "I love all of you. Here." She kissed behind Sadie's ear, below it, lightly bit at her lobe. "And here." She kissed and nibbled across the nape of Sadie's neck. "And here." She gave her right ear the same attention.

Her touch trailed up and down where Sadie was getting more and more damp, more and more swollen. She pressed her ass into Joan's core, lightly rubbing to bring her pleasure, too.

"I love your fashion sense and love of color," Joan said. "You're never afraid to be who you are. You're unapologetically you."

"That I am," Sadie said.

Joan's hands snaked under her pink T-shirt. "I'm mesmerized by your body, but no one could blame me. Your skin is so soft, it feels like it goes on for miles."

"Do you want to touch more of it?"

"I want to touch all of it."

Joan gathered the poly-cotton blend and tugged. Ah, so this was not gonna be a little below-the-undies situation.

That felt even naughtier.

She pulled the shirt off, tossing it onto the desk chair. "Look at these arms, and these shoulders. Boxing has really defined your muscles."

Yes, look at that and not the plainest white bra I own. Dressing for work this morning had meant unsexy undergarments.

"You're so strong," Joan continued. She slid her hands up Sadie's arms. "You've been working hard to be as strong physically as you are mentally."

She traced her fingertips around Sadie's shoulder blades. The gentle pressure, her murmured words of appreciation, the fact that she could see the changes to Sadie's body that she was pretty proud of as well, caused delighted tingles to burst and pop.

"Beautiful," Joanie murmured, trailing her touch down the length of Sadie's back.

Her mouth stayed against Sadie's ear, which was hot and a bit maddening. Torture of the very best kind.

"So beautiful and strong." Joan ran her hands to Sadie's stomach. "Your core, literally and figuratively. How you stand strong." She grazed the little rainbow on the left. "And your cute tattoos you don't share with everybody. They're your secret that only a privileged few get to see."

"All for you," Sadie said, her voice breathy from the oxygen rushing through her blood.

Joan played a little longer around her torso, her touch whisper-light. She moved to the front of Sadie's shoulders, her chest, faintly over her breasts. The padded barrier denied Sadie, making her wriggle.

"You have the biggest heart." Joan rested a hand there. "You're so kind and considerate, and you're always thinking about other people. And animals. Everyone wants to be around you because you exude how much you genuinely like and care about them."

Her other hand danced over Sadie's breasts, deliberately finding the skin peeking out from the cups.

"This is your favorite part of me," Sadie teased.

"I've made it known how much I love the girls. But just in case, I, uh…" Joanie shook her head. "I have to show you. Words won't do justice."

She unhooked the bra, Sadie gladly shaking it off so it could join her shirt. Joanie yanked her own T-shirt off.

"You read my mind," Sadie said, reaching behind Joanie to undo her plain neutral bra. "I need to feel your skin against mine."

"I know that's what you want," Joan said, and dropped the bra to the floor.

"I know that's what *you* want." Sadie appreciated her love's small, round breasts, her taut muscles, those abs she never, ever got enough of.

Joan turned her around, then folded her arms around Sadie and pressed her warm chest into Sadie's back. She brushed her fingers over Sadie's nipples, making her moan. It was so light, Sadie held her breath waiting for another stroke. When the next one came, and the next, they sent hard throbs to her clit that quaked all the way down her legs.

"So perfect," Joan rasped in her ear.

"Thank you, babe." She really meant it. She'd admitted early in their relationship that she was sometimes self-conscious of their size, of the stretch marks. Joanie had simply kissed the shimmery pale lines and insisted she was perfect.

She toyed with the sensitive skin, whispering words of love, while Sadie gripped Joan's shorts.

"Can we get all these clothes off?" Sadie said.

"Nuh-uh."

Joanie rarely denied her, so it was a turn on for her to control the pace. Though even she couldn't stay away from returning one hand to Sadie's pants.

Her touch remained steady, unhurried, gentle. The rush of want racing through Sadie made her lean her head back, sighing as Joan dragged a finger up her center.

"The way you feel..." Joan shifted, her nipples rigid against Sadie's back (and oh, how she wanted to nibble on them).

"Tell me," Sadie breathed. "This is so hot."

Joan cupped her through her pants. "I love that I know your

special places, and I love finding new ones. They're different some days, and with my hands versus my mouth." She husked a small laugh. "And my teeth versus my tongue, or just sucking on your —Oh, fuck."

She undid Sadie's pants.

"Turned yourself on too much with that one?" Sadie couldn't help giggling.

Joanie said nothing. Just shimmied Sadie's pants and purple panties down. Sadie kicked her rainbow-print sneakers off so she could step out of everything plus her socks.

She reached to help Joan get her shorts off. Her cute dinosaur-print boy shorts were the next to go, then her own footwear.

Sadie drank in the full beauty of Joan Malone, all hard planes and angles, her softness on the inside.

"I need to touch you," Sadie said, sliding her hands around Joan's taut ass.

"I'm not done with you. Turn around."

The command in her voice held a touch of Spark's firm tone. *Fuck.*

"Yes, ma'am," Sadie obeyed.

"That's my line." Joan's hands went back to work, teasing one nipple and sliding through her very wet folds. "Jesus, Sadie. You get so wet for me. I love... I just love touching you. Feeling you."

Sadie gasped as Joan hit a sensitive spot.

"Like that. Feeling you right here."

She did it again, making Sadie jerk and moan.

Joan held her in place, one stroke below, a pinch or twist above, her words encouraging and deep.

That Spark voice. Whether she knew she was doing it or not, it was—

"Oh my god, you have to speed up so I can—"

Sadie cried out, the sudden orgasm rising inside her.

Joan was still whispering low, still refusing to move any faster, making the release intense, long, exquisite. Sadie grasped wildly at whatever parts of Joan she could hold onto, yelling strangled nonsense.

"That's right, my love," Joan murmured. "Own your power. You're doing this for yourself."

"You're doing it to— Fuck, Joanie, this is—"

She all but screamed, owning her power as a second orgasm crashed hard and racked her whole being.

"You're so powerful and beautiful." Joan's voice was positively sinful. "Look at you. I've got you, baby. Don't stop. You're so fucking hot right now."

She whispered more wonderfully dirty things Sadie only half-heard through her thudding pulse and moans and sighs. She came down, chest heaving, her sweat making her slide against Joan's chest.

This couldn't stop. Would not stop.

Utterly feral, she stepped over to the desk and grasped the edge.

"Here," she begged.

She stuck her ass out, but Joanie already knew what she wanted. She moved behind Sadie and bent her over the piles of paper. Sadie steadied herself on quivering legs.

"I want you to think about this every time you sit at this desk," Joan growled.

Sadie whimpered and dug her nails into the wood.

Joan snaked a hand to Sadie's left breast. The other slid between her legs. When her fingers filled Sadie, she threw her head back. No slow caresses this time. She made sure of that by pumping against Joan's hand, getting well and truly fucked.

Joan adjusted her stance so her legs clamped around one of Sadie's.

Sadie reached down and rubbed at her deliciously sensitive clit. Joan released a low groan and said, "God, I love it when you touch yourself."

Sadie'd lost the ability to form words, only guttural sounds.

Joanie's fingers curled into just the right spot. "There," Sadie choked out. "Right there."

"You're so powerful. Make yourself come, baby."

She dragged her fingers lower to gather more wetness, then circled the place where a deep glow was growing.

Joan's legs tightened, and she moaned. She ground against Sadie's hip, having her own release.

Sadie pressed into her so she could give her better contact. The new position made Joan's fingers slide out, but she deserved to feel just as good.

She'd barely finished her orgasm before she adjusted Sadie over the desk and reentered.

The fresh pressure brought new jolts of pleasure. Sadie found the right spot again and circled it with intention. She clenched against Joan's fingers to sate her hunger.

Joan encouraged her, praising her when she bucked and twitched. She bit at Sadie's neck, dragging her teeth, causing desire to ripple down. It merged with all the wonderful sensations buzzing through her body.

Wild heat blossomed. Sadie rubbed feverishly as her insides convulsed. Joan slid in and out, each thrust a gift.

Stars shattered behind her eyelids as she struggled to breathe. No sounds, only the sensations spilling over.

She rode through the length of the orgasm, pulsing with wave after wave of pleasure.

Joan slowed her pace, her touch coming back to gentle caresses. She placed soft kisses on Sadie's upper back.

"You're amazing, Sadie Eagan," she whispered.

"You… *You…*" Sadie waved a limp hand.

A final shiver rippled through her. She sighed deeply.

Joanie pulled her hands back to rest on Sadie's hips. Sadie blinked at the lust-filled haze clearing from her eyes.

Next week's shift schedule came into view, and the security camera feeds with one square blacked out, and the pile of invoices she had to deal with tomorrow.

But right now, the only thing she was going to deal with was giving Joan the appropriate thanks.

She turned around to smile at her gorgeous girlfriend, all tousled, her eyes burning bright amber. "That was one hell of a confidence booster," Sadie said, her voice thick.

"I'm glad, sweetheart." Joan brushed Sadie's too-long bangs back.

"You didn't even have to use your warming abilities."

"I used my words."

"Yes, you did." Sadie slipped her hands up Joan's incredible abs, letting her thumbs graze Joanie's hardened pink nipples. "I want to use my tongue."

CHAPTER 16

In casual Friday morning chats with the press at City Hall, the name of the game was *friendly*. Superheroes conversing with journalists who generally wrote favorably about them, sitting around the meeting room with its heavy wooden furniture evoking a "Do take tea with us" vibe.

Joan and Mark were handling this one with Otis. These were by far her least favorite, performative wastes of time. She could practically hear Gus griping as she thought about all the other things she could be doing to actually help the city.

She would also much, much rather be fingerbanging her girlfriend against the desk at her place of business. Then getting the supreme joy of Sadie kneeling in front of her, looking up with those big brown eyes and a wolfish smile as she licked and fingered Joan into oblivion. And then Sadie thoroughly embarrassing her the entire drive home by listing everything she loved about her Joanie Maloney.

Joan adjusted in her tight bodysuit. The memory of Sadie's touches, her mouth, her *tongue*, lived happily rent-free in her head. Nights like those reminded her to put up with the annoying aspects of heroism for Sadie to have everything she deserved. She loved that woman with a depth of feeling a former Supervillain didn't know humans could feel.

Because she was human, unlike what some douchehats thought.

And unlike her Supervillain days, she had to face shit head-on. Running away and hiding for a few months was not an option when you were on the city's payroll.

A hero sacrifices for the greater good.

"Have you seen Iris's latest video?" one reporter asked.

"We have," Joan said. "I appreciate her bringing attention to the crisis in that town that's been without clean drinking water for almost a year. That's bullsh—baloney."

"What about her threats to the chemical production plant that allegedly contaminated the groundwater?"

"It's better for everyone if the state regulatory commission stands up and does its job. If their local Superheroes don't get involved, I'm sure we could find some that would."

Mark grinned and leaned in. "I'm not sure if melted ice would make suitable drinking water, but I'd donate it to be filtered."

Appreciative chuckles echoed throughout the room. If the smaller city near that town lacked the superpower or resources of, say, a Vector City, why didn't they reach out?

"Supers should be working together more," Joan said. "It's ridiculous how they just worry about what's happening in their area. If one of us has a skill that could help somewhere else, why wouldn't we do it?"

Otis gave her a tight smile, his brown eyes telegraphing she was overstepping again.

"I'm putting the word out to Iris," said Mark. "If you want my help, just say the word. Let's work together to fix the problem."

"To be clear, I don't agree with her methods," Joan said for Padma's benefit. "But I understand how she wants to make things better. Supers should listen more. Do more to help with everyday issues."

"Such as?" a thin white dude said.

"Being a part of the community. Taking a modest salary and not costing the city so much."

"Yeah," Mark said. "More volunteering, too. Race has done a phenomenal job at the queer youth center. Catch loves doing school visits."

"What are you two doing for your volunteer efforts?" the dude asked.

Joan hesitated, still feeling weird about taking credit for something that wasn't entirely creditworthy. "I've donated most of my pay to cover repair costs for what happened during the big battle earlier this year."

A short dude who'd been fairly quiet stood at the opposite end of the table. "Destruction that would have never happened if you people weren't allowed to go unchecked."

Oh great, an asshole had gotten in.

"Destruction as recently as last weekend when you and Lunk trespassed onto property you were barred from."

Padma quickly moved from where she'd been standing in the corner. "I think that's enough for today."

"No," Joan said directly to the asshole. "We were on a public sidewalk that was being blocked. Lunk was just doing what we do and trying to help."

"Unauthorized access," he continued, undeterred. "And more damage to a citizen's livelihood."

"Which we have paid for and then some."

"You can't keep throwing money at problems as a temporary solution to a permanent problem."

"That's enough for today," Padma repeated behind a forced smile. "Thank you all for coming and having coffee with our Heroes today."

Ugh, Joan *hated* when she somewhat agreed with these assholes. Paying for damages was a bandage, but the solution was not to ban powers. Accountability was.

"I take responsibility for what I've done," she said. "And I promise all of you I'm going to hold more Heroes accountable. And stop Supervillains who put people's lives in danger."

"Like you did?" the asshole said assholeishly. "Like Iris causing an even greater environmental disaster if she destroys the chemical plant?"

"We are not aligned with Iris," Otis stated. The gaze he flicked at Joan and Mark was a warning against bad optics. "We fight for you, Vector City."

With that, he left the room. Padma motioned for Joan and Mark to follow.

Frustration wound its way through Joan's bloodstream. Healthy criticism was a good thing. Why wasn't it okay for her to point out what most norms didn't like about the superpowered? Why couldn't these Citizen jerkwads work with them rather than against them?

Thank god they'd flown there so she could burn this off on the way back to HQ.

They normally took their time out of City Hall, but Otis turned to Padma at the main entrance and said, "That'll do for today."

The look on her face said she totally got it. "You might want to go out the back. There's a small gathering…"

Faint chanting in front of the building resonated forcefully. *"No to superpowers! Yes to human power!"*

"For crying out loud," Mark grumbled. "We *are* human."

Not about to hide, Joan shoved one of the heavy wooden doors open.

It wasn't a large group—maybe twenty-five or thirty—holding signs with Citizens for Human Power slogans. Their chants quickly turned to angry insults at the three Superheroes.

Joan stared them down, a dare to say something directly to her. They didn't—it was just regurgitated crap about the need to control freaks of nature.

She stepped to the edge of the wide cement stairs, then very deliberately blasted roaring flames from her palms. She swooped over them, arguably a hair too close by the way hats and hair blew around, before shooting up.

"You should be in prison!" one voice carried above the others.

She passed an office window with a Super Supporter sign in it. Then another one in a different building. That gave her strength to ignore the kerfuffle below. This was just a vocal minority.

Mark and Otis joined her. "Was that necessary?" Otis said.

"No, but it was fun," Joan said.

"Why do things to make them distrust you when they already distrust you?"

"I could rescue a roomful of puppies and they'd distrust me."

You should be in prison. Nice to know her single biggest fear was alive and well.

Why would they stop at banning superpowers? Next, they'd make using them a felony. It'd be easy to lock up anyone with a criminal past, or go after Iris to make an example out of her. Weren't they all just a bunch of domestic terrorists to these assholes? To them, Spark was still actively involved in thievery.

She let Otis pull ahead (he was a better flyer, being Flight and all) and said to Mark, "We need to talk to Iris again. I don't think she realizes what could happen to her if these assholes... What are you doing?"

Mark's propulsion slowed as he shot ice from one hand and checked his phone with the other. "Waiting for word on the vote. Zee said they'd text when the board announced the results."

Zee was at the youth center to see if they'd be allowed to stay or have to go. "I've got my fingers crossed," Joan said. "But not literally because, y'know, I'm flying."

Her brother started rapidly losing altitude, so he put his phone away to blast with both hands. Once with Joan again, he said, "We can reach out to Supers with powers that could help this town. You weld shit. Darlene can absorb shit. Nuance isn't our biggest fan, but maybe he can pretend to be the water safety whoever to get it cleaned up."

They spitballed other Supers as they landed on the roof at

headquarters. It wasn't about helping Iris. This was righting the wrongs of a norm-created problem. Hell, most of what they did lately was fix norm-created problems.

Mark tugged a glove off and set his palm on the biometric pad. Joan smirked to herself. They didn't use roof access all that often, so this was probably how Greta had gained access once or twice.

"Otis didn't wait for us," Mark noted as he held the door for Joan.

"I foresee a lecture in our future."

"I think he's more upset by the protestors. He hates not having everyone fawn all over him."

"True." She also got the sense that he didn't want to let the fine citizens of his city down. He had the bland routine Hero statements down pat, but he mostly believed in what he said.

Masks and gloves were removed as they took the stairs down to the control center to check in with Ward. Mark looked at his phone again.

Amiable conversation came from that usually darkened room. Today, the lights were bright, and an unmasked dude in a light gray bodysuit accented with black laughed with their sidekick.

"Hey, friends," Trav said. "Surprise."

"What are you doing here?" Mark said, dropping everything so they could hug.

"I'm doing a few things in the U.S." Trav patted his back. "Great to finally meet you in person."

After they broke apart, he gave Joan a big squeeze. He was a bit shorter than she'd thought. "Why didn't you let us know you were coming?" she asked.

"This was kind of a game-time decision."

"Mr. Blip has only been here for a few minutes," Ward said. "I was just about to get him a coffee."

Trav nodded at him. "I'm getting the lowdown on being a sidekick in this city. I have mad respect for sidekicks."

Ward looked so taken aback at getting recognized that he

stammered a bit before managing, "Thank you, Mr. Blip," with a weighted earnestness.

He hurried to the doorway, then turned. "Sorry, would either of you like anything?"

Joan asked for a mineral water, and Mark said he'd take some coffee. "I didn't sleep well last night," he said.

"Ah," Trav drawled knowingly.

"Nothing fun. It's 'cause of this vote thing."

Mark filled him in as Joan set her things on the counter below the monitors. Live feeds across the city and SuperWatch weren't raising any red flags. The crowd at City Hall was dispersing on one screen, thankfully without audio of their "No to superpowers" chant.

"That sucks," Trav said. "Sorry Zee's going through that."

"I was making them nervous, so they didn't want me there unless…" Mark scooped his phone off the floor. His mouth hung open as he read something on his screen, then widened into a relieved grin. "It didn't pass. Close vote—too close, but it didn't pass."

"Thank god," Joan said. "I needed some good news."

"I think we all needed good news."

"Tell them I'm here and we can celebrate," Trav said.

Mark waved a hand and angled away to type his reply.

"What are you telling them?" Joan said.

"None of your beeswax."

Trav's brown eyebrows scrunched together. He hopped through the wall, then reappeared through it behind Mark.

"He's typing *I'm going to give you the biggest hug*," he read over Mark's shoulder.

Mark jumped in surprise. "Dude!"

"Aww," Joan said.

"Don't sneak up on people. That's creepy."

Trav blipped through the wall again to reappear where he'd been previously standing. "That never gets old."

Joan laughed at the sneaky streak still lingering inside a fellow former Villain. "Why are you really here?"

"Partially because of Iris," Trav said. "I got the same result you did, only in DMs."

"That would've been easier," Mark said as he sent his text. "Less nature."

"It's mostly to see if I can do anything about Dale. I doubt I can change his mind, but maybe I can cool off his approach."

"Good luck," said Joan. "We want to reach out to Iris again."

"You can try DMs, but she'll probably block you." Trav slid a finger beneath the tight neckline around his throat. "I may go to that chemical plant if it doesn't make the situation worse. Kinda depends on how my dealings with Dale go."

"We'll help in any way we can, but we're fresh off villainy. There's a lot of mistrust of us."

"Ward!" Otis yelled from the third floor stairwell.

A few moments later, Ward's voice echoed up the stairs from the kitchen. "Yes, sir! Coming!"

"We can go tomorrow," Mark said.

Joan started to agree, then: "No, wait, I can't tomorrow. That's Sadie's dad's birthday dinner."

"You don't have to go. Iris liked me better anyway."

"I want to, though. Shit."

"Then we'll go Sunday."

"No, the sooner the better," Joan said. "Maybe we can go today."

Trav gestured at the monitor with SuperWatch on it. "We don't know exactly where she is. It could take some time."

A blur of movement flew past the doorway—Zee. They whizzed into the room and grabbed Mark, picking him off the floor in the biggest hug.

"Real quick," they said. "Then I have to get back."

"God, I'm so-o-o relieved," Mark said, his voice bouncing from being held aloft.

"Me, too." Zee set him down, said, "Dinner's on you," and zipped out of the room.

Mark laughed with pure joy.

Trav laughed, too. "So that was Race?"

"Super speed comes in handy," Mark said. He caught Joan looking at him. "Don't."

"That was adorable," she said with total sincerity.

"As much as we—er, I want to celebrate, the fact that this vote even happened is a blister on my ass."

"More places are gonna start banning us."

"Then let's do a video urging Iris to lean into the peaceful part of her pacifistism." Mark made a face. "Pacifistology?"

"Pacifism?" Trav suggested.

"Nonviolence," Joan tossed in.

Mark leaned out the doorway. "Ward, buddy," he called. "Whenever you're free, we need your technical expertise."

"Yes, Mr. Ice," Ward chugged out from the back stairs. "I'm still getting your beverages as well."

"Ward!" Otis barked from somewhere by the changing rooms.

"Almost there, sir!"

"I see your sidekicks aren't treated much better than mine," Trav said.

"Ward's the best," Mark said, unzipping his suit. "We try not to bug him too much, but the others…"

"Why is everyone yelling?" Kade's baritone bellowed down the stairs.

"Hey, do you wanna meet Blip from Yanton?" Mark hollered back.

"Yes!"

After a few moments, Mark snorted. "Now? He's here."

"Oh! Yeah! I'll be right down."

"Control center, big guy."

"This is what the norms should see," Joan said to Trav. "We're just as awful at communicating as they are."

Chuckling, Trav said, "My coworkers and I will text each

other around our headquarters. It's peak laziness, but I actually think they just hate it when I blip in and out to tell them something."

"Yeah, we're technically not supposed to use our powers on each other. But…"

"But…"

A slow grin tugged at Joan's mouth. Trav copied the knowing smirk.

He laughed harder, then chucked her shoulder. "I'm so glad to hang out with you two. Nobody gets what it's like to live the lives we have."

"I'm sure we could weasel our way into Mark and Zee's dinner plans."

"If we're in town," Mark said. "We have to figure that out first."

"Bring Sadie if we do," Trav said.

Joan nodded. "Of course."

He started to say something, then seemed to change his mind.

Thundering footsteps ran down the hallway until Kade appeared in fitted workout gear. "Blip! Hi! I'm Kade. Lunk. Whatever you prefer."

Trav's eyes widened. "Hey. Travis is fine. Or Trav to my friends."

"Trav. Cool." Kade crushed his hand in a wince-inducing handshake.

They exchanged pleasantries as Trav toyed with the mask dangling behind his neck. Villain Blip had worn a more black than gray ensemble. Trav had mentioned that when he turned over a new leaf, he'd wanted a fresh start all around. Hence the reversal of colors.

Joan glanced down at her reliable Spark suit. She loved it, but maybe she needed a design refresh, too. Maybe she could flip the red and black? Even though she really did like the black with slashes of crimson.

"Good news," Mark said to Kade. "The vote didn't pass."

"I'm so happy to hear that," Kade said with genuine happiness. "Is Zee okay?"

"They will be."

"I'll tell Nyah." To Trav, he said, "That's the woman I'm seeing. I don't know if we're officially dating yet, but I think maybe? Or that's where we're heading. I'd like to be dating. She's great. Do you want to see a picture of her?"

"Sure," Trav said.

Sadie should probably be told, too. Joan unzipped her suit to get her phone from an interior pocket. There was already a text from her girlfriend.

> I'm still struggling to stand properly. Good thing I can sit at this desk in my office 😉😅😶

Joan smiled to herself. That was indeed a good thing.

Kade looked up from patting his jogger pockets. "I think my phone's upstairs. Hold on, I'll be right back."

He trotted out of the room. Trav tilted his head, rather obviously checking out Kade's ass.

Mark shook his head. "Straight."

"Really?"

"Yeah."

"Damn."

"I know, right?" Mark elbowed him. "And you're an upstanding guy in a serious relationship."

Trav murmured a "Yeah."

A SuperWatch news notification popped onto Joan's screen. Several alerts chimed from a TV monitor.

> New Report: Dale Terwilliger announces multi-city speaking circuit. The Citizens for Human Cities Tour will begin in Vector City before moving to other major cities.

"Your timing's right on the money, Trav," Joan said.

CHAPTER 17

Joan went over to the touchscreen monitor to see about the other alerts. One included a video just released by the Citizens.

Ugh. As much as she hated wasting brain space on this shit, she had to stay informed. Her brother and Trav flanked her as she tapped to play it.

Hokey metallic-style graphics burst across an American flag. An overly dramatic voiceover lauded the efforts of the Citizens for Human Power and talked about this thrilling speaking tour for those who wanted to take back their cities from "the biggest threat to our way of life."

Dale Terwilliger's smug face appeared, not a dark hair out of place nor a speck of dirt on his navy-blue blazer and tie. He sat behind an imposing wood desk.

"My friends, we are in a national crisis," he said gravely. "For too long, so-called superpowered people have been running rampant through our streets, bringing fear and destruction in their wake. Fellow citizens, *we* are the true superpowered. We must take our power back from these domestic terrorists."

Joan's fingers curled into tight fists.

"I bring you this message of hope for better, more just living conditions in our great nation's most affected cities. Destine, Oceanview…"

"What, none in Canada?" Trav drawled as Dale listed a few other major cities.

"But there is one that far outweighs the others in its shameful decline." Dale looked straight into the camera.

"Vector City?" Joan guessed.

"Vector City. They were unable to stop Big Quake from large-scale destruction multiple times. He returned to cause further damage with Villain allies. This is also the city that allowed two former Villains to escape proper punishment and become…" He made air quotes. "Heroes."

Mark flipped him off with both middle fingers.

"This is the city we must take action in first. I look forward to sharing the stage with special guests and key members of the Citizens for Human Power. We will bring you the truth because we don't hide behind masks."

His smirk turned downright sinister. "We're working on big things. I can't wait to share those with you. We will restore equitability and decency and the true American way of life.

"Let's not look to people flying through the sky, but to our national symbol for strength and freedom."

The shot faded into a bald eagle soaring across snowcapped mountains as patriotic music swelled. It ended on a link to get tickets for the Citizens for Human Cities Tour.

"Human cities," Mark growled. "We are *fucking human*. Why do they keep using that language?"

"They're dehumanizing us," Joan said, the realization hitting hard and heavy. "It's intentional."

Shuffling came from behind them. Kade had returned, arms crossed, his usually jovial face wrinkled in a scowl. "I don't like that guy," he said.

Joan shook with contained emotion. These assholes really didn't value their lives or experiences as human.

She hit the link. "Where are they hosting this in… Vulture

Stadium? Do they really think they'll get enough people to fill an entire ballpark next Saturday?"

"God, I hope not," Mark said.

If that many people were against superpowers... "And I thought the Vultures' home record was the worst thing there," Joan said.

"Of course he picked Vector City first," Trav muttered. "It's the only major city with no active Villains. He wants to start where there's no real threat."

Mark grumbled in agreement.

"He's such a coward," said Trav.

Joan bristled at the c-word.

"Is this our priority now?" Mark asked.

"It's not for a week," Joan said. "I still think Iris is more pressing."

"I don't like the way he talked about restoring equitability. That means taking our powers away."

"They won't give up on that."

"Nuance could still be misleading him," Trav said.

"We can find out from Aura." Joan shrugged out of the top half of her Spark suit, letting the arms dangle. Her sleeveless gray tee offered little to cool her boiling frustration.

Kade frowned at the screen. "Big things for them are never good things for us."

Waving a hand, Trav said, "He's probably just writing another book."

"I wish it was something like that," Joan said. "But I doubt it. The look on his face was..."

She wiped at her forehead, trying to erase the image of the chilling gleam in Dale Terwilliger's eyes. Like he got genuine enjoyment out of ruining lives.

"I need a drink. Of water," she clarified, though something stronger could help ease the stress building in her head. There was so much right now. So many critical fires to put out. And she was much better at setting them.

"I could use that coffee Ward got pulled away from," Trav said.

"I can show you to the kitchen." Joan looked to the other two. "You guys want anything?"

Mark changed his order to a mineral water, and Kade an energy drink.

As they walked down the hall, Joan said, "Will you be extending your trip to attend this exciting display of humanity?"

"I might have to," said Trav.

She couldn't hold in a grunt. "I'm so annoyed. This shit keeps us from doing actual important things."

"Let's focus on what we want versus what we don't. Put our energy there."

"Very philosophical of you."

He got distracted by the portraits, particularly the large ones at the landing of the current Supers. "These are…"

"Gigantic? Ridiculous?"

"Kind of. Where's yours?"

"I don't have one yet. Still on probation." Joan scratched at her ear. "I don't think I want one. They're weird and pretentious. And I love art, so these are doubly offensive to my tastes."

"We sit for official photographs. I remember being really proud that day of everything it took to get there." Trav considered her. "Maybe that's what it'll mean for you."

She shrugged, then continued to the stairs.

He fell in step with her. "Hey, can I ask you something?"

"Sure."

"It's personal. I hope that's okay."

"Of course. We're friends." A little frizzle crackled in her chest. It was nice to have friends.

"Sadie's a norm, right?"

"She is."

"Did she know who you were when you started dating?"

Joan chuckled to herself. "She always knew I had powers. There were some, uh, growing pains at first."

"She knew you were Spark as a Villain?" Trav said.

"Those were the growing pains."

"How does… How did you deal with that? With all the complications?"

"We had to talk, a lot. We had to build trust. I promised to always be honest with her. She keeps my secrets and those of everyone around me."

"See, that's the thing." Trav stopped at the bottom of the wide staircase. "So, my girlfriend and I decided to take a break. That's the real reason I wanted to get out of Yanton for a while."

"Sorry to hear that," Joan said.

"It's for a couple of reasons, like any relationship. But mainly it's the constant lying. It's really rough on her."

"I'm assuming she knows you're Blip."

"Yeah, but she didn't always know I was Travis." His mouth quirked. "She's a journalist."

Joan raised her eyebrows. "Dude."

"I know, I know. She's curious and likes digging into things, and she always wants to get to the truth. We fell for each other professionally before we got involved."

"So she knew what she was getting into?"

"Yes and no. She knew about my past, and she knows the man I've become. Things were pretty good for a while, but it's gotten harder. She quit working at the newspaper because she could no longer be objective in her coverage of Superheroes. She likes where she's at now—it's an independent health journal. But I hate that she had to give up the career path she was on."

"I get that," Joan said.

"How do you two deal with all the lying? I never had trouble bending the truth before."

"Me either."

"But *she* has to lie, and I don't like that. And she doesn't like it."

"Sadie…" Joan cringed and admitted, "…doesn't really have a

problem lying. When she's doing it to protect someone she cares about, or herself."

Like with her family.

"Oh." Trav nodded slowly. "That's good, I suppose."

"We have a few norm friends who know, which is helpful. And she's been welcomed into this world." Joan gestured at the airy lobby.

"We've had to keep our lives very separate. That's been tough."

"That would suck. And like, Sadie's family doesn't know. They think Mark and I run a Brazilian steakhouse. We have to get our story straight every time we talk to them."

"I'm an investment banker." Trav's eyebrows quirked. "I don't actually know what investment bankers do, so I just say my job is good."

"I'm sure you invested in many banks in your day," Joan joked.

"I invested a lot of time and effort into them. Just not while they were open."

"I guess the big thing with me and Sadie is that we don't lie to each other. We don't always have the best communication, but we're working on that. Trust is big for us."

"Yeah, that's a big one for me, too."

She hadn't had the chance to talk to anyone about this who might understand. "I used to worry a ton about her safety. Do you do that?"

"Oh yeah, for sure. It's a part of keeping my Super life separate. I don't want anyone coming after her."

"Sadie's been learning self-defense techniques, so that's helped. But I don't think I'll ever not worry a little."

Trav lifted a shoulder. "I think of it like any couple. There's always a tiny part that doesn't want anything bad to happen to your partner. It's just most people don't worry about Supervillains holding their loved ones for ransom."

"Dude, that happened to Sadie."

"I know. It's not surprising you worry. But you trust her. That's really great." Trav shuffled his feet. "Maybe I'm not all the way there yet. I'm still a work in progress."

"Baby steps every day," Joan said.

"Every day," he agreed.

"You're a lot further along than I am. You're enlightened and shit."

"Lots of therapy. Lots of spiritual work."

Damn it, was she really gonna have to do therapy?

"Sadie has these meditations she listens to on the way to work," Joan said. "I could probably stand to be more zen. The, uh…" She flickered a small flame from her palm. "The fire thing isn't just physical."

"It couldn't hurt to try."

"It might hurt. You ever have a shit-ton of fire back up inside your body?"

"No, but I've had similar sensations. Not using our powers…" He shook his head. "I really don't want to think about what it feels like to not have them permanently. I've had them suppressed for weeks, and it's terrible."

"It's not right."

Trav ran his fingers through his brown waves. "I need to talk to Dale. I know Iris is important, but…"

"Let Mark and I deal with her. You try getting through to Soaring Bald Eagle Man."

Joan led him toward the kitchen. If she and Mark had to leave town, what excuse would Sadie come up with for missing Mr. Eagan's birthday dinner?

All the lying really did suck.

CHAPTER 18

Dad's birthday dinner always featured fresh veggies from his garden. This year, Mom had gone to great lengths to cook them because of Carrie's list of pregnancy no-nos. So it was veggie lasagna in the air-conditioned dining room because the early September heat wasn't good for any of them.

Sadie tucked up a wayward lock of hair that refused to stay in her ballerina bun while Joan fidgeted in her chair. Joanie and Dad had been talking about their gardens while Mom fussed over Carrie, since her husband was out of town at some accounting seminar.

Most people saw Mom's preppy style reflected in Carrie, right down to their matching shoulder-length chocolate-brown hair. Dad's breezy Hawaiian shirt was more on par with Sadie's carefree flair.

In home décor, though, Mom had won out. The renovated dining room was pretty but bland with its grays and blues. It needed pops of lemon yellow and raspberry to liven it up.

Across the rectangular table, Mark made yummy sounds. "Donna, this is delicious. I love the way you used the thin zucchini slices in place of noodles."

"Why thank you, Mark," Mom crowed. She adored Mark and his steady stream of compliments.

Joanie still struggled not to be so formal with "Mr. and Mrs. Eagan." It made her relax more when her brother was there to guide the conversation.

Sadie squeezed her thigh under the table. Joan and Mark were still reeling from Iris's sharp rebuttal to the emails they'd sent her. Using some of their old Villain know-how, they'd found a way to contact her directly rather than make a public spectacle. Her response was to go on social media reaffirming her way was the only way to bring attention to causes that had been ignored.

It wasn't great timing with that gross Citizens tour announcement. Joanie had been distracted all day. Though really since last night after getting home from hanging out with Travis. Sadie'd had to work late in order not to go in today, and she probably didn't need to hear former Villains trade war stories anyway.

She smiled at the melding of her worlds: Mark quizzing Mom about her recipe, Dad and Joanie weighing the pros and cons of pruning tomato plants, Carrie not missing any opportunity to talk about what was going on in *her* life. Even subtly trying to one-up her little sister when Sadie talked about her café (the one she owned, thank you very much) and starting the Super Supporters meetups.

Not that her family cared much for her efforts to support the superpowered.

Joan's phone buzzed in the front pocket of her olive-green pants. She apologized and pulled it out.

"Work-related?" Mark said.

"No, just Trav letting us know he made it to Destine."

To talk with his horrible former stepbrother.

"How goes the restaurant business?" Dad asked as he cut into his lasagna.

"Good," Joan and Mark answered together.

"It's been keeping them busy," Sadie said.

"Are you planning on opening something closer to home?" Mom asked.

"Hopefully," Mark said.

"Maybe a restaurant near Sadie's Café."

Sadie shared a grin with her mother. Her family's support was chipping away at the old worries that'd been holding her back. Mom finally recognized—and acknowledged—Sadie's badass business owner-ness, and it was awesome.

"It'd have to be a different concept," Mark said. "A Brazilian steakhouse would do better downtown. A casual Italian restaurant or an elevated burger place would be good for the Village."

Carrie studied him, then swung her gaze to Joan. "Doesn't Restaurante Falso mean something like false restaurant?"

Sadie coughed into her napkin.

Joan made a vague shrug and said, "It translates differently in Portuguese."

"Portuguese," Mark said, nodding. "It's a good time to start a new business in Vector City, so we'll see."

Joan cast a look at Sadie. They'd gone over the latest developments with the fake restaurant on the drive to West Vector. Then Joanie had taken her hand and said, "Sorry you have to keep lying to them."

The alternative was exposing her secret identity, and almost as bad, damning Sadie to a level of overprotective parenting the likes of which she didn't want to imagine.

Mom ripped an end off her garlic breadstick. "Did you hear that Dale Terwilliger is starting a speaking tour in Vector City?"

"Ew, Mom," Sadie said. "That guy's disgusting."

"He talks about things a lot of people feel."

"I thought you didn't watch Badger News."

"I don't usually," Mom said. "I've seen him in some interviews. It's about time people stood up to these menaces."

Sadie gripped her fork tight. She darted a look at Mark. His expression didn't change, though his irises swirled slightly in varying shades of blue.

"Having abilities is part of who they are," she said. "Calls to restrict them is like telling tall people not to be tall. It's in their DNA."

Dad speared a bite of lasagna. "I don't think they should be restricted or their powers taken away. But they should be more considerate and think about what they're doing before they cause so much damage."

"Vector City is the most logical place to start." Mom waved across the table with her breadstick. "You three should want that after what happened to your food truck."

"Yes, someone with powers crushed it," Sadie said. "But more people with powers saved the city. There's so much good that comes from—"

"You're such a Superhero apologist," Carrie said, then took a sip of water.

"I've seen firsthand what they do. You haven't."

"I've seen the dangerous world my baby is being born into. Things are scary enough without the added stress."

Mom and Dad agreed.

Sadie wanted to jump on the table and rage. "Just don't ever mention Dale Terwilliger. He's a hatemonger who preys on people's fears."

She shared a sad, understanding look with Joanie.

Mark cleared his throat. "I'm sure the city's Heroes appreciate things like you did, Sades, with the signs and hashtags."

"Thanks," Sadie said while her sister said "Apologist" again. That made her blood boil. "So what if I advocate for them?"

"Even the ones who were Villains?" Carrie sniffed distastefully.

"Especially them. Spark and Ice are good people. Breeze is, too. They all helped when I—"

Whoops, that almost slipped out.

Carrie narrowed her eyes. "When you what? With the food truck? 'Cause, uh, that got pulverized."

Sadie glanced at Joan. Her wonderful, wonderful Joan. "How

can I properly support the Supers when I can't even tell my family what happened to me?" she murmured.

"With the..." Joan gazed into her eyes. "On the roof?"

"Yeah."

Her lips parted.

Sadie sucked in a deep breath. Blew it out. Stared down at her plate, gathering the strength to look at her parents.

"Remember last year when Trick, Volt and Hide got captured? They kidnapped someone and had them on the roof of that skyscraper. All the Heroes banded together to stop them and rescue that person."

Joan set a steadying hand on her upper back.

"That was me. I was the hostage."

Mom's mouth curved in disbelief. "What? No you weren't."

"My identity was never released because I didn't want you to worry. But yeah, it was me. Trick used mind control to get me up there. But then Spark—and everyone else—rescued me."

Dad sat up, realization spreading over his face.

"They were really kind," Sadie said. "They made sure I was okay. Spark in particular was... They were all concerned about me, but Spark was really nice."

"Oh my god," Carrie breathed, her brown eyes large and round.

"So I don't want you thinking badly about the former Villains. They—"

"Sadie Jane Eagan!" Mom's hands fluttered to her chest. "You were kidnapped by Supervillains and didn't tell us?"

"I didn't want you freaking out."

"Why didn't you tell us after it happened?" Dad said. "We should have been there for you."

"I had Joanie." Sadie's lips trembled as she smiled at Joan. "She took care of me."

Joan gave her a tiny smile and rubbed her back. Her forehead was wrinkled in concern.

"You told Joan but not your parents?" Mom looked like she was about to erupt.

"She was my neighbor. It was just—"

"You are so dead," Carrie muttered.

"Sadie." Dad raised stern gray eyebrows at her. "You do not keep something like that from us. You must have been terrified. Were you hurt?"

"No, I was fine," Sadie said. "I was under mind control, so I don't really remember it."

Mom stood and buzzed around her chair. "Why you? What did…?"

"I don't know why they took me. Wrong place, wrong time."

Joan's hand clamped protectively around her shoulder.

"The whole experience brought Joan and I closer together." Sadie patted Joan's hand, telling her she was okay. "It was one of the good things to come out of it."

"I've told you time and time again living in that city is dangerous." Mom tossed her hands. "And I thought the scariest thing was that food truck incident. Little did I know you…you…"

Now Sadie felt bad as Mom's eyes filled with tears. "Please don't cry. It was fine."

"It was *not* fine! You were just minding your own business when these Villains decided you were disposable."

"No, it wasn't like that. I, um…"

"It wasn't random," Joan said quietly.

Mark whipped his head to gape at her. So did Sadie.

"I know why they took her."

"No, Joanie." Sadie leaned in and set a hand on Joan's knee. She was not going to expose herself to spare Sadie.

Joan pulled her arm back to clasp her hands at the edge of her plate.

"Joanie…?" Mark's voice held a question as much as a warning.

"Why, then?" Mom spluttered. "Why did my daughter attract the attention of Supervillains?"

"You don't have to," Sadie murmured.

"Yes, I do." Joan gave her a tight smile. "We can't keep lying to them."

"Are you sure?"

"Yeah."

"Are you sure?" Mark said.

Sadie held her breath, the room suddenly cramped and hot.

Joan stared at her hands. "The reason they took Sadie was to get to me. They wanted to get my attention…because I'm Spark."

The words floated in the air like they were waiting to be exhaled.

Sadie couldn't let her hang out to dry, so she said, "It's true. I've always known. I knew when she rescued me."

"I knew you were hiding something," Carrie cried.

Mom pressed her fingers to her mouth, eyes glassy as she gazed at Joan like seeing her for the first time.

"Don't be mad," Sadie said.

"I'm the same person you've gotten to know," Joan said. "The foodie who's madly in love with your daughter."

Sadie nestled her hands atop Joan's and squeezed them.

"I guess I want you to know all of me. Sadie kept this from you to protect me. I'm sorry we lied to you."

Dad looked like he was gradually processing the information. "Then you knew… Sadie, you know she was a criminal."

"I do," Sadie said.

"She broke the law for many years."

"She broke a lot of everything," Carrie chortled. Was she enjoying this, or masking her fear with humor?

"I did a lot of bad things," Joan said, which just about broke Sadie's heart.

She scooted closer. "But she did a lot of good things during that time. Remember when we got an anonymous ten thousand dollars at Vector City Coffee? That was from Joan."

She kept waiting for Mom to explode in a furious freakout. Or Dad to tell Joanie she was no longer welcome.

They just kept staring at her like they weren't sure what to do.

Carrie pointed at Mark. "Then who are you? Are you really her twin brother?"

The insinuation hung heavy.

Joan looked at her brother, her face telegraphing *It's up to you.*

Mark shrugged. "Ah, hell. Yes, I'm Joanie's brother. You might also know me as a plucky guy who goes by Ice."

He twirled his hand to toss ice shavings in the air. They dropped on his plate.

"Oh my god," Carrie said.

"Oh my god," Dad stated.

"Oh my god!" Mom's hands flew to her cheeks. She turned to Joan and said, "Show us how you..."

"Do you really want me to?" Joan shared an uneasy look with Sadie. "It can be a little unsettling."

"*Do it.*"

Joan slid her hands free. She flicked a tiny spark between two fingers.

"No, really do it," Mom said. "I need to see this."

Joan exhaled, then circled her hand so a flame rose from her palm. She let it flicker for a few seconds before waving it out. Showing everyone she could control it.

Dad sat statue-still in his seat. "Then you two are Spark and Ice," he said slowly. He nodded at Joan. "Spark." Then he nodded at Mark. "And Ice."

"Yup." Mark stuck a finger in his lemonade. The ice cubes crackled as the glass frosted over. "If you need me to cool down your drink, that's my specialty. Joanie can heat up your coffee if it gets cold."

"Spark, and Ice." Dad repeated his head nods.

"Then there is no restaurant," Carrie said.

"No. It's our cover story." Joan's lips quirked. "It does mean fake restaurant."

"I knew it," she hissed with a certain amount of glee.

Sadie pushed her chair back, getting concerned that her mom wasn't moving. Was she in shock? Should they call an ambulance?

"Mom, are you okay?" she said, rising on unsteady legs.

"Sadie…" she whispered through her tears.

Joan stood, and they laced fingers. "Mrs. Eagan, I swear to you I would do anything to protect Sadie."

"She already has," Mark added. "We all look out for her. She's probably the most well-protected person in Vector City."

"That's true," Sadie said. "I spend a lot of time at their headquarters. That building is indestructible."

She left out that Quake and Company hadn't been able to topple it.

"I'm friends with the Superheroes. Lunk—he's huge, nobody messes with him. And Race is really great."

"Sadie." Now Mom's voice had some weight to it. "I… I…"

Sadie steeled herself for the inevitable.

"Well, I guess it makes sense."

"Huh?" That was not at all what she'd been expecting.

"We wondered about a few things, didn't we, Stuart?"

"There were some things that never quite added up," Dad said.

"We figured there was trauma in your past you didn't want to talk about, Joan, and we respected that. Sadie told us how you're estranged from your parents. We could see you'd turned your life around. And you've been wonderful with Sadie. You've been the best partner she's had in a long while. Maybe ever." Mom shook her head. "I'm trying to reconcile the person we know with…"

"A menace?" Joan said softly.

Mom and Dad looked at each other.

"I guess we never considered who was behind those masks," Mom said. "The sort of people you might be."

"Your lives outside of being Superheroes," Dad said.

"Or Villains." Carrie grinned with big sister superiority. "If anyone would date a Supervillain who became a Superhero, it'd be my sister."

Now it was Sadie's turn to have trouble processing what was going on. Her parents really liked Joan. Had just said she was the best partner of Sadie's life, which was true. They didn't even seem distressed.

Clapping her hands together, Mom said, "We do have some serious complaints about the actions of the superpowered, though."

"So do I," Joan said.

"Me too," Mark chimed in.

"We're happy to listen to them. We're trying to make positive changes to the system."

Sadie's gaze ping-ponged between her parents. "You're not upset?"

"Oh, I'm extremely upset," Mom said. "And I have *a lot* of questions. But we owe it to you to try and understand."

"We like you, Joan." Dad smiled at her, then Mark. "You too, Mark."

"Thanks, Stuart," Mark said.

Sadie ventured, "Maybe in time, you'll like Spark and Ice."

Holding up a hand, Mom said, "Let's take this one day at a time."

"That's fair," Joan said.

"You can't tell anyone," Sadie stated firmly. "Nobody. I mean it. Not a soul."

"It's for everyone's safety." Mark glanced at Carrie.

"Obviously." Carrie cradled her belly. "I don't want anyone coming after me or my baby."

That alarmed Mom. "Do you think that would happen? Should we be worried?"

Joan screwed her face up and said, "All the Villains I fought are now in prison. That sends a pretty strong message not to mess with the people I care about."

"Yes." Mom frowned at Sadie. "Why didn't you tell us about getting kidnapped? Did you have that pepper spray you're supposed to carry with you at all times?"

Dad wagged a finger at her. "You had your earphones in and weren't paying attention."

"Earbuds, Dad," Carrie corrected.

The focus turned to Sadie's untruth. Not Joanie's. Not Mark's. A normal amount of parental concern.

They were more upset about Sadie's fibbing than her living with a woman who shot fire out of her body.

Holy shit.

She started giggling ridiculously. Joanie quirked her eyebrows like *What the hell?* Then she seemed to get it and started chuckling.

Mark got in on the realization and laughed, too.

Holy shit, what a relief. It crested off her in waves. Joanie too, with a whoosh of heat.

Her parents knew. Her parents *knew and didn't care.*

Well, they cared, but they were being remarkably not terrible about it.

Poor Joanie, though. Her girlfriend's parents were aware, but not her own.

Ignoring her family's questions, Sadie tugged Joan into a hug.

"I'm proud of you for telling them," Joanie whispered in her ear.

"They deserved the truth," Sadie whispered back. "Why did you expose your secret identity?"

Joan's arms tightened. "Trav and his girlfriend broke up from all the lying. That's not going to happen with us."

Sadie caught Mom watching them, nerves wrinkling her forehead. But her mouth was tilted in a small display of pleasure. She could see that Joan Malone was the right person for her daughter, even with those dreadful superpowers.

Pulling back so she could say it directly to the love of her life, Sadie promised, "That's *not* going to happen with us."

CHAPTER 19

Despite decades in the criminal element, Joan hadn't spent much time in sewers. She looked down at the sludge coating her Spark suit. At least it was a storm sewer and not a sanitation one because *that* would be as shitty as the rest of her day.

It'd started out a pretty good Tuesday with a quick breakfast with Sadie. Her parents had still not combusted after the "Happy birthday, your daughter's dating Spark" bombshell. She'd driven Sadie to the café and gotten coffee for her coworkers. Darlene had patrolled late last night, so she hadn't baked (and thus potentially burned) anything yet.

Then there was a second attempt at reaching out to Nuance. This time, he'd video called back to tell Joan that Dale Terwilliger had stopped communicating with him, and had she done anything about Greta since it appeared she was still free?

And then Trav had reported that Dale had rebuffed him, telling him this movement was not about revenge, it was about righteousness. It'd ended with an ominous "Wait and see what we have coming."

And *then* Ward had gotten word about a broken line in the main sewer system that Spark surely could help weld back together. Only it turned out storm sewers were made of cement.

And the long, low crack could only be repaired via more cement. No firepower needed.

So Joan had taken one for the team in her sturdy protective bodysuit to kneel in the muck and help patch it up. The slime clung to the latex like a long-lost lover.

The public works crew couldn't help chuckling as Joan clomped toward ladder. At least that was made of metal.

Ward owed her for this.

"Thanks again," the foreman or crew chief or whoever said. "I'd shake your hand, but…"

"There's a hose up top?" Joan said.

"Pretty sure there's a fire truck up there."

If not, she was going to fly into the city sky trailing gunk and flecks of cement. That would do wonders for her reputation.

She climbed the ladder to a chorus of thanks from the crew. Nice folks, though her willingness to assist had probably quieted any qualms they had about her.

Bright daylight greeted her as she climbed out of the manhole. The street had been partially blocked off.

There was a police cruiser, two public works trucks, and exactly zero sources of water.

"I thought we were friends, firefighters," she muttered.

Clicks from phone cameras and laughter came from looky-loos and passersby. Ah, hell. Let 'em share Spark helping her city.

Joan mustered a smile and small wave. "All in a day's work."

"Did you shoot any fire down there?" a goofy white dude asked behind his phone.

"Didn't have to."

"Can you do it now? I wanna see if all that toxic sewage on you ignites."

"Why would you want that?"

The guy laughed like a hyena. He held his phone closer. "Come on. Do it."

"No."

"It'd be so cool. Come on, Spark."

"Dude, nobody wants that smell."

He kept demanding to see if toxic sludge would burn. What a douche. *Light yourself on fire to see if you burn, Spark.*

She wasn't letting this guy go viral, so she flicked excess muck off her gloves and shot into the air. She kept her speed slow—not that it mattered, as the sludge loved her suit. The cement was rapidly crusting onto it.

It was unnerving to have norms provoke her into shooting fire. They used to avoid it at all costs. Were they getting more comfortable with her, or more comfortable poking the bear to see if it attacked?

She used the rooftop entrance at HQ and went straight to the changing rooms. "Ward!" she barked, sounding like Otis but not giving a damn. "You owe me a thorough suit cleaning."

"I think he's out with Otis," Mark's voice came from the gym.

"Shit."

"We were supposed to work out together."

"Got called into action."

"What did…" He stepped out of the gym, took one look at her, and burst into a fit of giggles that quickly morphed into horror. "Is that what I think it is?"

"Storm sewer mess and cement?"

"Oh thank god. You smell like shit."

Joan peeled off one glove, then put it back on to unzip the gross menace.

"Perry wants to see us at the warehouse."

"Why?"

Mark shrugged. "Maybe he wants to lecture us about coming clean to Sadie's parents."

"I didn't tell him we did that."

"Yeah, better let him find out accidentally. Preferably when he's in a good mood after seeing Gus." He plugged his nose and waved her away. "Speaking of coming clean…"

Joan stalked down the hallway. "I'm going!"

"Do you have workout gear? We can see if today's the day our old punching bag completely disintegrates."

"Let me shower first."

"Just take your suit off. You'll get all sweaty anyway."

"*Shower.* The stench is trapped in my nose."

She did, in fact, wash the stink off her person and changed into black leggings and a loose blue tank.

The warehouse. Hmm. In all the madness lately, she'd forgotten about that weird afternoon where Perry gave Gus a tour of it. That could be what this was about.

After leaving a not altogether polite note for Ward in the control center about the mess he needed to address upstairs, Joan met Mark in the garage.

His sports car was nowhere to be found, so she said, "Guess I'm driving."

"I got a ride to work," Mark said, a private smile on his lips.

"A very quick one, I imagine."

"Beats sitting in traffic."

"Don't you get sick? I get super nauseous when Zee races me somewhere."

Mark headed toward her sedan, saying, "I've gotten used to it."

"I'll bet you have," Joan drawled suggestively just to piss him off.

As they buckled in, she mused, "You've been spending a lot of nights together."

"So?"

"Like, actual full nights. You didn't go home when we got back from West Vector. You went to Zee's place."

"So?"

"So, the Mark Malone I've known my entire existence wouldn't have even texted when he got home. You went all the way across town."

Mark slid his sunglasses on, poised for a comeback, but then stayed silent.

Joan focused on getting out of the garage and onto Leyton Avenue. "All jokes aside, you know how much I like this for you."

After a long pause, he said, "I know."

"You two have some serious feels, don't you?"

"It's…whatever." Mark squirmed in his seat. "Feelings are gross. Zee thinks feelings are gross. We enjoy each other or whatever. Good company. They occasionally make me laugh."

"Come on." Joan sent him a knowing look. "You hardly talk about them. I've been the unlucky recipient of every sordid detail of your love life since you made out with Jimmy Galliano freshman year."

"It was Timmy Galliano, and yes, I suppose…" He scratched at his ear. "I suppose talking about it makes it more real."

"It *is* real."

He groaned and blew a puff of cold air on the passenger window. Drew a frowny face in it with his finger.

"You're falling for them. Just admit it."

He groaned louder and slouched in his seat.

"Why is that a bad thing? Zee's great. They keep you on your toes, and you do the same."

"I *might* have feelings for them," Mark said, so falsely indifferent Joan almost laughed. "But we have a contentious past. There's still lingering resentment on my part for the years of freebies from the norms. Zee's like what would've happened with us if we'd fought for the good guys from the start. They got handed everything on a silver platter."

"And we had to steal the silver platter." Joan nodded. "I get that."

"I had to work really hard, and I'm still working really hard. We have to keep proving ourselves and starting over. It's sometimes annoying to see how easy it was for them. Not that it's always easy for them."

Mark rolled his head to look at her. "We don't get a lot of the microaggressions they do. We're cis and white. We mostly get a free pass when we're not in our Superhero outfits."

A pang cramped Joan's chest. "You're right. Zee gets hit from all sides all the time."

"They had to publicly come out as nonbinary. That was a whole thing."

"I can't even imagine."

"Seriously," Mark said. "Being a Superhero and having to explain what that means a million times over. Truth be told, I always admired how they handled it all with grace."

"You got their pronouns right away," Joan recalled.

"Yeah. I was a Villain, not an asshole."

She smiled and flicked the turn signal on at a red light. "Do you think that's why the youth center situation was so awful for them?"

"It definitely was. They really feel like that's a place for people to belong. Being excluded would've been a giant slap in the face."

"Shit." Joan glanced at her brother. "I kinda feel like an asshole for all the crap we gave them."

"Don't feel too bad," Mark said with a half-smile. "They gladly took some of the freebies as a *fuck you* to douchey people."

They laughed, but Joan still felt the twinges of guilt. Otis probably had more than one norm treat him like shit, in and out of Flight gear. And Sherrelle, and Zee, and…

"If we think it's hard to gain respect, it's gotta be a thousand times worse for superpowered people of color."

"White privilege," Mark sang, swaying his arms in a white boy dance.

"Well, if anyone's mean to Zee, I'll kick their ass. As Spark or not."

"Thanks. I think they know you would."

"And what would you do to defend their honor?"

He tapped his chin, then narrowed his eyes. "Remember what you did to Melvin when he took Sadie?"

"Of course."

"Like that."

"Wow. You *do* like them, buddy."

She reached over to mess up his hair, but he blocked her. So she opened her mouth to joke that therapy seemed to be helping. Nah. Therapy wasn't a joke. And it apparently *was* working. He was seeing outside of his own experiences, thinking of someone else's needs.

Still, she was his big sis, so she teased, "Mark and Zee, sittin' in a tree…"

"Watch the road, jerkface."

Knowing her brother was doing so well improved her mood. Sure, it was a little weird that Mark wasn't coming to her for everything, but not an unwelcome weird. This had to be how he felt when she'd started dating Sadie. Why he always stopped by before Zee entered the romantical picture. Joan had changed their slightly codependent dynamic first.

As they approached the warehouse, Mark remembered Perry had said to park outside. She pulled up near the concealed side entrance. Always secret entries to secure places. Even an access card and alarm at home. Some parts of her life—her version of normal—would always be this way.

It wasn't surprising to find Gus sitting at the table with Per, both of them looking over a spreadsheet.

Joan did a double-take as she passed a few stacks of boxes and large crates. A wrapped sculpture. Several framed paintings, including the Flemish landscape that had been in Perry's living room for years.

"Doing some remodeling, Per?" she asked.

"You're late," Gus said. "Join us over here."

"Joanie had to shower." Mark cringed. "Trust me."

Joan focused on what was definitely three paintings that once graced the walls of Perry's condo. "What is all this?"

Perry stood and walked around the table. "When our former associates left their homes, they left what they'd taken. A lot of items would have been seized and neglected, or sold for a fraction of their worth at some auction."

"We've been collecting it, but we need a place to store all of it."

Gus waved a hand at the boxes. "Hence our need to repurpose this space."

Scratching at his hair, Mark said, "You're stealing already stolen goods? Should we report you for dual thievery?"

"We're not keeping them," Gus stated sharply. "We are giving them back to their rightful owners."

Joan blinked. "Sorry, I think I misheard you. You're giving them back? All of them?"

"Yes."

"But what about..." She walked over to the paintings. "Per, these are yours. You're giving back what you took?"

His mouth twisted a few times before he said, "I don't need them. They'll be better served in a museum or on public display."

Mark squinted and peered at him. "Did you sustain a head injury? Should we be alarmed?"

"What, I can't turn over a new leaf, too?"

Joan touched a stormy seascape. "But these are your pride and joy."

Perry crossed his arms and leaned toward her. "Did you know Ethel had a supposedly lost VanderHooven?"

"No." Hard to imagine boring Ethel with anything of real value. "Which one?"

"*Still Life With Roses.*"

"Really? That's been missing for decades."

Perry smirked with delight. "It was."

Excitement dancing through her veins, Joan said, "Where is it?"

"In my den."

"Nice."

Gus narrowed her eyes. "That was the only sticking point I had to concede to get everything else."

Ah. It made total sense that Gus was the driving force behind this. An artist and former defender of good wanting stolen art to be returned.

Shit, she was gonna go after Joan's stash, wasn't she?

"How are you going to give it all back?" Mark asked. "Put it on the steps at City Hall with a big note?"

Perry nodded at the spreadsheet on the table. "We know where a lot of it came from. It will be delivered anonymously, like we used to."

Mark jutted a thumb at Joan. "Haven't you heard? Spark and Ice take credit for their past good deeds now."

"But not our past misdeeds," Joan pointed out. "We can't be the ones who return all this."

"This isn't about credit," Gus said, shuffling toward them. "It's about righting some wrongs."

"Except for the VanderHooven," Mark snickered.

Perry leveled him with a *You should know better* glare. "It's a *VanderHooven*."

Gus raised a displeased eyebrow at him.

Perry gave her a look in return. "I'm keeping the mystery of what happened to it going a little longer."

Joan headed over to the table. Being so close to a pile of loot she could very easily get her sticky fingers on was quite the temptation. "We'll help you however we can. I'm assuming that's why you wanted us here."

"Not exactly." Perry followed her. "You shouldn't be linked to this."

Gus grumbled about everyone sitting down right after she'd gotten up.

Once they were settled, Perry said, "This is going to be a somewhat legitimate operation. You can still come here, but you have to remove anything personal. Anything to connect yourselves. The workout stuff, the—"

"You said we could leave that here," Joan said.

"You can't use it whenever you want. We'll be in and out with new items and moving vans. You'll be in the way if you're working the punching bag."

"That thing needs to be thrown away," Gus sniffed.

"Nooo!" Joan and Mark cried.

"We carried that all the way from this gym that was getting rid of it," Mark said. "It's one of the only things we legally obtained as young Villains. It's sentimental."

"It's falling apart," Gus said.

"Then I'll keep it at my place. I'll rent another warehouse. I'll…"

He tried to figure out an alternative as Joan's emotional tornado consumed her. The warehouse was their safe place. It had been for years. Where they'd hung out, planned heists, celebrated after them, dreamed of and had their food truck, where they'd grown up…

It was like losing their childhood home all over again.

Perry sighed loudly. "You'll still be able to come here. We have to remove any trace of what this place was used for."

"We have to say goodbye to it," Joan whispered, her throat itchy and tight.

"You're both being very dramatic. Just get the gym stuff out. Anything in the changing room you left behind."

She met Mark's gaze, silently lamenting the same thing: This was the last time they'd truly get to hang out here.

Perry shuffled his papers. "I didn't think this old place meant so much to you."

"Whatever. It's fine." Mark shrugged a shoulder, Mr. Nonchalance.

This was one more thing slipping away from Joan. Perry could —and should, it was a good idea—use the space for something better. He'd been the one to start reimbursing the norms for loss and damage, so such benevolence wasn't out of left field. But it sucked.

"Can we at least store the workout stuff in the changing room until we find a place for it?" she said. "We need time, and this is low on our list of important shit right now."

"Temporarily, fine," Perry said. "Or get rid of it. You can exercise at your headquarters. Joanie, your building has an entire workout center."

But she didn't want neighbors or spinning classes or whatever they did there. She wanted to lift weights with her brother and heat up the dumbbells so they shocked him when he grabbed them. Or spar with Sadie and maybe Greta again someday. This was *her* fucking space and she wanted it.

She just didn't want to lose it.

Mark elbowed her. "We'll move it all today and find a permanent home in between guarding the city and trying not to get our powers taken away by ignorant shitheads."

"Yes." Gus's thin lips pursed. "How is it going with your efforts to curb that awful group? Other malcontents have come and gone over the years. What concerns me about this one is their mobilization. Your computer doohickeys make it easy to spread lies and rhetoric."

"Plus this one's trying to access technology that suppresses our powers," Mark said.

"The only thing all Supers seem to agree on is that they're bad news," Joan said. "I've even seen a few Villains post on Super-Watch speaking out against the Citizens."

Her brother laughed. "The one thing Heroes and Villains can band together on. Our mutual hatred of Dale Terwilliger."

Villains got to voice their disdain with language Joan wished she could use. Padma had expressly told her she couldn't say "This fuckin' guy."

"What about the young one? What's her name?" Gus looked to Perry. "The one who keeps saying she'll blow things up."

"Iris," Perry said.

"She's gaining a popular following. Is she speaking out against this group?"

"I think so, but it's one of her many grievances."

Gus touched one of the lists. "She could help return stolen goods."

"Is that noble enough?" Mark rolled his eyes. "She only does large-scale noble causes."

"It's noble to those who will get their possessions back."

Joan shook her head at the idea. "Overall public perception of her isn't great. Plus I don't think she'd help you sneak around. She likes the spotlight."

But she knew someone who craved the spotlight in a different way—from her excellent skills at sneaking around. Someone who needed new challenges, who would relish the skill-sharpening, who…

Who was on a Superhero's shit list and needed a good deed to get Nuance off her back.

"What if Greta helped you?" Joan said.

Mark burst into a loud laugh.

"Nuance is on my case. I at least have to pretend like she's being punished. What if she does one, maybe two jobs for you— really tricky returns. I make it seem like she's reforming her ways. Then everyone's satisfied."

"Everyone but Greta," Mark chortled.

"This could be the only way out of her predicament."

Gus raised a blonde eyebrow. "Can she be trusted?"

"We always have," Joan said. She looked to her brother and Perry to back her up.

"Greta does love a good challenge," Mark said. "And yeah, we trust her."

Perry picked up a different list of information. "I wouldn't trust her to babysit or lead peace talks, but for this, yes."

All Joan had to do was convince Grets this was the best olive branch she could extend. A thank-you for protecting superpowered people from the Citizens getting that damning tech.

It was worth a phone call to find out.

CHAPTER 20

It'd been a busy Wednesday so far at Sadie's Café. People were back to their post-summer routines. No food truck was parked outside, but a group of Super Supporters had commandeered the outdoor dining space to plan a protest at Dale Terwilliger's speech. They'd all ordered drinks and snacks and had tipped well, thanking the staff for hosting. That was awesome.

Less awesome, Sadie and Nyah had to have a Come to Jesus talk with Estelle that afternoon. She was one strike away from being fired. Nobody wanted that, but it was the crappy reality of needing to do what was best for her business.

Sadie glanced over at Estelle humming along to the glam rock Cam had won Rock Paper Scissors to get to play. She looked up from cleaning some spilled almond milk to greet an incoming customer.

Ugh, this conversation was gonna suck.

Sadie stepped behind one of the tablets and smiled at the skinny white dude. "Hi, welcome to Sadie's Café. What can we get you today?"

"Sadie," he said.

"Yes, I'm Sadie."

"I heard you opened a coffeehouse."

She blinked and really looked at him.

Oh god—it was Ferret Guy, one of her not so illustrious exes.

"Oh hey, hi," she said. "How are you?"

"Good. Good. Nice to see you."

"Nice to see you, too." Oh god, what was his real name?

He eyed her up and down. "You look great. Really great."

"Thanks. So do you." Well, he looked how she remembered: sort of bland. That was why she'd given him a chance—he was a remarkably unremarkable guy with a steady job. A change of pace…until it'd been time to pet-sit his three ill-behaved ferrets.

"You've been busy, huh?" Ferret Guy said, glancing around.

"Very busy, yeah. We opened in the spring."

"That's great. Hey, we should hang out. It's been too long." He grinned. "The babies would love to see you."

Nope. No way. Not a chance. "Thanks, but I have a girlfriend."

Ferret Guy processed that, his grin widening a hair too much. "That's right, you… Yeah. Okay. No worries."

"She's actually stopping by shortly. She's so supportive of this place."

"Cool. She sounds great."

Sadie smiled to herself. "Yeah, she's super."

They engaged in chitchat before she took his order. (A plain black coffee she suspected he got because it was the cheapest possible thing.) Then she let Cam fulfill the order so she could "get back to work" by clearing tables.

Ugh, Ferret Guy. Thank goodness she had her Super girlfriend now. Even if she was a little miffed at Joanie.

Greta was coming to meet with Joan to discuss her proposition. A proposition that—*hello!*—Sadie had suggested but gotten quickly rebuffed. She was still annoyed by that and let Joanie know last night.

Joan had been contrite, but this new development with Gus and Perry somehow made it different to her. It wasn't working *with* the Supers, but giving the illusion of it.

Which again was what Sadie had suggested, but whatever.

Part of her wanted Greta to say no. A tiny but vengeful part, probably stoked by hanging out with Perry.

Her phone vibrated with what she already knew was another check-in from Mom. The shock had worn off, so now it was questions like "Are you ever scared she might burn you?" And Carrie sending screenshots of Joanie covered in sewer muck with gleeful LOLs.

It was still a million times better than how she thought they'd react. A few worried texts and phone calls with intrusive questions ("What about when you're...*you know*..." from her mother, ew) were the best possible outcome.

Alexis came out from the back, ready to start her shift in the black café T-shirt and twin French braids trailing down her shoulder blades. She checked the dwindling art supplies. Customers were really into creating signs either for the café's windows or their own.

"We're almost out of everything," Sadie said. "I have to make another trip to the store."

"That's so cool," Alexis said with a smile.

Nyah poked her head out from behind the Progress Pride flag, giving Sadie a look that said *Let's get it over with*.

Sadie nodded glumly. She paused with her handfuls of plates and mugs at the edge of the counter. "Estelle, can I borrow you for a minute?"

"Sure thing, boss." Estelle high-fived Alexis on her way by.

Sadie set the dirty dishes in one of the sinks, then gestured to the office.

Estelle saw Nyah already in there. Her face fell. "Uh-oh. An office meeting."

"Go in and have a seat, please." Sadie used her Boss Voice.

Estelle slunk into the rolling chair in the corner.

Sadie closed the door and said, "We need to have a serious discussion about your future with us. We all love having you here, but you need to be here on time and ready when your shift starts. And after lunch."

She nodded, her lower lip trembling. "I really am sorry. I know I keep messing up."

Sitting in the other chair, Sadie said, "Is there something we can help you with? Do you need better transportation, or a different schedule?"

"No, it's not the schedule. There's been a lot going on, but it's not like anything out of the ordinary for my life."

One skill she'd learned from Joan, and even Gus, was the importance of listening. Giving someone a chance to air their concerns. So Sadie leaned in. "Nyah and I are here for you if you need help."

Estelle's gaze swung to Nyah, then back to Sadie. "I've been worried about my cousin and our auntie. They've had some stuff going on. I have to keep going between their homes to help out. It makes me be late, and my anxiety and ADHD doesn't help with that. That's not a good excuse, I know."

"Family's important," Nyah said. "You know my schedule's dependent on my aunt's medical treatments."

"Their health is good. It's just, uh, work, for my cousin. And, uh, other stuff. Justin runs this medical clinic that's had a lot of extra stuff this year."

"Justin?" That pinged Sadie's antenna. "Your cousin's name is Justin, and he's a doctor?"

"Yeah," Estelle said. "You might have met him. He's stopped in a few times."

"Justin Devers?"

"Yeah."

"Yes, I know him. I didn't know he was your cousin."

They stared at each other, assessing the situation. Estelle apparently knew Justin was…

Oh, wait. His aunt was a retired Hero. The same one as…

"And your aunt?" Sadie said.

"She doesn't live around here. Things have been a little rough with, uh…" Estelle scratched her nose. "She's pretty upset by the Citizens for Human Power."

"Why?" Nyah asked.

Sadie gave Estelle a subtle eyebrow raise. "Because she champions human rights," she pulled out of her butt. "She cares about the mistreatment of targeted groups of people."

"Exactly," Estelle said, nodding.

How much did she actually know? Joanie and Mark's secret identities?

Nyah half-sat on the edge of the desk. "What's really going on? What do you two know that I don't?"

Shit.

Sadie exhaled, then gestured at her friend. "Okay, let's be real. I know what Justin does because I met him at Superhero headquarters. And I've been there because—"

"Joan is Spark," Estelle said like it was no biggie. "And the rest of them. Nyah's dating Lunk."

"What, who, what?" Nyah looked around, mouth hanging open.

Sadie swiveled her chair to better see both of them. "Justin is the doctor for all the Superheroes in this region. Their aunt is a retired Superhero. No, I don't know which one. I guess Justin talks about it with his family."

Estelle nodded. "Yeah, I've always known about you and the twins and everyone. Justin's the one who told me about the job opening here. He said I'd be safe here."

Nyah said something, only Sadie's antenna pinged harder on Estelle's words. It all made sense now.

She asked anyway. "You have powers, don't you?"

The young woman scrunched her neck in toward her shoulders. "Yeah," she said slowly.

"What?" Nyah's eyes widened. "You're a Superhero? Which one?"

"No. I have powers, but I don't control them very well. I keep them a secret."

"What do you do?"

Nyah leaned in. Sadie did, too.

"I can teleport," Estelle said.

"You can teleport." A bark of laughter escaped Sadie's mouth. "You can teleport and you're always late?"

"I know I know I know." Estelle tugged on her black T-shirt's neckband. "I get someplace and lose track of time. And then I have to go somewhere private to do it, and sometimes I end up in the wrong place. Like I go home instead of back to work if I have lunch with my auntie. She's in a different time zone, and that always messes me up."

Sadie couldn't stop laughing. Nyah even snorted at how hilarious it was.

"You think it's only the people in spandex who have abilities? There are more of us who choose to live under the radar."

Like Perry had tried to do.

"It doesn't always work, though," Sadie said. "Keeping it hidden."

"Not always," Estelle said. "That's why I'm extra careful."

"I figured there were superpowered people out there we don't know about," Nyah said. "Why don't you want the fame and glory?"

"That comes with scrutiny and blame and a whole lot of junk. I've got bad anxiety. I couldn't handle it."

"I understand," Sadie said. Then a new thought sprang to mind. "Wait, does Justin have healing abilities or something?"

"No, he's a norm." Estelle raised an eyebrow. "But I think he's pretty super."

It was funny hearing her say *norm.*

Nyah tucked her hands in the front pocket of her hoodie. "Well hell, where does that leave us? You're still tardy too much. Don't teleport close to your work hours, or at lunch?"

"Not that we're asking you not to use your powers," Sadie quickly added. "Please do. But consider your unique limitations. Set more alarms in the right time zone?"

"Yeah," Estelle laughed, then sobered. "Since we're being

honest, I'm scared about all the talk about wanting to restrict powers. I haven't been sleeping well. That's messing me up."

Sadie set a hand on the North Star tattoo on Estelle's forearm. "I'm so sorry. I wish you'd been able to tell us that sooner. It's really bothering Joanie, too. Er—sorry, it felt weird to say that in front of you. I'll have to remember you know things."

Estelle looked at Nyah. "I'm surprised you know so many things."

"Are you kidding? Have you seen her when Lunk's around?" Sadie did a fake giggle and batted her eyelashes.

Nyah swiped at her, similarly giggling. "Okay, so, keep tabs on your teleporting. How else can we support you? Host more Super Supporters events? Are those worthwhile?"

"I think so." Estelle had gradually been sitting more upright. Now, she was bright and animated. "Can we close the café to attend the protest? We all kinda want to go."

"Absolutely, yes." Sadie nodded emphatically. "Done and done. I'll do some posts on the socials that we'll be closed and why. Thank you for the suggestion. I'll pay whoever's scheduled that day, of course."

"Thanks."

"Perry's gonna love that," Nyah muttered.

"Some things are more important than profit," Sadie said. "I think Perry would agree this is one of them." She took the opportunity to add, "And in return, we really do need you here on time, ready to go. If you want to have lunch with Justin at Superhero headquarters, you can take the bus."

"Yeah, I know," Estelle said with a smile. "I was late that one time because I went to Italy to get us authentic pasta."

Sadie just shook her head.

"Is it okay to let the people we know know that you know that..." Nyah's eyebrows bunched together. "That's a lot of knows."

"I guess it's fine." Estelle made a face. "I just don't want them to try to recruit me. Or do like they're doing with Iris and give me a bunch of lectures."

"Sure thing," Sadie said. "Joan and Mark are very understanding about things like that. If you ever want to ask someone about how to better control your powers, you can talk to Joan."

"Okay, yeah, thanks."

Sadie grinned, feeling a weight lifted off the whole office. Hopefully, sharing the truth was what Estelle needed in order to thrive.

It wasn't workplace appropriate, but she reached out and hugged Estelle. Estelle squeezed tight like she was grateful to be rid of the weight, too.

"Just to be crystal clear," Sadie said when they broke apart. "No one else here knows. And if they suspect anything, I don't encourage it. Please don't encourage it either."

Estelle clucked her tongue. "If I told people, they'd want me to take them all over the place. And I can't teleport another person."

Nyah crossed her arms. "But for real though, that's a cool power to have."

"It is," Sadie agreed. "Like if I had to choose…"

"I like it," Estelle said. "It's better than some of the other ones, like that dude who screamed a lot. Or, no offense Sadie, but shooting fire seems pretty terrible."

Sadie smiled to herself, glancing where she'd gripped the desk in the throes of passion. Even if Joanie hadn't directly used her heat, her warmth was always naturally present and very welcome.

"It has its advantages," she said, and tried not to laugh.

CHAPTER 21

Greta stared at Joan across the table against the exposed brick wall. They'd kept their voices quiet, not drawing attention from the other café patrons or staff. Sadie and Nyah were in a meeting in the back, which was probably a good thing.

Leaning over her lavender latte, Joan said, "What do you think? Two good deeds and not pulling any big jobs for a while? Stay under the radar a little longer?"

Greta toyed with her to-go cup. "Can you just tell them that's what I'm doing?"

"Gus won't lie for you. It's better to do two jobs to prove it wasn't a one-and-done."

"And how do you propose I spin this so it doesn't reek of working with any of you?"

Several retorts sat on her tongue, but Joan said, "You could be honest. Explain what happened, and how you're getting out of it."

"That's a great idea," Greta drawled. "You know how understanding and forgiving my associates are."

"You already made it known Spark and Ice are protecting you."

"That was for the benefit of…" Her lips twisted in frustration from her dealings with Nuance.

"You also know what will happen if you don't do this."

Greta sipped her complicated half-caf beverage.

"This is what I can offer you," Joan said, then added, "The best I can do for you."

Her friend set her cup down, staring at it contemplatively.

"Think of it as a new challenge. Keeping your skills sharp. If you want to tell people you're screwing around and returning things for the hell of it, do it. It'll add to your rep."

Greta stayed quiet for several long moments. Finally, she met Joan's eyes. "I need assurance that Perry's taking the lead. I will only communicate with him."

"Okay," Joan said. "He'll have detailed information for you."

"Too detailed," Greta grumbled.

Joan cracked a smile. Grets looked like she was trying not to.

"And then we're square. We go back to our regularly scheduled activities."

"We can." Joan shrugged a shoulder. "Or we could check in once in a while."

Greta raised an eyebrow and said, "You haven't heard more about that group thinking you and I are the same person?"

"I haven't. If we're lucky, that means they moved on." Joan shifted in her chair. "But they're coming to Vector City first, so maybe Spark has something to do with it."

"They're coming here because you have no Villains," Greta said.

"That's what Blip said."

"Blip." She half-smiled. "Now *that* was a Villain I wish I'd gotten to meet in his heyday. The way he could get into a building without regard for its security measures…"

"He's a changed man. I don't think you'd want to hang out with him now."

They shared an uncomfortable look—a question as to if *they* could hang out.

Joan would have to be the one to make the effort. "You stuck your neck out for me. I do appreciate that."

She waited for Greta to reciprocate. Giving kudos was not her strong suit.

Greta tapped her coffee cup, then said, "Thanks for dealing with Nuance. And watching out for me. You didn't have to. You could have written me off."

"I protect everyone in Vector City," Joan lightly joked. "Even those who don't want it."

"Supposing…" Grets tilted her head. "And I mean just supposing we hung out. What would we do? Our hangouts were never normal."

"What, everyone doesn't help their friend break into the penguin habitat at the zoo?"

"You were the one who wanted to pet those stinky, disgusting birds."

"We could go to the zoo when it's open."

The suggestion landed like a metaphoric thud.

"That sounds boring," Greta said.

"It does," Joan agreed.

"We could spar. I haven't kicked your ass in a while. You probably want to kick mine."

"I kinda do," Joan admitted. "I've learned some things from Darlene."

"*Please* tell me you're joking."

Joan schooled her face into a noncommittal expression.

"That's foul, Joan."

"Is it?"

"Yes." Greta retched in revulsion.

"Maybe we should start here." Joan raised her mug in a toast. "With coffee. See how it goes."

She nodded slowly. "Coffee."

They drank in silence, a tentative truce. If one of them didn't storm off in a huff, it'd be progress.

"Your hair looks good," Greta said.

"I like it." Joan ran her fingers through the short layers. "A lot."

"You were always afraid to cut it short. Said it'd draw too much attention."

"Having longer hair made me feel like I could hide behind it." She raised a foot to show off the neon yellow of her sneaker. "Did you see these?"

Greta chuckled. "Definitely not hiding anymore."

"I'm really not. Either as Spark or Joan."

She'd missed having Grets to talk to so, so much. One of the very few people she could really open up to.

"I told Sadie's parents about me," Joan said.

Greta stared at her like she'd lost her damn mind. "How did that go?"

"Not bad. I think it helped that they like me. And they know I'll always protect Sadie."

"Always, huh?"

"Yeah," Joan said. Then she grinned and voiced what was in her heart. "Yeah, I think it's gonna be always."

Her oldest friend couldn't hold her smile back. "I'm glad you met her."

"Me, too. She changed my life."

"For better or worse."

"It's for better."

Grets looked like she wanted to say something, then changed her mind. "Have you taken her flying?"

"Not yet," Joan said.

"I'll bet she'd like it."

"I've mentioned it, but we're not sure how we'd do it without anyone seeing her."

With a slight shrug, Greta said, "Go to the middle of nowhere."

"Yeah. Maybe if we take our New Year's island vacation. We could do it along the beach at night or something."

Nyah came out from the back. She spied them and hurried over to Greta. They fist-bumped and instantly fell into talk about a special edition announcement for *Sea Voyage Five*.

Sadie pushed past the Pride flag, looking cheerful and beautiful.

Joan's heart pulsated with loving warmth. That was the woman she wanted for always.

Sadie checked with Alexis and Cam before coming over. "Hi, honey," she said, wrapping her arms around Joan's shoulders from behind.

"Hey," Joan said.

"I have something bananas to tell you later," Sadie whispered in her ear. She exchanged hellos with Greta, lightly rubbing Joan's upper back.

Her happy heart swelled watching her friends gush about OchoStrike's new arsenal of swords. Sadie smiled at them, then Joan.

This was the life she'd been fighting for, and would keep fighting for. Could she dare to dream that everything was going to be okay?

Sadie bent over to sample Joan's lavender latte. "Mmm, that's good."

"Never as good as when you make them."

"How did it go asking…" She shielded the side of her face to say, "About the thing? I'm guessing okay."

"I think it'll happen," Joan said.

"Really? Oh, good. That's so great."

"It should satisfy all parties."

"Hmmm." Sadie tossed her ponytail. "It's almost like someone already made that excellent suggestion."

"Yeah, yeah."

"So you admit you should've listened to me in the first place and not dismissed my suggestions?"

"I didn't dismiss you," Joan said.

"It felt like you did."

"Sorry babe, but at the time, we didn't have a good solution. This is a solid plan."

"Still…" Sadie raised her hands, palms out. "I'm expressing my feelings."

"I appreciate that, but—"

"No buts when I tell you how I feel." Her eyes narrowed to irritated slits.

Ugh, feelings.

Joan tried again. "I appreciate that, *and* I hear you expressing yourself. I too am expressing myself. This is a lie that's not really a lie because—" She darted a gaze at Greta. "—is actually doing the thing."

Sadie's mood was visibly souring. She tapped her dark pink nails together.

"What?" Joan said.

"Hang on," Sadie muttered. "I'm taking a moment to breathe before responding like my meditation app says to do."

Joan waited through the moment, taking a breath, too.

Sadie closed her eyes, opened them, then said, "A lie that's not really a lie triggers a hot button in me from…"

Ah, okay. "From when we first met."

"Uh-huh. Hearing you say that reminded me how easy it is for you to justify a lie."

"It's kind of easy for you, too," Joan couldn't help pointing out.

"Well, you're not right, but you're not wrong. I usually do it to spare my parents more worry, or to protect myself or the people I care about."

Joan turned to fully face her. "That's what I'm doing. Not that it was always why I did it, but…"

Though the lying to Sadie had been all about protection.

"I think we've been doing the same things for the same reasons."

A play of emotions danced across Sadie's face.

"You okay?" Joan asked.

"I am processing that information," Sadie said in a measured voice. "It's a little hard to hear my actions are similar to a Supervillain's."

"Former Supervillain."

"I meant what you did as one, not what you're doing now."

Damn it, things had taken a turn. They agreed but were annoyed with each other. Why was it so hard to communicate these days? One minute, promises not to let anything stand in their way. The next, butting heads about…agreeing?

Greta and Nyah had stopped yammering and were watching them. Sadie noticed and took a step back.

A young Black woman with soft corkscrew curls approached her. "I just wanted to thank you again."

"You're so welcome," Sadie said, mustering up a smile. "Anytime you want to have a Super Supporters meeting here, our doors are open."

The woman gestured at a group of eagerly determined folks gathering their things outside. "We're looking for a few places to donate drinks and snacks for the volunteers at the protest if you're interested."

"Sure, we'd be happy to."

Protest?

Joan looked to Nyah.

"They're coordinating a protest outside that Citizens for Human Cities talk," Ny said.

"No kidding," Joan said, mostly to herself.

"Our Heroes have a lot of support." Nyah nodded to the dozens of Super Supporters signs taped inside the windows.

Joan glanced up at Sadie. She had the best support right next to her.

Sadie walked with the woman toward the exit, her movements confident and in charge.

"She sure is bossy," Greta teased.

Joan raised an eyebrow at her. "I've always been attracted to bossy women."

Nyah planted a hand on her hip and said, "It'd be cool if our city's Superheroes showed up to that protest."

Joan had planned on being as far away as possible from that hate-filled gathering, but this alternative might not be so bad. "That would be cool," she said. "I'll let them know about it."

"It would freak the Citizens out to see a shitload of Supers outside the ballpark." Greta's smirk was laced with a glimmer of vengeance. "Can you put the word out to other cities?"

Snorting, Joan said, "Normally I'd say why bother, but this might be the thing that could bring us together."

"The enemy of my enemy and all that."

"We're not enemies, but we need to play nicer and not be so insular."

Something on Greta's face said that wasn't what she'd been referring to, but Sadie rejoined them.

Greta focused her attention on Sadie. "How's your training? Still not punching anyone?"

"We've been so busy lately, I haven't had the chance."

"I'll meet up with you at the warehouse when you're ready."

Joan's guts twisted. "We can't use the warehouse anymore. That's where Perry set up his operation."

"For what?" Nyah said.

Damn it, there were too many fricking moving parts and too many people involved in varying degrees.

Sadie waved a hand. "I'll tell you later."

Greta studied Joan, then said, "That must be hard for you."

She knew exactly what it meant to lose the warehouse as a hangout. "Yeah," Joan said. "I didn't think it would be that big of a deal, but Mark and I are really sad."

"That was your home base for a long time."

"I guess it's time to move on."

"It's still a bummer," Greta said. "We had fun there."

They shared a look that said they'd talk about it another time. That was really nice.

Sadie seemed a little confused, which Grets picked up on. "I've got a place to work out, Sadie. Joan knows where it is. You can both come."

"Why does she get to see where you live and I don't?" Nyah said, crossing her arms.

"If you want to learn proper fighting techniques, ask that guy you're spending so much time with."

Nyah giggled and blushed and took Greta's ribbing.

As cool as it was for Grets to invite Sadie to her spacious loft (something she never ever did), she couldn't have Nyah over because of her connection to Kade.

Joan touched Sadie's arm, trying to bridge the literal and figurative distance between them. "Are you going to this protest?" she asked, keeping it light so it didn't come off as overprotective.

"I'm planning on it," Sadie said.

"What do you think about Supers showing up? Lending support to the people giving us support?"

A small smile spread across her face. "I was actually gonna ask if you wanted to come."

"I do. Count me in."

At least they could agree on that.

CHAPTER 22

The rest of Wednesday and all of Thursday were a blur of Sadie working and helping plan a protest and barely seeing Joanie. Which sucked because something was off again with them. This was the longest relationship either of them had ever been in, so it was uncharted territory.

She flicked the light switch with her elbow to turn on the bedside lamps while rubbing in her thick hand lotion. It was after midnight, and she had no idea when Joanie would be home. Might as well keep her thin wrap on, since her silky lilac-colored mini slip didn't afford a lot of warmth against the air conditioning Joanie desperately needed.

She stepped on the toes of her ankle socks to remove them, then placed them in the hamper.

Couples hit rough patches and worked through them. Their love was strong. Their support was strong. Their communication was getting better. So what was it?

She'd just pulled the covers back when the alarm beeped, then beeped twice to signal it had been reset.

"Hi, babe," Sadie called.

A tired groan was the response.

As she settled under the thin sky-blue blanket, Joan plodded into the bedroom.

"Long day?" Sadie guessed.

Joan groaned again and flopped facedown onto the bed. Her sleep schedule was all messed up because of the odd shifts she kept getting assigned.

Sadie cooed and sat up to rub her back, eliciting more moans.

"Did I wake you?" Joan's muffled voice said.

"Nope. Just climbed in."

This week's big story was Iris and the chemical plant situation. The state regulatory commission had finally stepped in, probably because she'd exposed some bribery and gotten an elected official kicked out of office. There were also likely shady dealings at the top of the company. It wouldn't be surprising if some executives got the boot as well.

"Were you doing damage control because of Iris?" Sadie asked.

Joan turned her head so she was cheek-down and facing in. "She's doing this one the right way. Maybe we've gotten through to her."

"Maybe." Sadie scooted closer and breathed deep, catching a hint of citrus and ginger. "You smell nice. No sewer system?"

Her Super girlfriend made a pained face. "No more sewers."

Of course Joanie wasn't obligated to talk about her work. It was just nice to have a "How was your day?" conversation.

"We're almost set for Saturday," Sadie said, kneading the knots out of Joan's neck. "Nyah and I are using Kade's truck to deliver the refreshments late morning. We're closing the café at noon. I'm meeting up with everyone at the volunteer hub around one."

Joan hummed in reply.

"Do you know who's coming on your end?"

"Everyone. We had a meeting about it. All voted yes."

"That's good."

"Trav's gonna be there." She moaned when Sadie found a particularly tight knot. "I reached out to every major city. A few of the nearby minor ones. Not sure about them. I think Sherrelle will show."

"What about Nuance?"

"Far as I know, he's only interested in Grets doing those jobs for Perry."

"You mentioned posting a video on SuperWatch calling other superpowered people to action."

"Otis vetoed that," Joan mumbled.

Before she could say it, Sadie said, "Bad optics."

"It could look like we're trying to bully the norms with a massive Super presence."

She snorted. "Not like they're not trying to bully *you* with their presence in our city."

Joan muttered something into the blanket Sadie couldn't make out.

"What's that?"

"Nothing. How was the rest of your day?"

"It was really good," Sadie said with a smile. "We've got this month's trivia and open mic nights locked in. Did I tell you Nyah and Greta came up with gamer nights? Not like videogames, but tabletop games. There could be board games, and those fantasy card games to bring in your friends the LARPers. Wouldn't that be cool?"

"That's great, babe," Joan murmured. She patted Sadie's thigh.

"I think that's something you'd like to attend. Something legal for you and Greta to do for fun."

"Love that."

Her grin widened, and she moved her touch down Joanie's back. "My mom only texted twice today, and one was a link with tips on how to protest safely. I asked if she wanted to come but didn't get a response other than *Oh, Sadie.*"

"Baby steps," Joan said. She slowly pushed her way up to sitting, wincing at the effort. "Being okay with one superpowered person isn't the same as supporting all of them."

"They support *two* of you."

Joan slid off the bed and went over to the dresser. "Kade was distracted working out and sent the rack of dumbbells crashing toward me and Darlene. We had to jump out of the way. Darlene threatened to bake muffins and force him to eat one, which was the highlight of my day."

"Darlene?" Sadie laughed. "Being funny?"

"It was pretty funny. Then Kade felt bad and got apologetic. I had to spend the next twenty minutes assuring him it was okay."

"Is he still being self-conscious about his Superhero name?"

"Oh, yeah."

This was all so normal. Why was a cloud hanging over the room? She could practically feel it.

"Just checking in," Sadie said, folding her hands in her lap. "Everything okay? I know you're tired."

Joan pulled her ultra-soft cotton black tank and shorts from one of the drawers. "Tired. A bit overwhelmed."

"Can I do anything to help?"

"Snuggles."

"Coming right up. Just get that cute butt back over here." Sadie bared one shoulder out of her wrap to show off her skimpy slip.

"Yes, ma'am," Joanie said with a half-smile.

She went into the bathroom to wash up. Sadie's phone buzzed with the daily summary of sales. She grinned at the numbers. It felt so amazing to not dread them.

"I'm proud of you, Sadie," she told herself.

Joanie would be proud too, so she hopped up and went to share the good news with her key investor. That would cheer her up.

"Babe, you're actually gonna see a return on your investment. Look at this."

Joan had changed into her jammies and was reaching for her facewash in the medicine cabinet. She glanced at the total profit and said, "Nice. Way to go, boss lady."

"I'm going to reach out next week to a couple of job applicants. It's time to add to the Sadie's Café family."

"Go for it."

Sadie couldn't help hugging her phone and swaying with happiness. "I feel like I'm finally in control for the first time in my life. I know exactly what I want, and I have exactly what I want. It's mind-blowing."

"Yeah," Joan said.

A shadow crossed over her face. At first it looked like it'd been cast from the light above the medicine cabinet, but no. Something was bothering her.

"What's on your mind, honey?" Sadie said.

Joan gripped the edge of the sink and stared into it. "You…" She cleared her throat. "You feel in control for the first time. I feel like I've lost control of everything."

"You do?" Sadie stepped closer.

"I have to go to a damn committee for everything. Why did we even have to vote on going to the protest? That should've been a no-brainer."

She set her phone on the sink, giving Joan the space to express what had been building up.

"Mark doesn't tell me shit anymore. And we can't hang out at the warehouse. Perry's got this new thing with Gus. I have to make deals. So many fucking deals to appease everyone." Joan pushed off the sink. "I knew there was going to be an adjustment when I switched sides, but I didn't expect the level of vitriol I'd have to deal with."

She ran a hand through her short waves. "I can't seem to get a grip on anything. Not Iris, not the Citizens. Nothing I do is working, and the whole fucking world thinks I'm a domestic terrorist."

"That's not true," Sadie soothed.

"If it's not Supers threatening me, it's the norms." Joan tossed a wild hand gesture. "These people want me to go away. They want me in prison."

"You're scared that might happen."

Her gaze locked onto Sadie's, anguish written all over her face. "I'm never *not* scared about that. One false move, or one law gets passed, and that's it. Life behind bars. Or else getting stripped of my powers. How can that fear ever really go away when I'm constantly being threatened by one thing or another?"

"Oh, sweetheart," Sadie murmured, her heart aching at Joan's pain. "I'm so sorry."

"I'm so happy for you, babe. I really am. It's just been hard spinning my wheels and being frustrated all the time. I was more chill as a Villain when I could do whatever I wanted. But a hero sacrifices for the greater good."

Sadie frowned at that. "Is that a Gus-ism? That sounds like something she would've told you."

"It is, but it's one I agree with."

"You can't sacrifice your well-being." She almost felt silly bringing it up, but she said, "One of the things the business-women have taught me is the need for self-care. You have to take care of yourself. Put your oxygen mask on first, y'know?"

That wasn't the major issue plaguing Joanie, though. Sadie touched her cheek. Joan's skin was hot, her fire bubbling under the surface.

"I hear what you're saying about the relentless worry. That must be so hard."

"I just…" Joan rested her hand on Sadie's. "I want what we have, but everything's changing, and I'm helpless to stop it. I guess I like things to stay a certain amount of constant. Having so much upheaval at once is messing with me."

Ah, that was a lightbulb moment. Joanie did like everything just so. The apartment clean, her shoes lined up in the closet, her recipes just right, the plants on the balcony pruned a specific way. The things she could control.

"You need stability," Sadie said. "You like to have a handle on things."

"Yeah."

What did that mean for them?

She slipped her hand free and gave voice to what had been gnawing at the back of her mind. "There's been a weird distance between us lately."

"Yeah," Joan said. "What's up with that?"

"I'm not sure, but it's been bugging me."

"Me, too."

"At least we've both felt it." Sadie scratched at her ear, then tucked her hair behind it. "Now I see where you're coming from. I've just been a little put off by the distance. Worrying about it has made it worse."

Joan leaned against the sink. "It hasn't been intentional."

"I didn't think it was. And we've been busy and distracted. That can't be helping."

She agreed quietly.

Hmm. They'd been together for over a year. The shiny newness of dating had muted into a comfortable connection. Everything wasn't intense with big, exciting emotions.

This was reality. Who they truly were, separately and as a couple.

"Do you feel like our dynamic has shifted?" Sadie asked.

"Kinda. Maybe."

She stroked Joan's cheek with her thumb. "I think it's evolving, in a good way. We've both grown a lot, and have had a lot of growing pains. It hasn't always been easy, but we've had each other as a constant."

Driving that point home, Sadie cupped Joan's face in both hands and said, "*We* are the constant. You're mine, I'm yours. No matter what."

Joan wrapped her arms around Sadie's lower back. Her chin wobbled and her mouth curved like she was fighting back tears.

Sadie gave her a gentle kiss. "I can't pretend to know how you're feeling. I'll never know what it's like to have superpowers, or have someone threaten to take them away."

"It sucks," Joanie said. "The threatening part."

"You've experienced not having them. That feeling of being

powerless. That's how the norms feel. Is there a way to make them feel more…empowered? Less un-powered?"

"I don't know. Probably not."

"You empower me. You *really* empowered me last week in my office."

Eyebrows scrunching together, Joanie said, "Not sure Spark can apply that same technique. Nor would I want to."

"Nor would I want you to." Sadie moved her hands down to Joan's shoulders. "It's just an example of how good you are with people. Maybe there's a way to channel that into something that benefits society. A way for you to take back *your* power and sense of control." She shrugged. "I dunno. I just want to help. I always want to help."

"I appreciate that." Joan chewed on her lower lip, then said, "Some things, you can't help with. Other than listening, and snuggling, and being my forever constant."

"Always."

Sadie tugged her into a hug. Then Joanie's words sank in.

My forever constant.

Forever never seemed real before. She'd liked the idea of forever but didn't think a girl who attracted all the wrong people could have forever.

She could very well have it with Joan.

Grinning against Joanie's neck, she said, "This is one of those times it's okay to say 'Sadie, I love you, but stop trying to fix everything.'"

A soft chuckle rumbled in Joan's throat. "Well, we *are* talking about feelings and junk."

"You're expressing yourself really well. I hear you and what you need."

"Have you expressed everything you need to?"

"I think so," Sadie said. "Acknowledging how we've been feeling is helpful."

Joanie's arms tightened, filling her with warmth. "Everything you're doing with the Super Supporters has been really great. Thank you for that."

"I couldn't sit around and do nothing. It was an easy decision."

Joan pulled back slightly. "Would you still love me if I didn't have my abilities?"

"Of course."

"And if I wasn't a Superhero?"

"I loved you as a food truck operator, so obviously yes."

Her mouth slanted into a smirk. "If I go to jail, will you come for conjugal visits?"

"Joanie," Sadie chastised. "You're not going to jail. I won't let it happen."

"But if it does?"

"I'll bust you out. Greta and I will sneak in and rescue you."

Joan's eyes swirled like amber whirlpools of love and affection. "You two together might be dangerous."

"I think I *will* box with her," Sadie said. "In case I have to take out a few guards."

"Sadie," Joan laughed. "Jesus."

"At any rate, you are not going to jail. There are more people backing you than not." She kissed Joanie's cheek. "Good always triumphs over evil. Love wins."

Tilting her head, Joan said, "Our love will always win."

Sadie nodded in complete agreement. "That's another constant you can count on."

CHAPTER 23

Vulture Stadium sat near the southwestern edge of Vector City. Getting there was often a traffic nightmare, so Joan was grateful for the ability to fly.

The parking lot was packed with vehicles, people entering the facility in Citizens for Human Power T-shirts, and a crowd of protestors gathering behind the temporary barricade with signs supporting superpowered people's rights.

She stood with Mark on one of the long wings of the light-up vulture perched atop the outfield scoreboard. It was turned off, given the sunny afternoon and the fact that it wasn't game day. At least for the baseball team. It was very much a day for Supers to be alert and aware for whatever might be tossed in their direction.

The general din of noise had grown steadily over the past ten, fifteen minutes. Angry anti-Super voices were getting more insistent. Competing chants from allies clapped back. A chorus of "Kumbaya" had started up.

Joan had to laugh at something she never thought she'd hear as Spark. "Even hippies like us," she mused. "I figured they wouldn't be into the 'Punch first, ask questions later' approach."

"They're here for Iris." Mark pointed out a cluster of people with a banner declaring *We Stand with Iris*.

"She wasn't clear about whether or not she's coming."

"She is. She wouldn't miss the chance for this much exposure."

Joan made a vague noise in agreement. She scanned the lot for any signs of trouble. Otis wanted them to be there as much for their usual duties as putting in an appearance. It wasn't likely, but a Supervillain could use this opportunity to do something big. Or even Iris—she did like threatening to blow stuff up.

It was a small comfort that the ballpark was less than a third full. The rally outside was pretty well attended, all things considered. A few thousand people spilled out onto the plaza, the sidewalks. Social media and windows throughout the city were filled with Super Supporter hashtags. Businesses were using the signs as a way to combat the No Superpowered Activity rider and tell Supers where they were welcome.

She spied Ward and Padma by Otis as he scribbled his autograph and posed for photos near the small temporary platform/riser thing erected just off the barricade. Kade was planning on staying close to Nyah and everyone from Sadie's Café. Joan trusted him to look out for Sadie. Plus, some of Sadie's friends, their food truck friends and Amit had planned on coming today.

Zee and Darlene circulated on ground level. They were all gonna gather before the rally started to show a united front. Any other superpowered in attendance would join them, which as far as she knew was Sherrelle and Trav.

"Do you think Perry's coming incognito or as Breeze?" Joan wondered aloud.

"I don't know," said Mark. "He likes his privacy these days."

"It'd be nice to have another redeemed Villain show these jackholes we aren't all bad."

"Eh, if he wants to be Péricles Barbosa, let him be Péricles Barbosa. He deserves to be known for who he is."

Joan gave him a sidelong glance. That was an odd way of phrasing things.

A body flashed through the metal roof. Trav walked over in his Blip gear to the tip of the vulture wing. "I found Dale. I got into the dressing room he's holed up in and was forcibly removed. Security is tight."

"He didn't want to have a family reunion?" Mark said.

Trav shook his head. "He yelled something to his security detail about getting me out of the building. It felt kind of desperate, like he didn't want me in there for a specific reason."

"Then we should be extra vigilant," Joan said.

"And ready for anything."

"We should tell the others. It's about time to meet up. I think Flight wants to say a few words."

The first scheduled speaker was already in the wings of the stage. The backdrop was done up with large swaths of red, white and blue material with a C, H and P on them. Stars-and-stripes-inspired flats flanked the sides.

The podium had a soaring bald eagle painted across it in gold. "Why do the Citizens use a bird for their symbol when their whole deal is human power?" Joan said.

Mark snorted. "Because a powerful human would be a picture of Lunk flexing his muscles."

Saluting, Trav said, "See you down there."

He blipped through the roof again.

Joan and Mark stepped off the vulture and blasted slowly around the stadium. Otis had instructed all of them not to showboat.

Phones trained upward to capture their movement. Cheers and whistles greeted them, which was nice. There was a tense police presence, and Joan couldn't say it was full of friendlies.

She caught a glimpse of the volunteer pop-up tent just off the plaza. Sadie was over there handing out refreshments in her black café T-shirt. *Be safe, my love.*

After landing, Joan waved to the crowd, forcing a smile. She turned around to mutter close to Otis, "Blip tried talking to Terwilliger. He didn't want Blip to see something. We need eyes on him."

Otis nodded once.

Surprise rippled through the crowd. People parted near the platform.

"Holy shit," Mark murmured.

Sherrelle appeared in her flowy gold-and-white Aura body-suit. And Flux from Destine in her purple ensemble. And then Ray Jay and two other Oceanview Supers, all in oceanic hues.

And then it was like a bizarre Superhero parade of names and outfits Joan sort of recognized from some of the smaller cities.

The crowd went nuts. She and Mark had to keep scooting closer to the platform to make room for the twenty or so new arrivals.

Adrenaline surged through her. This was fucking great.

"Whoa," Trav said as he came up behind her.

"Guess your message was received," Mark said to Joan.

A smile tugged at her mouth. "Guess so."

Several young people dressed in business casual trailed the group, all chatting into earpieces and tapping on screens. *Sidekicks.*

A big roar went up. Even the other Supers started whooping and clapping. Joan couldn't see what had caused it until they shifted.

Amazing Woman and Breeze.

Joan's hand flew to her chest. *Gus.*

The expression on her face said *I can't believe I'm still fighting this shit.*

Perry caught Joan's eye and gave a subtle nod. She nodded back, sending him major thanks.

Darlene and Zee came over, and Kade lumbered through the crowd. The Supers who knew one another high-fived and fist-bumped. Joan shared greetings, some less enthusiastic with her and Mark, some more pleasant.

Kade stage-whispered against her facemask, "Everything's okay at the volunteer tent."

"Thanks," she whispered back.

She took a moment to study the scene. Sadie was the one who

could bring norms together, but Joan had brought Superheroes who generally stayed on home turf to Vector City. Showed them how working together could thwart the bad guys. Pretty frickin' cool.

"I thought there'd be more people," she overheard Ray Jay say.

Zee answered, "You should see the gatherings across the city. Friendship Park has a huge one going on right now."

"How do you know?" some dude in red said.

Zee just gave him a look. "Super speed."

Loud patriotic rock (if that was a genre) blasted inside the field. A baritone voice did a welcome message for the Citizens for Human Cities Tour. The protestors booed loudly.

Padma clapped her hands. "Thank you for coming. All Superheroes to the stage, please. Let the crowd know you're here. And remember to smile!"

Ward looked up and down in a manic rhythm while furiously one-handedly typing on his tablet.

Supers shuffled and jostled for position on the platform. A few of the ones who could fly floated above it to make things easier. They all waved to the appreciative crowd.

Now there was backup should they need it.

The video feed on the scoreboard jumbotron was visible from their vantage point. A short white guy in a dark suit and red tie had stepped behind the dais to cheers inside. He clasped his hands victoriously overhead.

"It's a great day in Vector City now that we've arrived," he said to their delight.

The protesters booed even louder.

The speaker gave an animated speech using buzzwords that meant nothing but to incite anger. Joan tuned it out to visually sweep the scene around her.

Otis suddenly shot into the sky, heading for two spandex-clad figures sitting on the overhang facing home plate.

"Is that…" Mark said, craning his neck.

A spray of what looked like pink fireworks sparkled against a puffy white cloud. The person in black and bright purple unfurled a small banner that said *We can't with these guys*. The one in lime green and black popped a sad face in firework form.

"Thunderdash and Magique," Joan said.

"It's cool, man, it's cool," Ray Jay said. "We called a truce for the day."

Another flying Super in blue and white shot up.

"They're not here to cause trouble," he yelled after her. "They want to protest with us."

Really though, those two weren't so much Villains as playful tricksters. The total opposite of Prowl and Ether.

Joan's gaze crossed paths with Darlene's. She was gripping her arms tight enough to break them.

"Fucking Oceanview," she ground out.

Thunderdash made a *Timeout* T with his hands, saying something to Otis and the other Super. After a few conversational moments, TD gestured to the banner. Magique twirled a twinkly pink halo over each of their heads.

The other Super waved for them to get down. TD raised his hands, then grabbed the banner. He conjured a lightning bolt to guide him down as Magique sparkled a path toward the ground.

"I see we've attracted a few out-of-town guests," the speaker said.

Joan snorted. He didn't know about the Supers packed together outside the...

"We should spread out," she said. "I don't like that we're all in one spot."

Darlene cast a sharp eye at the situation. "This is not ideal. We should be covering the whole building."

"They're planning something hinky," Trav said. "We need eyes inside. I'll go."

"I can go." Sherrelle wiggled her fingers. "Make that crowd a little more into love and respect for their fellow man."

"We can't use our powers on them," someone said from the

other side of the platform. "It would only prove what they're accusing us of."

"Anyone do invisibility?" a deep voice asked.

"I shapeshift." This came from Alter, a fortysomething Super lady from a small Midwestern city.

"I can absorb that ability," Darlene said.

Joan pointed at them. "Okay. You three go in and blend in."

"I don't blend so much as blip," Trav said. "But I'll let you know what I find."

Flux touched her ear. "What frequency do you run your comms on?"

"What comms?" Mark said.

"Your comms." She tapped her ear. "For communication."

"We don't have those. We have Ward."

Ward, whose fingers were in danger of cramping up from extreme overuse at the foot of the steps.

"Oh my god," Flux huffed. "Then yell really loud if you find something."

"Break off in teams of two," Joan instructed.

Otis rejoined them. "Thunderdash and Magique said they only want to take part in the demonstration. They will return to Ocean-view tonight."

"Yeah, man, it's a one-day truce," Ray Jay said.

Most of the other Supers grumbled their objections.

Mark nudged Joan's arm. "You'd think Superheroes had never made an alliance with Villains before."

Good point. She raised her voice to say, "This affects them, too. We shouldn't exclude people with powers who want to speak up. Let's be better than those trying to divide us. Let them stay."

"They'd be fools to try anything with all of us here," Trav added.

"Says the former Villains," some dude snickered.

Joan's internal flames sparked. "Yes, says the former Villains who've been able to uphold a truce. Give them the benefit of the doubt."

She directed a little fire to her eyes so they could see how serious she was. Or be freaked out—either worked.

The Supers backed off and mumbled about pairing up.

Patriotic rock blared again as the speaker left the podium to raucous applause. Joan and Mark made their way a little closer to the volunteer tent. If any shenanigans occurred, she wanted to be near Sadie.

They studied the crowd and peeked at the jumbotron as the next speaker stepped up. A middle-aged white woman with bleached-blonde hair whose favorite word was "suspect" judging by how many times she used it.

Joan's phone vibrated rhythmically against her chest. Gut instinct told her to answer.

It was Trav. "Flux is right," he said. "You do need comms."

"Did you find something?" she asked.

"There's an unusual amount of private security walking around. Dale's on his way to the field. Catch and Alter are trying to get close to him as guards. I'll keep you posted."

"Thanks. Things are good out here."

As they ended the call, laughter rippled through the crowd. TD's banner shot up on a thin bolt of lightning.

"Don't ruin this for us," Joan muttered.

She told Mark about Trav's Terwilliger intel. "What is that dickhole up to?" he said.

"We should be in there."

"We're supposed to be peacefully protesting."

"I'd feel more peaceful if we knew what was going on."

She caught a flash of red hair under the volunteer tent, and her heart drummed harder. What if this was all some ploy to get Supers in one place to arrest them? What if Sadie had to watch her get hauled away, or Joan had to fight her way out and end up a wanted woman again?

The blonde speaker finished her irritating discourse. More Ameri-rock blasted throughout the ballpark.

Joan checked her phone. No updates. She figured there'd be

another warm-up speaker or a break, so she was surprised when the crowd inside erupted.

Dale Terwilliger's smug face filled the jumbotron as he smiled, waved, pointed. A rousing chant began: "*No to superpowers! Yes to human power!*"

The protesters made an opposing ruckus.

Joan's hands curled into fists.

Otis flew up for a better view, and the Super who could climb like an insect scuttled up one side of the stadium.

Dale positioned himself behind the podium and held up a *Settle down* hand. "My friends," his voice boomed. "My dear friends. I'm coming out a little early, I know. We'll still get to everyone else's inspiring, important words today. But I had to share some disturbing news with you."

Mark flicked ice shavings from his fingers.

"I have been informed that just outside these walls, our enemies have congregated. Superpowered menaces not just from your city, but from across our great country."

The crowd reacted with outrage.

Dale looked up toward the press box. "Can you switch to those cameras?"

Moments later, the jumbotron cut to a shot above the plaza and temporary platform. A few Supers were still on it, and Kade-as-Lunk and Ray Jay were visible to the side.

"There some of them are," Dale said. "More are around the building. If you look up…" He pointed to Otis-as-Flight. "One of them is right there."

The camera swiveled to him.

"I happen to know some supposedly former Villains are in attendance. Can we get a shot of them? Where is Blip? He's probably breaking into your cars. Find Blip."

That was pretty fucking personal.

Then Joan saw herself and Mark onscreen. She blinked and had to force herself not to step into a fighting stance.

The people around them waved signs and cheered. A few gave

the camera the finger.

"There's two of the Villains," Dale's voice echoed. "Do you trust these criminals to walk free? We should lock them up."

"There's literally two real Villains over there," a guy in the crowd said. He pointed to where TD and Magique were.

The threat roiled inside Joan. She struggled not to blast into the sky and set the stage's backdrop aflame.

Dale said something about the Supers that had been sitting on the roof, and the camera found TD and Magique on the street. They bowed comically as if being recognized for some great achievement.

"Do you see how they disrespect us?" Dale said, which made his followers shout in agreement. "No regard for what's right. They are deviants. Our so-called Superheroes are letting them—"

"Dale Terwilliger," a somewhat familiar woman's voice resounded from a different microphone. "Bring the cameras back to Dale Terwilliger."

The jumbotron returned to showing the stage. Dale clammed up, looking all around him.

"Citizens for Human Power," the woman said. "You are spreading hate and lies. This has to stop."

A hush settled over both crowds.

Iris walked out from behind one of the flats holding a wireless microphone. *Oh, fuck.*

A collective gasp rippled across Vulture Stadium. Iris's supporters hurrahed.

"The biggest threat to our world isn't the superpowered," she said. "It's ignorance and misinformation."

Dale waved to his security team. "Get her! Get her! She's here to destroy us!"

"Shit," Mark said.

He and Joan blasted up at the same time a few other Supers did.

Iris deftly avoided the guards. "We're not perfect. We've not done our best. We're flawed humans, just like you."

"Do it!" Dale yelled. "Deploy it now! Now!"

Joan had just reached the roof overhang when her fire cut out. She landed hard, Mark tumbling beside her. Resounding thuds and cries said they weren't the only ones who'd...

Who'd had their powers suppressed.

She caught a glimpse of men in dark suits swarming and taking Iris down.

"Don't worry, my friends," Dale said at the podium. "We are safe. I have neutralized the superpowered threat."

Joan scrambled with her brother to the edge to watch the scene unfolding onstage. That odd sense of not having firepower weaved through her body.

"I was going to surprise you with this later, but they forced my hand." Dale looked at Iris, now pinned to the stage and yelling. "Thanks to the generous support of our allies in the prison system, we were able to procure unprecedented access to some very exciting technology. Have you ever wondered how Villains are unable to use their powers in there? There is a particular low frequency that suppresses them."

Dale proudly raised a hand. "We have deployed it, and look! Nobody's flying, nobody's shooting off fireworks, as God intended."

"Allies from the prison." Joan shook her head in short, jerky motions. "These assholes just walked right in and got it."

"Fuck those guys," Mark seethed.

If the prison system was corrupt... That spelled disaster for her biggest fears being realized.

To his cheering crowd, Dale said, "We were prepared for this sort of attack." He gestured at Iris as the security guards pulled her up. "She wanted to take us out."

"No, I didn't," Iris said loud enough for his mic to pick up. "I just wanted to talk."

"This girl has repeatedly threatened lives and property. She came here to inflict carnage upon us, and we stopped her."

"I'm a pacifist! I would never hurt a living creature. I wanted to engage in a dialogue with you."

Joan's phone buzzed like crazy in her pocket, but she didn't dare take her eyes off the stage. Were the guards coming for them next? Was that why there was so much security? She and Mark could make a break for it, but what about Gus? Or Perry?

Dale looked into the stands. "Don't you feel safer, my friends? Look over there at Flight." He chortled. "He's not flying anymore."

Otis stood on the field, a little dazed from his long fall.

Dale said something else, but Joan glanced down at her legs. She felt extra fireless. Unusually suppressed, like there was barely even a whisper. The prison's system had to be dialed up much higher than the one they used at HQ, since this was reaching beyond the walls of the ballpark.

Was this how it felt to be imprisoned? Was this what it felt like to be a norm?

"I say we start by locking up this terrorist Iris where she belongs. And then…" His smile turned downright mean. "We get the other ones who deserve it."

Trav ran onto the field shouting, "Dale, stop it! That's enough!"

Joan caught the momentary flash of recognition in Dale's eyes before he resumed his cocky smirk. "There's another one that needs to be put away. That man is a wanted criminal in four Canadian provinces. What do you say? Should we extradite him to face charges?"

Trav's reply was lost in the crowd's bellowing.

The shouts oddly petered out. Dale swayed slightly, as did his guards. People bent over, their words morphing into confused murmurs. The microphone warbled with feedback, and the camera feed shook.

"What's going on?" Mark said.

Otis and Trav met on the field, looking around like they'd noticed something was awry.

Voices started to pop up outside the ballpark with variations of "What's happening?"

Joan stood to scan the parking lot. People seemed confused and disoriented. How was Sadie?

What *was* happening, 'cause it sure as shit wasn't from any of her brethren.

She called for Mark to follow and slid down the far edge that led to the upper deck. No one was sitting this high up, so they ran to the nearest stairwell.

The closer they got to the lower levels, the louder the noise.

Dale's voice echoed with unconvincing assurances. "Stay strong, my friends. This is another coordinated attack on us."

Joan paused when they hit the main level to look at one of the TVs. Iris had regained her microphone and was sprinting off the stage. "This isn't from superpowers. I don't know what's going on."

The people milling about the concessions—mostly employees —clogged the area as they struggled to move or even stand upright. One young guy looked dangerously close to puking.

Joan and Mark weaved their way between ever more panicky norms.

"They must have planted some sort of countermeasure," Dale said. "Something to cause us pain."

"We didn't," Iris insisted.

"This way," Joan said to Mark.

She headed down the aisle that led to the seating closest to the home team dugout. The energy in the stadium was just weird—a mixture of anger and fear and static in the air.

She spied Dale in the flesh barking to his guards to get him out of there. "Be strong, my friends," he said quickly into his mic. "Humans have the power."

Then he ran like the chickenshit he was.

CHAPTER 24

Sadie rubbed at the pressure in her head. Something had gone wrong since they'd turned on that power blocking. She'd been around it before and had never suffered ill effects. Norms weren't supposed to feel anything, and didn't it not have a wide radius?

She'd stepped out of the tent along with everyone else. Now her staff was holding onto the flimsy metal bars. (Other than Estelle, who looked confused but otherwise well.) Nyah wobbled beside Wren and Beth-Ann. Amit braced himself against Morris, who braced himself against Tenia.

She wanted to tell Joan but knew looking at her phone was the last thing on Joan's mind. Where was she? Her power had cut out mid-flight. Was she okay? Her Super suit had probably absorbed most of the impact, but still.

The protestors were starting to murmur about a Villain attack. Some nearby Superhero gave reassurances in a deep voice that it couldn't be from superpowers because they were being suppressed.

She blinked up at the jumbotron. The stage was now empty. The camera panned to the three Superheroes on the field—Spark and Ice not among them.

Travis-as-Blip reached for Iris's microphone. "It's the power-blocking technology," he said. "It's not working right. Turn it off."

Dale was being whisked across home plate by his handlers. "That's what they want you to believe!" His words were subtly picked up by the mic. "Don't touch it!"

"That has to be it," Iris said.

"That is *not* it!" Dale cried.

The camera rolled and landed on a crooked shot of the crowd. People were trying to get up, trying to get out of there.

Something that felt like an electronic wave pulsed across the plaza. Sadie's knees buckled, and she reached toward the nearest body.

Estelle.

She steadied Sadie. "I think Blip's right," she said. "I'm not sick, but I can't…"

"I think it just got turned up," Sadie said. "I feel worse."

Now the sensation was unsteady with a distinct uptick in the jitters. The norms had to get out of there.

She chugged in a ragged breath and said as loudly as she could, "The frequency is making us sick. Get away from here and you'll feel better."

She managed her way past the tent, relaying the message to her friends and employees. Estelle nodded in understanding and went the other way, urging the protestors to clear the plaza.

Even though her head was killing her and her throat scratchier with every shout, Sadie got as far as the main gate. Rally attendees were starting to stumble their way out. She caught a glimpse of a TV screen inside that showed the field. Cops were yelling near the stage at Blip and Iris and Flight.

"What do you want us to do?" Iris snapped at them though the mic. "We're not controlling this. Turn it off, damn it!"

"You're creating the problem," Blip said.

Another jittery pulse shot through Sadie. That seemed to make the people leaving the stadium even more frantic. They bobbed and weaved, frightened and nauseous. One man in a Citizens tee tottered to a trash can and threw up in it.

Where was Joanie? She could take care of herself, but what if she was stuck in a swarm of unfriendlies? What if the crowd took their frustrations out on her? Was Mark with her?

She'd want Sadie to get to safety, but the protestors needed to know what to do.

"Everyone move away from the stadium," she called, waving weak arms. "The frequency is making us sick."

A Superhero with a voluminous black cape saw what she was doing, then started to do the same with the rally attendees streaming through the main entrance. Helping them despite their aversion to the superpowered.

Loud clangs and bangs sounded from inside. People were yelling at each other, yelling in general.

Sadie reached the sidewalk but got stuck in a jam of protestors unable to go anywhere. "Keep moving," she said. "Get away from the stadium. You'll feel better."

Iris was telling people not to panic. "I swear, we're not pulling one over on you. I wanted to engage your leader in conversation, but he left."

Her pleas for a peaceful resolution were drowned out by crowd noise and more metallic clangs inside.

Sadie walked past a news camera capturing the chaos. She turned her head to hopefully not be identified. Best not to open the door to questions or Super connections. Plus, having her parents see her on the news was not a great way to ease their concerns.

She just hoped their newfound support didn't include installing SuperWatch on their phones so they wouldn't know about this growing fiasco.

Instead of getting onto the field, Joan found herself swept up in the rush of Citizens trying to get out. She didn't know where Mark was. All she could hear was crashes and booms as people knocked over trash cans and things around the concession stands in their haste.

Then people started getting bowled over. *Shit.*

She pushed her way to a woman clutching her purse and covering her head on the cement floor. Joan hauled her to her feet. The woman looked petrified, and Joan was tempted to be an asshole.

"Be careful," she said instead.

The woman nodded, eyes wide.

Joan left her to assist a man and woman with two crying little girls against the wall. Who the fuck would bring kids to something like this? The poor things were in hysterics.

She softened her approach. "Hey. There's an exit just over there. Stay close to the wall and you'll make it out. Let me help."

She blocked some of the swelling crowd so they could get closer to the gate. The dad picked up the girl with the tear-stained face and crooked pigtails.

The kid stared at Joan over the man's shoulder. "Thank you, Spark," she said with a tiny wave.

Joan waved back, giving the kid a small smile so she didn't grow up fearing the superpowered.

Fuuuuck. She had to help these people whether they wanted it or not.

A faint jolt hit her body. Then a familiar heat started building in her gut. It wasn't full fire, but definitely coming back.

She spotted an older white man and a woman with a walker getting bounced around by people desperate to leave. She shouldered her way over to them. "Can I lend you a hand?"

The man batted her away. "You did this to us!"

"No, I didn't. I'm trying to get you out of here."

"Let her help, Harv," the woman said. "That's the least she could do."

Joan carved a path for them, calling for people to take it easy. "No one needs to get hurt today."

Strange looks and unwelcome comments followed her, but she got Harv and his lady through the exit. They deliberately moved away from her.

Not that she expected a thank-you, but their quick disregard was annoying.

Wait a sec… She tapped her fingertips against her palms. *There you are, old friend.*

Her fire was back, so hopefully they'd turned that shit off.

Only that meant the norms' strength and speed had returned, too. The stampede out of the ballpark gained momentum.

Joan shot into the air. She searched the crowd for Mark and the other Supers, but also for anyone who might need help.

She was on the opposite side of where the volunteer tent was. *Kade, please find Sadie.*

Two thirtysomething women had climbed up a streetlamp but didn't have a clear path down. Joan flew over as they cried out for rescue.

"I can take you one at a tiiii—"

The women launched themselves at her, tangling their arms around Joan's neck. She only managed to outstretch one arm to blast the necessary fire to get them to the middle of the street.

They landed in a heap on the blacktop. The women rolled onto their backs while Joan sprang up.

"Thank you!" they chorused.

"We love our Superheroes," the brunette one said.

"So much," said her fair-haired friend.

Joan nodded at their gratitude.

"Spark!"

She looked up to find Mark hovering above her.

He jerked his head toward the stadium. When she joined him, he said, "We need to get Iris out of there."

"What about—"

"The others are helping out here. *We* need to get to Iris before they do."

She caught his meaning: *Before the other Supers apprehend her.*

They soared into the ballpark. The jumbotron had gone black, and it didn't sound like the mics were live anymore. A few dozen faithful attendees were sticking it out in the stands.

Otis had backed Iris against the stage. Trav wasn't there—probably gone after Dale. The remaining private security and cops were realizing they felt better.

"Distract them," Joan told Mark. She couldn't due to not wanting to burn the grass on her favorite team's field.

He sprayed the turf in front of the stage to make it too slippery to walk on.

Joan landed next to Iris. "Hurry up and get out of here," she said quietly.

"We can't let her go," Otis commanded.

"We can't let her go to jail."

"She's an active threat."

"She was never going to hurt anyone."

Iris's eyes sparkled as she looked all around them. "I was never gonna blow up a building. I'm kinda surprised everyone kept calling my bluff. I hate violence, but what else was I supposed to do?"

Joan gave her a look. "Not threaten to blow stuff up?"

"People probably think this was your fault," Mark said. "It's pretty much your M.O."

"I swear, I didn't do it." Iris gazed up near the press box, eyes flashing. "There are two men in the broadcast control room with walkie-talkies waving their hands around. A third one's gesturing at a computer." She tilted her head, eyebrows meeting in the middle. "That's weird."

"What is?" Mark said as he shot a thicker layer of ice between them and the cops.

"There's a woman in the ceiling."

Joan's throat tightened. "A woman?"

"Dark hair in a ponytail. She looks petite. Has a laptop and a backpack."

Joan and Mark stared at each other.

Greta.

Iris started to say more, but the three Oceanview Supers came running onto right field with their sidekicks in tow. She dove under the stage.

Joan glanced between where her friend could very well be and the threats surrounding her. Did Greta... Was that why...

"Iris," Ray Jay called. "We've gotta take you in."

"You can't," Joan said, blocking his path. "She can't go to prison. Especially not right now."

The Oceanview Supers protested.

"You heard what Terwilliger said. They want to make an example out of her."

"We'll keep her at our HQ," Ray Jay said.

"What if we keep her at ours?" Mark said. "She's already here."

Tingles quelled Joan's fire. She tried to form a fireball and got a few small sparks.

"Damn it," Otis said, hopping up and down but not getting air. "Not again."

The nearby norms groaned and clutched their heads and stomachs, sliding on the ice. The sidekicks crumpled against each other.

Joan gestured at the control room. "Our priority is finding out what's causing this. We can talk about Iris after."

Iris, who was making a break for the bullpen. *Ugh.*

One of the Oceanview Supers sprinted after her on his long legs.

Joan said to Ray Jay, "You can't throw her to the wolves. Let us protect her."

"She's, like, our problem," he said.

Iris screamed as the guy grabbed her around the waist. They wrestled and struggled.

Joan jumped over the edge of the ice to…well, she didn't know what, but she had to try.

She pulled them apart. "Hang on. Iris, tell him what you told us."

Iris looked at the rest of the Supers walking over. "Come on. You guys know me. You know I'd never hurt anyone. I came here to talk to Dale Terwilliger."

"Did you sabotage their equipment?" Otis asked.

"I already said no a million times. I wouldn't even know how to do that."

But I know someone who would, and probably did.

"We can't let you go," Ray Jay said.

"You're to blame, too," Iris said, tears in her eyes. "You let me down. You all let me so down."

Mark stepped over to her. She jerked and moved back. "Would you like to be held at our headquarters until we figure out what to do with you?" he said.

"Why are you giving her a choice?" the tall Oceanview Super demanded.

Mark glared at him. "Because she hasn't felt like she's had a lot of choices."

"We'll watch her," Joan said. "You have our word she'll be safe. We know you don't want anything to happen to her."

Iris clasped her hands beneath her chin, eyeing Mark warily. "You swear you're not just gonna throw me in jail forever? You said I could trust you."

"You can," he said. "We believe in second chances around here."

"I just wanted to make the world a better place."

"Maybe you still can."

She nodded slowly. "Okay. I'll go with you, on my terms. Let me do a livestream explaining…"

Iris's words, the Supers' rebuttals, dulled in the background.

Joan looked into the upper deck again. Three men in dark suits congregated around the control room doorway. Even sickness wouldn't stop these guys.

So not having her powers wouldn't stop Joan.

She turned to Mark. "You've got this?"

"Yeah. Go get whoever else you can to put a stop to..." He twirled his hand and unsuccessfully produced ice. "This."

CHAPTER 25

Sadie finally made her way back to what was left of the volunteer tent. One of the legs had buckled, and most of the people had cleared the area in favor of the neighboring streets.

She rubbed her stomach, the pain and weakness having come back. The A/V had gone out, so she had no idea what was happening inside.

The barricades had been knocked down or moved. She spied Kade's huge frame as the steady stream of people let up outside the main gate. She started over to see if he'd taken care of their mutual friends.

Several people sat on the edge of the makeshift stage. One of them was Ward, pounding a frustrated fist on his tablet. Justin was taping a white bandage to his temple. He and a woman in an EMT jacket were treating several minor injuries.

"You're going to need stitches," Justin said.

"I don't care. I must get to Mr. Flight!" Ward let his tablet slide from his fingers. Oh—the screen was shattered. He pulled his phone from an inside jacket pocket.

Sadie changed course to check in with them.

"Excuse me." Padma shooed at her. "This is a triage station for Superhero sidekicks. Please move along."

Sadie opened her mouth, then realized she'd never actually met Padma. "Sorry," she said. "That's, uh, my friend, Dr. Devers."

"Your friend is busy," Padma said.

Justin looked over. "It's okay. Everyone got out safely. You should get out of here."

"Not until I know…" *That Joan is okay.*

Her aches subsided again. People began to move faster. Loud honking from the parking lot started up in earnest. A few moments later, Zee raced over.

Ward adjusted his glasses, even though one of the lenses was cracked. "Mx. Race! What do you need?"

"Where's everyone else?" they asked.

"Mr. Lunk is over there, but I don't know about the rest. I got knocked to the ground, and—"

Zee took off again.

The Super who could climb like a bug scrambled down the side of the ballpark. "Thank god," he said to someone on the ground. "I've been stuck on top of a stadium light."

Thunderdash coasted down on a lightning bolt. Magique burst handfuls of pink sparkles and met him halfway.

"Oceanviews are occupied in there," Thunderdash said. "They've got Iris."

"Our cue to leave," Magique said in some sort of European accent.

"It's been real, Vector City, but we shall take our leave." Thunderdash saluted, then waved. "Oh, hi Spark!"

Sadie whipped her head around, searching the sky until she saw the familiar black-and-red suit and dark wig silhouetted against the sun. Relief rushed through her bloodstream.

The Oceanview Villains flew past, calling "Down with the Man!" above the dwindling crowd.

Joan landed a few feet away. Sadie instinctively moved toward her, her strength steadily returning.

Joan took one step, then stopped abruptly. "Is everyone here all right?" she asked, addressing Sadie in her Spark voice.

I'm okay, Sadie telegraphed. *You're okay.*

Padma strode forward. "A few of the sidekicks are a little banged up."

"Nothing too serious?" Joan said.

"Cuts and bumps. There was a rush out from the stadium."

"Ms. Spark!" Ward limped over. "I'm so sorry. Is Mr. Flight still inside? Does he need me?"

"No. Take it easy."

The other sidekicks scrambled off to find their Heroes.

"Something went very wrong with the device they're using," Ward said. "Is it turned up too high? Is that how it's reaching outside?"

"That's what I'm about to find out. Lunk!"

Kade looked over, then started trotting toward them.

Sadie wanted to ask all the questions. Was Iris in custody? Where had Dale Terwilliger gone? Did they have any idea how to stop this on-and-off power blocking?

"Ward, what happened to your head?" Kade said, his voice thick with concern.

"I'm fine, Mr. Lunk."

"I need your help inside," Joan said to Kade.

Ward nodded. "Whatever you need."

"No. You're injured."

"I'm all right."

She planted her hands on her hips. "Then go back to HQ and prepare for a guest."

"Did you apprehend a Villain?"

"Sure." Joan waved for Kade.

"Spark," Sadie said.

Joan turned.

"Can I do anything for you?"

Her lips quirked. "Get to a safe place."

She flared about a foot off the ground before her flames spluttered out. "Goddammit," Sadie heard her sigh.

Her own sickly symptoms were rapidly making a comeback.

Kade rotated an arm, then grimaced. "This is so annoying."

Zee jogged from around one of the ticket windows, visibly irritated at how slow they were moving.

And then Perry-as-Breeze walked over. Alone. To the worried faces shot at him, he said, "Amazing Woman is fine. She wasn't staying around in case a building fell on her again. What are we doing about this?"

Joan murmured to them, eliciting nods in response. A few other Superheroes trickled over. They huddled up, making it impossible to figure out what they were talking about, but Sadie thought she saw Joan looking at her phone.

She fought through her nausea to stand beside Justin. "I wish I knew what was going on," she whispered.

The jumbotron suddenly burst back to life. Shaky camerawork zoomed in and out until Dale Terwilliger came into focus. He was onstage again, dark suit jacket off, profusely sweating and surrounded by security.

His words weren't audible until the sound on the wireless mic kicked in. "...integral information to share," he croaked. "Can you hear me now? Are we back?"

"This fuckin' guy," Justin muttered, summing up Sadie's thoughts exactly.

"We've been sabotaged! This is the work of a deviant we've had our eye on. The Supervillain Spark. She's also a computer hacker who goes by Greta."

Sadie's hands flew to her mouth as she sought out Joan.

"She knows how to control this technology." Dale winced in obvious pain. "She wants us to suffer."

A black-and-red blur ran toward the nearest entrance, followed by Zee, Perry and Kade.

Followed by Sadie. She wouldn't let Joan go down for this.

Dale's lies continued as she moved as quickly as possible through concessions. It was a sticky, stinky mess of knocked over stanchions and garbage cans, spilled condiments and beverages, popcorn, hot dogs, and Citizens for Human Power paraphernalia.

The sickly feeling was definitely stronger inside. By the time she made it to an aisle leading to the field-level seats, Joan was standing on the pitcher's mound, hands on hips.

"Say that to my face," she shouted at Dale.

His security tightened around him. Several other norms were clustered in one corner of the stage. A swath of ice covered the outfield, more people spread along its edges.

Joan held her arms out. "I'm not whoever you think I am. As you can see, I'm not doing a damn thing."

"Don't insult us with your lies, *Greta*," Dale said, his voice raspy. "You're controlling this."

"With what?"

"You obviously installed a virus or planted a bug. You could be using a remote control or your phone."

Joan stared at her empty gloved hands, then held her palms out for inspection.

"Then you have an accomplice."

"It's Iris!" an angry voice screeched behind Sadie. Several others agreed.

Only Iris was with some Superheroes against one of the bullpens.

Dale grasped the podium, struggling to stand straight. "You're using some kind of superpowers."

"Dude, I shoot fire. And uh, nothing's coming out now."

"Arrest her!" Dale yelled, pointing at Joan. He swung toward Iris. "Arrest her, too! And find Blip!"

"I'm right here, Dale," Travis said as he strolled onto the stage.

"You have to be her accomplice," Dale seethed.

"No. We protect people, not do this to them." Travis gestured at the sweaty, swaying guards.

Mark stepped onto the mound and said something to Joan. Sadie reached for the railing in front of the first row of seats for support.

"You're doing more harm than we are with this faulty equipment," Travis added. "Shut it down before more people get hurt."

"I won't." Dale pushed off the podium, wobbling on unsteady legs. "That's exactly what you want. To get your powers back and misuse them."

"All right, but you're the one making the people who trust you sick."

Sadie spotted Catch and—who was that, Alter?—standing at the foot of the stage stairs. Both women had their arms crossed, lips pursed. At least it looked that way from this distance.

Her nausea lessened, and she gulped in a deep breath.

Joan twirled her hand. A small flame ignited from her palm just as Mark shot ice shavings into the air.

"None of us did this," Joan said.

Dale jumped behind the podium, bumping the wireless mic and causing ear-piercing feedback. "Turn the suppression back on! Protect me from these menaces!"

"Protect *you*?" Darlene-as-Catch said loudly. "What about all the citizens who will be affected?"

Sadie saw but didn't hear Mark say, "Bad optics."

"You're out to get me." Dale cast wild gazes at the various Supers. "You're all out to get me."

Travis shrugged broadly. "No one's out to get you. Not like your crusade to get rid of us."

That was when Sadie noticed every Super—all the ones in attendance—had converged onto the field. Not in a stalking, threatening way. Gathering in a show of solidarity.

The Citizens onstage and police on the ice and grass didn't seem to know what to do. The audience didn't either. It was their worst nightmare: a whole lot of superpower in a contained area.

Otis walked over to the pitcher's mound, holding up a congenial hand. "We won't be using our powers unless it's to assist anyone in need."

"Dale looks like he's in need of an enema," Mark snorted loud enough for Flux to shush him.

Okay, it made sense now, what they were doing. Calmly proving *they* weren't the threat. These Citizens were the real threat, and it was being broadcast across SuperWatch and social media based on how her phone was buzzing in her back pocket.

Kade stepped onto the ice, hands fisted at his sides. He clomped toward the stage so hard, it cracked beneath his feet.

"I don't like you." His voice thundered across the stadium. "You're mean, and you made my friends sick, and my sidekick got hurt, and my strength keeps going in and out, and I'm…I'm *pissed off*."

He stopped at the foot of the stage, glaring up with an intimidating scowl. Dale staggered backward until he hit the tall red curtain.

Darlene hurried over to Kade. "Lunk won't hurt you," she stated, the mic picking it up. "He's a kind person."

She took hold of his arm, then jerked like she'd absorbed his strength.

"I, however, would love to exact justice on you." She pierced Dale with a penetrating glare. "But I won't because I have sworn to protect the people. All people."

Oh, damn. Sadie covered her laughter. Joan and Mark exchanged a *Holy shit!* look.

Dale dropped the mic and ran offstage rambling about conspiracies and Greta. He almost careened straight into Ray, the other Oceanview Supers…and Iris.

He startled and took off in the opposite direction. Iris held her phone up, talking like she was doing a livestream. Good. This deserved to be shared with the world.

"Arrest them!" Dale cried. "Arrest them all!"

"You can't arrest people who aren't doing anything," Travis said, leaning against the podium. He was very much enjoying this.

One of the men onstage waved his arms, shouting for the cameras to be shut off.

Dale covered the side of his face as he dashed past a fuming Darlene and Kade. Then he slid onto the ice, slipping and skidding and falling on his butt.

"Here, let me help you," Joan called to him. She stepped to the ice and set her hands on it. Flames coasted over the surface to Dale's right, causing steam to rise and the ice to melt. It very quickly became a shallow pond.

Joan stood and gestured toward the press box. "Apologies to the Vultures organization. Lifelong fan. I'll pay to have the field resodded."

She was very, *very* much enjoying this.

Sadie breathed a sigh of relief.

Dale flopped around, his once pristine white shirt streaked with mud, his always perfect hair a disheveled mess. He found his footing and splashed to his feet, making his way across the baseball diamond.

"My faithful friends!" He waved a dripping hand at the stands. "Help me!"

A few of his truly faithfuls hurried to the railing, reaching toward him. They pulled Dale up, assuring him they had his back.

Oh, hell no.

"These freaks ruined our beautiful event," Dale said, smoothing down his filthy tie. His gaze crossed paths with Sadie's as he hastened in her direction. "They must be controlled like the animals they are."

She clenched her hands, stepped into a fighting stance, and jabbed hard, snapping a blow just below Dale's nose.

His head flew back and he landed against a burly supporter's chest.

Oh, shit.

She stood frozen as time skidded to a halt.

Then she shot through the aisle, up, stopping abruptly inside one of those fancy private suites.

Her body and brain bobbled back and forth. A sturdy arm supported her. Zee's masked face came into focus.

"Holy shit, Sadie," they said, then laughed. "Stay here."

They zipped away, probably to make it seem like they barely left.

Pain sizzled through her knuckles. She rubbed at them, replaying what'd happened several times in her mind.

"I just punched Dale Terwilliger."

She stumbled toward the wide windows facing the field. A swarm of people surrounded Dale, dazed and bloody-nosed.

A man in a black ballcap gestured to the left. Several cops headed toward the aisle in that direction. The opposite direction of where Sadie had gone. Zee was back by Mark and Joan, and they were all muttering behind their hands.

"I'm in so much trouble," Sadie whispered.

Some of the Supers on the field looked thoroughly entertained. She'd done the thing they really wanted to do.

Travis had gone over to where his former stepbrother was being whisked away by his security detail. She couldn't read his expression, but no doubt it was filled with *Good riddance to bad rubbish.*

The man in the ballcap leaned over the railing and said something to him. Travis nodded, hopped over the railing, and blipped through the first tier of seats.

Sadie sank onto one of the crimson faux-leather armchairs farther back in the suite. The TV above the windows had *No signal* in one corner of the dark screen. Maybe the feed had cut out before her socking Dale in the face. Maybe she'd—

Someone flashed through the wall, making her scream and jump out of her chair.

"Sorry," Travis said, holding up a hand. "It's just me. Are you okay?"

She slapped her palm against her racing heart. "You almost gave me a heart attack."

"You almost gave Dale a heart attack." He chuckled. "Nice jab."

"Did everyone see that? Am I in really big trouble?"

"I don't think so. The cameras went out."

Hopefully, Iris or someone else livestreaming didn't get a good shot of her face. Or—oh god, the Sadie's Café logo on the back of her shirt.

"Alter sent the police away from here. They're looking in the wrong place."

"Alter?"

Travis jutted a thumb toward the dispersing group of attendees. "The person in the ballcap."

Oh. Sadie nodded. *Shapeshifter.*

She glanced at the field. Most of the Supers were gone. Kade was still by the stage watching the Citizens scurry down and make a run for it.

Ray and Otis were talking while Iris feverishly tapped on her phone. Otis said something to her, and she reluctantly handed him the device. Darlene scrutinized them, clutching her crossed arms.

"What's going to happen to Iris?" Sadie asked.

"I think she's going into protective custody," Travis said.

She flexed her sore hand. "Sorry your ex-stepbrother is such a jerk."

His mouth tilted in a smirky smile. "Thank you for reminding him not to be such a jerk."

A quick knock sounded on the door before Joan and Mark came in chattering with Zee.

Sadie took several strides to hug her girlfriend, only Joan stepped to the side. "Not here," she said.

Oh, right, of course. Windows and secret identities and all.

"How are you?" Sadie said. "I can't believe he tried to pull that crap and expose you."

"I'm okay. Stand over here. We need to block you."

She switched places with Joan, leaning against the corner in the tiny kitchen area.

"You are my hero, Sades," Mark said. He gave her a fist-bump, which knocked against her sore knuckles.

She hissed and covered her hand.

"You should ice that," Zee said.

"Here." Mark pulled a glove off, then set his palm on her reddening knuckles.

Ah, the cooling sensation felt good. "Thanks," Sadie said.

"You guys really do need comms," Travis said. "Texting is not the best way to communicate."

"I'll bring it up at our weekly meeting," Joan said. "But we got the word around. I think our calm, unified approach worked."

The door opened again. The superpowered readied to fight as Sadie crouched to the carpet, heart hammering.

Perry walked in and almost had the door closed when someone else slipped in.

Greta, wearing all black, a matching backpack, and a pleased little smile.

She tilted her head and sought out Sadie. "Now *that* was a good hit."

"Holy shit," Joan said. She shook her head, laughed, grasped Greta by the shoulders. "What did you do?"

"I hacked into their system and fucked with it."

Wait, what?

"Every time they turned it off and on, it corrupted the program more," Greta said. "It's totally fried now."

"How did you get it to make the norms sick?" Mark asked.

Greta gave him a look. "I'm very good at what I do, Mark."

Joanie shook her head again, laughed again. "Damn right you are."

She looked like she wanted to pull Greta into a hug. Greta patted her hands and grinned. A lovely healing moment at a very bizarre time.

Sadie stood slowly as the old pals separated.

"Thanks," Joan said quietly.

"You couldn't be the ones to destroy it," Greta said. "It had to look like *they* were making people sick. And I had a bone to pick with this particular group."

Travis inhaled sharply and stared at her. "Oh my god. You're Greta. *The* Greta."

"I am." She shot a finger gun at him. "You're Blip."

"You stole the Paulina Blue Diamond from that auction house eight years ago. Before I could. I was mad, but also really impressed."

"I'm a fan of your string of bank heists the summer before that."

He looked a little starstruck. "Thanks."

Zee put a hand over their eyes like *I'll pretend not to hear any of this.*

"Why were you here?" Perry said.

Greta moved into the little kitchen and opened the mini fridge. "To steal their fundraising donations. Then I caught wind of what they were about to do and changed course." She pulled out a bottle of water. "I still got the money, to repay the Citizens for all the kindness they've shown us."

Perry got his *Hooray for revenge* twinkle in his eyes. Definitely a revenge Sadie was not mad about.

Still, Joanie's safety was her priority. So she asked, "Do you think they'll try to trace it back to you? Or who they think you are? Like, Spark?"

Greta took a long swig of water, then said, "They can try, but do they need more bad PR? Mighty fishy to have lost all their donations."

Joan stepped closer to Sadie, heat radiating off her in waves. "What about you?" she said to Greta. "Everyone who knows you will know this has your fingerprints all over it. You protected a bunch of Superheroes."

"And destroyed a hate group with my dazzling skills." Greta's smile gleamed in the sunlight. "This will make me legendary."

The Heroes let that go, considering what she'd done for them. And herself. This was as much for clearing Joanie's name as bolstering her own, which was peak Greta.

"But man," she said, gesturing with her plastic bottle at the windows. "Terwilliger went above and beyond my expectations by publicly refusing to turn it off. Blip, the way you egged him on was a thing of beauty."

They shared compliments, clearly big admirers of one another's work.

Zee turned to the twins and said, "We should get the norms who committed an assault and several major felonies out of here."

"All justifiable," Perry said.

Joan reached for Sadie's hand. She ran her gloved thumb gently across the aching knuckles. "Does it hurt?" she murmured.

"Yeah. A lot."

"I'll treat it with arnica gel tonight."

"That would be terrific."

"We should have you work the punching bag with thinner wraps so you can build up a tolerance."

"For the next leg of the Citizens for Human Cities Tour," Sadie joked.

"Maybe they'll cancel it."

"They should cancel the whole damn thing."

Joan tenderly squeezed her fingers. "Thanks for punching an asshole for me, sweetheart."

Sadie leaned in, wanting so badly to kiss the woman she loved. "I will always fight for you, Joanie."

A smile tugged at her lips. "Who knew you meant that literally?"

Greta walked to the door. "Dinner's on me. Assuming you don't have to do annoying Superhero things."

"I don't," Perry said.

She paused with her hand on the doorknob. "Is this what it feels like to be a good guy?"

"Smug?" Mark said. "Self-satisfied?"

"No."

Joan laced her fingers through Sadie's. "That's real, honest pride, Grets."

"Ew." Greta shivered at the mention of honesty.

"It's okay. It grows on you."

CHAPTER 26

They had a lot to talk about at Monday's weekly meeting, and two guest attendees.

Kelsey sat in the corner rather than at the conference table, bored and twirling in her chair. Out of her Iris ensemble, she liked to wear loose-fit, eco-friendly clothes made with recycled materials and sustainable organic what-have-you.

Trav sipped his coffee in a silver Sadie's Café tumbler. He was heading back to Yanton in a few hours and had made sure to stop by the business of the woman who'd clocked Dale Terwilliger in the face. Not that the general public knew that—her identity had been carefully hidden.

Those who knew Sadie were damn proud of her. Joan happily drank the last of her Kick Me Up.

The big reveal of the power-blocking tech had backfired. Overall opinion and trust of the Citizens had taken a hit. Even those who'd previously spoken out in favor of restrictions were saying if it made regular people sick, it wasn't worth it. The next stop on the Citizens for Human Cities Tour had been postponed, and there was talk of the one after that being pushed back as well.

Dale was in full damage control mode. He'd of course said his erratic behavior had been caused by the faulty tech, and had also strongly suggested Super interference of some kind. Standing back and letting him ruin his own reputation was working out pretty well.

The Citizens for Human Douchery had been ordered to pay for the cleanup of Vulture Stadium by its corporate ownership. Which had proven difficult given the mysterious loss of donations collected at the event. Which was being looked into by more than one government agency for more than one reason.

Kelsey swiveled her chair, head lolling against the back. "Can I *please* have my phone?" she moaned.

"You're supposed to be locked in the basement," Joan reminded her for the twentieth time.

"But I'm *bored* and could be doing something to—"

"Would you like to be locked in the basement?" Otis leveled her with a glare suggesting she not ask again for phone privileges.

"I could be helping weed out the people in the prison system who sold us out," Kelsey said.

"It's being dealt with."

She crossed her arms and sulked. She really didn't grasp that this was as good as it was gonna get.

They were keeping her here while investigations at the prison were ongoing. Off the record, the inquiry was being headed up by Nuance and Alter pretending to be administration higher-ups. But really, anyone on every Superhero's shit list would be best served severing ties to a group that wanted to get rid of Superheroes.

The one thing Kelsey did understand was that if she ran away, Iris would be a wanted fugitive. Whoever caught her next would not be so understanding.

"We'll keep an eye on what you asked us to," Mark said to her.

"Make sure the puffins have safe habitats to nest in before winter."

"Where?"

"*Everywhere.*"

Zee chuckled under their breath. "No good deed, Mark."

"No kidding," he grumbled.

Kade got up to recycle his energy drink can. Ward struggled to his feet to help, but everyone yelled at him to sit down. Even Otis.

Their sidekick gave an apologetic smile. "I'm so sorry. I'll be back to normal tomorrow, I promise."

He fingered the small row of stitches on his forehead above an old pair of glasses. He seemed pretty proud to have a battle scar, but happier to have made it through so they didn't have to go looking for a new sidekick.

"All in all, we accomplished our goal," Otis said. "We strengthened ties with our allies and supporters while weakening the opposition."

"But we didn't stop them," Kade said. "We should have won. The good guys are supposed to win."

"I don't think this is a win-lose situation, buddy," Mark said.

"What if they get that thing that squashes our powers again? I'm scared about that."

"We have our secret weapon," Joan said. "Greta would be happy to further mess with them."

She expected Darlene to voice concerns about that, only Darlene was unusually subdued today. Probably from the fact that a notorious criminal had saved their asses.

Kade wasn't having it. "I just hate that the bad guys are still out there."

"Then we keep fighting," Joan said.

Zee nodded in agreement. "For as long as it takes."

"We didn't stop them," Mark said, "but we sure as hell dented them."

It sucked that the Citizens didn't get their comeuppance, but this was still a victory. It looked like they could no longer connect Spark to Greta, which was a huge relief. Spark and Ice seemed to be more accepted as good guys thanks to their efforts to get people to safety. Plus they were on video showing restraint and working in tandem with established Supers.

Darlene shifted in her seat. "If they do host these rallies in other cities, there should be a strong Superhero presence."

"We'll be there," Joan said, jutting a thumb at her brother. "Pretty sure I can count on the rest of you."

"Some of us have to remain here to deal with local issues," Otis said.

"We don't have any Villains."

"Otis wants to go to the one in Destine," Kade said, then gave an exaggerated wink.

Otis ignored him.

"I'll go if I can," Trav said.

"Can I go?" Kelsey said while chair-twirling.

"No," everyone chorused.

"*Uuuggghhh.*"

Joan tried to placate her with, "Maybe someday if you get probationary status like we did."

Mark screwed his eyes up. "Are we still on probation?"

Otis considered that for a moment, then said, "No, I suppose not."

"Nice." Mark elbowed Joan.

She smiled at him. It *was* nice.

Trav elbowed her other side. "Get pumped for that portrait, Spark."

"Yeah, yeah." She was gonna put off the portrait as much as she put off therapy appointments. "One thing this past weekend showed was how cities have to start working together. Our mistrust and insular nature is hurting us. We have resources and different powers and experiences that could benefit all of us. There should be, I don't know, a league or assembly or squad of Superheroes."

"Think of the good optics," Mark said.

"I've wanted something like that for a long time," Darlene said.

"Really?" Joan said.

"Yes. The idea was always shot down."

"Let's do it."

"I have specifically wanted a mentorship program for women

Superheroes." Darlene subtly raised an eyebrow—enough for Joan to understand. It was the support Gus had needed, and what Darlene had needed from Gus.

"That would be cool," Kelsey said, her back to them.

Darlene narrowed her eyes at the former Super. "Then perhaps young Heroes will have someone to talk to before they turn to a life of crime."

Before Kelsey could respond, Joan said, "Or young people might be given a chance rather than be left to flounder and turn to villainy."

Darlene nodded like it was settled. "I will start planning mentorship opportunities. Spark will continue connecting cities and their Heroes."

Oh, okay. Guess that was a thing and it was happening.

She stood abruptly and said, "I'll be right back."

"This is good," Zee said. "It'll create more trust with the public. If they see us working together…"

"Acting like friends," Kade added as he sat.

"Being proactive."

"Approving more SuperWatch claims," Mark tossed in.

Lord, all Joan felt like she did some days was work on Super-Watch claims. But they were important. "We have to get those approved more efficiently. Don't they have someone at City Hall who can do that?"

Otis shrugged.

"Maybe *we* can hire someone to go through all the claims, get our okays and whatever information they need from us…"

A lightbulb went on in her head. She turned to Mark to see him lightbulbing, too.

"Someone who loves mountains of mindless paperwork," Mark said.

"Who wants to help people."

"Who loves making Superheroes do stuff for him."

"We've got the perfect candidate," Joan said with a grin. "He has an MBA."

"Who?" Kade said excitedly.

"Perry."

Joan blinked, surprised it was Otis who'd said that.

"Who's Perry?" Kelsey said, swiveling around again.

"Is that okay with you?" Joan asked Otis.

"If it's all right with him," he said.

Joan smiled at Mark. He smiled back. "I think he'll be amenable to it," she said.

Ward conferred with Otis on how to notate that in the meeting minutes. "Ms. Joan, will you be reaching out to Mr. Breeze about this?"

"Sure." Joan pulled her phone from her front pants pocket.

There was a bank notification about a deposit. A $24,000 deposit. What?

She clicked on it, her mouth quirking at the memo.

GET A NEW SUIT ALREADY

Greta. Joan had mentioned at dinner the other night she wanted to replace her Spark suit. And Grets had recently come into some money she was looking to donate to a worthy cause.

She shook her head and went into her texts.

> I thought you were going to stay out of trouble for a hot minute.

Laying low and doing the agreed-upon jobs for Perry and Gus's pet project was to ensure Greta stayed off the Supers' radar. Making a large anonymous deposit was...

Well, it was how Greta showed she cared. Giving money stolen from the Citizens to someone they had wronged.

Her response was, predictably:

> I am

Then she sent a selfie of her in front of the counter at Sadie's Café with Sadie and Nyah grinning and waving behind it.

Joan's heart warmed, but then a prickle of concern tickled the back of her neck. Sadie and Greta together could be more trouble than she'd considered.

"Catch is coming back," Kelsey said. "She's carrying a cake."

Joan and Mark shared an uneasy look.

"Yum," Trav said.

Mark gave him a headshake that said it was not yum.

Darlene entered the room carrying a round, chocolate-frosted cake on a white stand.

"You made a cake?" Kade said, unable to hide the trepidation in his voice.

"Yes." Darlene set it on the credenza.

She went about cutting pieces and placing them on the small snack plates. Ward went about discussing the schedule for the week.

Joan nearly cried tears of joy at having no scheduled appearances. Hopefully Sadie could sneak out on Wednesday or Friday for them to have a date day. Maybe not to work out, with Sadie's healing hand, though she'd expressed that she was looking forward to jabbing and uppercutting at the HQ gym.

Darlene slid a plate in front of her. It was a two-tiered white cake. It looked fluffy, with a good ratio of cake to frosting, but looks could be deceiving. Especially with Darlene's pastries.

Trav, being a genuinely nice guy, was the first to take a bite. He chewed, his eyes widening until he swallowed. "Wow, that's really good."

"Really?" Kade said, getting a glare from Darlene as she set his plate down.

"Yeah." Trav went in for another bite.

Mark was the next brave soul. "Oh my god," he said around a mouthful of cake. "It *is* really good."

Okay, Joan had to taste it to believe it.

A pillowy-soft sponge with a delicious, silky chocolate icing, and ooh—a slight hint of sea salt to balance the sweetness.

"Darlene, this is a fantastic bite," she said.

Darlene nodded from the head of the conference table. "I had a few missteps, but I learned from my mistakes and improved."

"You really did."

The meeting was put on hold in favor of digging in.

"I want seconds," Kade said with a blob of frosting on the side of his mouth.

"I want seconds and thirds," Mark said.

Darlene crossed her arms, then uncrossed them. "I made it because I have an announcement. I am moving to Oceanview to join their Superheroes."

Joan's fork clattered to her plate. "You what?"

"They have a need for another Superhero, since…" She made a vague gesture at Kelsey.

Kelsey deliberately licked the frosting off her raised middle finger.

"Vector City is in good hands. Oceanview needs a top-to-bottom overhaul. Things are far too lax there."

Nobody knew what to say. Vector City without Catch?

"I will still get the mentoring program together," Darlene continued. She nodded at Joan. "We will work together. You have picked up on the fight for justice."

"Um…" Joan swallowed, the cake suddenly dry in her throat. "I don't think anyone fights for justice as hard as you do."

"Which is why I'm going to Oceanview. It's a new beginning. A new challenge." An eager glint lit her brown eyes.

Kelsey scooted her chair closer to the table and set her plate on it. "You have your work cut out for you."

"I'm looking forward to it."

Ward stared at Darlene, eyes sad, fingers motionless on his laptop keyboard.

"Well, Darlene," Otis said. "I speak for all of us when I say you will be missed. You've been the most upstanding Hero I have ever worked with."

"Thank you." The compliment added a little color to her cheeks. "You'll have five Superheroes in a city without Villains. And two retired allies who step in when needed. You will be all right."

She looked at Joan again, then added, "You will all be all right."

Never, ever in her thirty-six years on this planet did Joan think she would *not* want to have Catch in Vector City. But she found herself saying with total sincerity, "We'll really miss you, but we'll stay in touch."

Darlene's eyes softened. Then she straightened—it was getting too sentimental in the room. "Yes, for future professional collaborations."

"Darlene," Kade said, wearing a very serious, very worried expression. "Is this because I have a girlfriend?"

She shot him an incredulous look. "No."

"Because we had a thing, and now I'm dating someone else."

"I don't care," she said.

Relief erased his concern. He broke into a huge grin. "Did I tell you guys? Nyah and I are officially dating."

"Aww," Mark said.

"That's great, buddy." Joan sacrificed her hand for a high-five across the table.

Zee and Trav and Ward offered their congratulations. Darlene truly couldn't care less.

"Way to go, the Strong Man," Joan said.

"You can call me Lunk," Kade said. "I'm reclaiming it."

She tilted her head, not sure if…

Ah, hell. Let him have it.

"The best Lunk I know," Joan said.

"Hey Darlene, will you make another cake before you go?" Mark joked, scraping the icing off his plate.

Talk turned to when she was leaving, and packing and

moving, and Kelsey offering suggestions on places to live close to Oceanview HQ. Joan's heartbeat steadily picked up.

Another big change. Another adjustment, but ultimately a good one.

Maybe Darlene would find a better work-life balance. Probably not, especially with the monumental task ahead of her. But her work made her happy, and who knew—maybe the chill vibe of Oceanview would rub off on her.

You have picked up on the fight for justice.

Huh. Spark was making her mark by being fair, by trying to do right by most people. Unless they were total assholes. They could suck it.

Spark was kind of the new Catch. Not in demeanor, but in responsibilities. Being a positive role model, a strong woman, someone who didn't take crap. And if a person with abilities needed guidance, she would do what she could for them.

That was what a real hero did.

CHAPTER 27

Joan hugged Trav outside the conference room doorway. He had to get to the airport now that the meeting was over.

"You're always welcome in Vector City," she said.

"You're always welcome in Yanton," he said. "Take care of Sadie. You've got a good one there."

"I know it."

He hugged Zee, then Mark. Then smiled knowingly at them. "Lots of good here, too."

"Don't be gross," Mark said.

Zee shouldered him back into the room, then waved goodbye.

Trav laughed and said, "I don't think those two realize how much they like each other."

"They'll fight it tooth and nail," Joan said.

He sighed deeply. "I think I'm gonna give it another try with my girlfriend."

"You should. She sounds pretty great."

"She is." Trav shoved his hands in his jeans pockets and got all hunched up. "We at least need to try, right?"

"Right. You never know."

"Thanks for talking to me, and, y'know, for showing me it's

possible. Seeing how you and Sadie navigate things has given me hope."

"I'm glad." Joan chucked his shoulder. "And I owe you thanks. After we talked, I decided to tell Sadie's parents the truth."

"Oh god. How did that go?"

"Better than I expected. They see me as Joan. Maybe they'll see me as Spark and not be freaked out by that. Someday way, *way* in the future."

"That's great," said Trav.

"More hope for you, my friend. Keep me posted."

"You, too." He checked the time on his really nice watch that had to be a score from his villainy days. "Meet you at the next protest?"

"I'll be there," Joan promised. "Do you remember which changing room your stuff is in?"

"I've got it." He grinned, clutched his Sadie's Café tumbler to his chest, then blipped through the wall.

Joan jumped and muttered, "Damn it." That definitely took getting used to.

She headed into the conference room to see if Darlene wanted to hash out a few details for their respective outreach. Otis and Kade were fighting over the rest of the cake. Mark and Zee were in the opposite corner, murmuring close.

Mark made a face like he didn't want to do something. Zee whispered in his ear, then squeezed his hand with a small *You've got this* nod.

Hmm. That was worth investigating.

Joan joined them, saying, "Wasn't it cool hanging out with Trav?"

"Yeah, he's great," Mark said. He patted his navy-blue shorts pockets. "Damn it, I left my phone… Come with me."

She followed him out of the room. Zee did not. Ooookay.

As they walked down the hallway, Joan said, "Can you believe Darlene? Oceanview is in for it."

"Yeah."

"It's hard to imagine Vector City without Catch running around spouting about justice."

"It's a good move for her," Mark said.

"Yeah. And she's got a point. Do we really need six Supers in a city without Villains?"

He scratched at his hair.

They passed the landing and the large portraits. Joan considered the scant amount of open wall space. "So we're finally off probation. We should make Gus a spectacular dinner and ask her to paint our portraits. Which I still think is ridiculous, but if—"

"Hey, can we talk?" Mark said.

"Sure. What's up?"

He kept moving toward the lounge. Joan caught up, growing more concerned when her brother closed the door behind them.

"Everything okay?" she asked. "Did something happen with you and Zee?"

"It's not that." Mark perched on the edge of the couch, nervously rubbing his hands.

Joan sat beside him. "What's wrong?"

He swore under his breath, then said, "I don't know how to say this."

"Just say it."

"Y'know how Darlene said she wanted a new challenge? That things will be okay and are in good hands? That she feels like it's okay to step away?"

"I don't know that she said that last part, but okay."

Mark glanced at her. "Remember when you asked me if I liked being a Superhero and I said I did?"

"Yeah," Joan said, her heart thumping in anticipation of something really, really bad.

"I wasn't lying, but I wasn't…" He chugged in a breath. "I really miss the food truck. I loved it. That was the happiest I think I've ever been. I miss cooking, I miss planning menus, I miss it all. I want to be a chef. That's what I've always wanted."

Through the ringing in her ears, Joan heard herself say, "Okay."

"Wren and Beth-Ann found a place. It's on the northern edge of the Jewel District. Beth-Ann's gonna handle front of house." He avoided looking at her. "Wren and I have talked about her needing a sous chef if I was ever interested. Well, I'm interested. I told them I wanted to do it. They're keeping their food truck for special events and such. I'll run it for them. Maybe if they open a second location, I could run the kitchen there."

"What about working with people who don't know about your..."

"I've got a much better handle on that since culinary school. I don't *have* to use my powers, but they're there in case they might enhance a dish."

"A vegan restaurant?" Joan said, even though that was the least important bit of information.

"I can make vegan dishes. It's a cool challenge."

"Then you'll..." She couldn't bring herself to form the words.

"I'm giving up being a Super," Mark said. "You guys really don't need me. I'll still be here for emergencies, like Perry. Or at future protests. Ice won't go away forever."

"But it's Spark and Ice," Joan said, minorly panicking at the thought of... "It's always been Spark and Ice."

"I know, Joanie. I've thought so much about this."

"I want you to be happy, and I guess I've known you weren't all that happy, but..."

But she could see the excited light in his eyes. He loved to cook. He hadn't stopped scribbling research and development ideas in the notebook he'd used for Hot and Cold.

He glanced down, plucking at the couch. "I've always followed whatever you did. Which is my deal, and I own it. You didn't make me. But it's time I stand on my own feet."

Too much anxious energy was building inside Joan. She had to get up, had to pace it out. "I thought you liked all the attention. You're so good with the public. Way better than me."

"That's just playing the role of Superhero. Yeah, I do it well, but..." Mark shrugged. "Ice gets that attention. I want to be known for being Mark Malone. I've never gotten the chance to shine as myself."

He gestured at her. "You like having positive attention for Spark because that means people aren't afraid of you. Joan Malone has a happy private life. You've got what you've always wanted."

His insinuation floated between them. *Let me have what I want.*

Joan focused on his unusually confident calm. It wasn't Mark's blasé, *Everything's cool* indifference. He'd made a decision for himself. It was good. It was mature.

"I totally understand," she said, "and I get it. I was conflicted about not reopening Hot and Cold to become a Hero. It felt like I was making you abandon your dream in favor of mine."

"You didn't. I could have said no. And I mean, who would turn down the chance to be a Superhero?"

She didn't want him thinking she wasn't okay with his choice. Sure, it hurt, and she was surprised, but maybe not *that* surprised.

"I'll stand by whatever you do," Joan said. "I always will. And you're right. You should do what's in your heart. We don't have to stay joined at the hip forever. You were pissed when I moved away from you and Per, but that was something I had to do. I get it, I do."

But still, she was losing her other half. Losing her partner in crime, her partner in just about everything.

"Thanks, Joanie," he said with a small smile. "And you're not losing me. I know that's what you're worried about. I'll help with Kelsey's damn puffins. I'll still drop by at inappropriate hours and whine about how hard my normal job is and how much they're taking out of my paycheck for taxes."

They shared quiet laughter. She sat again to close the distance between them. "It's probably good that you and Zee won't work together anym—Wait, do they know your plan?"

"Yeah, they do." Mark smiled to himself. "We've been talking a lot about this. They helped me come to a decision after this past weekend. They're supportive of it. They pointed out I really want to build something for myself."

"That's great," Joan said. "You two can have grown-up conversations. And you have someone in your life you can go to for the important stuff."

He picked up on what she was suggesting based on the stink eye he shot her. "Yeah, it's been nice. We actually talk a lot, about a lot of stuff. 'Cause, y'know…"

"Because…"

Mark huffed. "Because we're dating, okay?"

"*Finally.*"

"Don't be so smug. We agreed we're a couple or whatever. It was so gross and mushy and feelings."

"But good?" Joan said.

"I guess," Mark said, trying and failing to squelch his grin.

"How gross and mushy? Did you use the L-word?"

"Nah. We're not there yet. We're in 'like a lot.' Exclusive 'like a lot.'"

"Note that you said you're not there *yet*."

"Yeah, yeah."

"I can't wait to meet their mom," Joan said.

"You'll like her. She's a pistol."

It was so nice to have partners with parents who were cool with them. Would their own parents like Sadie and Zee? Could they be open and honest about real jobs and secret identities?

Yeah no, that was not something she could deal with today.

She punched his arm. "I'm so happy for both of you. I mean, Zee could do a lot better, but—"

"Whose side are you on?" Mark batted her away. "You know Sadie could do a hundred times better than you."

"Oh, no doubt. I work every day to be on her level." Joan leaned in and joked, "Maybe someday, you'll be worthy of Zee."

"I'll try."

The glow emanating from him eased a lot of her big feelings.

Zee kept Mark on his toes. There wasn't another person Joan trusted with her brother other than the Superhero who didn't give up on the Malone twins.

"I talked about this in therapy, in case you were wondering," Mark said.

"I figured. Will you have to stop seeing the Super shrink if you're not a Super?"

"I haven't told her my decision, but I'd still see her even if I have to pay for it. It's important."

She studied the self-assured man her little brother had become. "I'm really proud of you," she said, her eyes filling with tears.

His softened with concern. "How are you, really? You've had a lot of upheaval lately, and I just dropped a bomb on you."

"It's all good things. I'll get used to it."

"But…?"

She couldn't hide anything from him. They'd gone through literally everything together: scared kids, misunderstood teenagers, rebellious Supervillains, redeemed Superheroes…

"I can't do this without you," she whispered, her voice thick.

"Joanie." Mark turned to fully face her. "You were born for this. You're really good at being a Super. It's what you were meant to do."

He glanced around the room. "This was never my dream. You gave me my dream with the food truck, and I will always love you for that."

His sincerity pushed her over the edge. She wrapped him in a gigantic hug, tears rolling from her eyes and sizzling on her cheeks.

Mark squeezed her tight, sniffling, "Damn it Joanie, don't make me cry. Fuckin' tears freeze to my face and it hurts."

They laughed and hugged a little longer. Then pulled apart so she could touch his icy tears and melt them.

"Shit," Joan said, then snuffled. "Are we gonna have a triple date with Perry and Gus before you start your new job?"

"Quadruple date," Mark said. "With Nyah and Kade."

"We'll get Otis and Sherrelle, and if Trav can patch things up with his girlfriend…"

"Maybe we'll just hang out at Sadie's Café at the next open mic night."

"It's where friends gather."

They got up, swiping at the remnants of their tears and mumbling about lunch.

Her loved ones weren't leaving her. They were forging their own happy paths, the same as she had.

If theirs were even a fraction as good as Joan's path, they were in for one hell of a good time.

EPILOGUE

Seven months later

Sadie fastened the heavy metal latch on the back of the rental truck. She moved around the side closest to the elevators in the parking garage loading zone.

"I think we're good," she said to Mark and Zee.

"Were there any more boxes?" Mark asked, wiping his forehead on a pale blue T-shirt sleeve.

"There's one more with cleaning supplies. I can put that in Joanie's car."

"Who's driving the truck over there?"

"I can."

Mark snorted.

"I know how to drive," Sadie defended.

He playfully cringed, to which she smacked his arm.

"I'd help more, but I have to get going," Zee said. No rest for the Supers, especially since Joanie had the day off.

"Why can't you just…" Mark mimed grabbing and throwing things really fast.

"Super speed, not super strength, Mark."

Sadie tugged her sock farther out of her tennis shoe. "The super strength is meeting us after Nyah's aunt's dialysis."

Kade was going to help with the move once he had Nyah's aunt home from her treatment. He liked taking her and keeping her entertained. She loved his company, and Ny loved having her sweet boyfriend always willing to lend a hand.

Holding his water bottle to block his mouth, Mark said, "Estelle could just teleport shit for you."

"She can't risk someone seeing her," Sadie said.

Estelle was still content keeping her powers to herself. She'd been talking a little with Joanie and a few of the other women from the Super support group. Learning ways to control her teleportation so she didn't end up going to the wrong places. She was feeling better about her abilities, and she'd only missed half a shift all year, so definite progress.

"Where's Greta and her big van?" Mark asked.

Sadie snickered. "Greta is not the friend who helps you move."

"At least not legally," Zee said.

"I think she's out of town on assignment."

Greta had discovered it was almost as much fun to break in and return things as it was to take them. She'd been working with Perry and Gus to give back more of the stolen artwork, jewelry, and other items. It kept her skills sharp, and she could be as crafty as she wanted as long as she didn't leave with anything new in her possession.

So far, so good, fingers crossed.

Sadie was looking forward to their next self-defense training session at Greta's place. They weren't worried about hurting one another, so she could really go for it. Greta definitely didn't hold back, which was the best way to learn quickly.

Sometimes Joanie and Greta would box, dissolving into laughter at the end. Their evolved friendship was a lot of fun, especially when they nerded out with Nyah at café gamer nights.

Mark checked his phone. "I have to get to my vodka sauce for the walnut ravioli."

"That sounds good," Sadie said.

"Get it while you can. We're swapping it out for a lighter springtime pasta dish."

"Thanks for helping. We really appreciate it. Pizza and beer on us the next time you're both free."

"Next Monday," Mark said. The restaurant was closed on Mondays, so that was usually his only day off.

Zee touched the back of their hand to Mark's chest. "We've got that thing at the youth center next Monday."

"Oh shit, that's right. Soon. We'll get together soon."

He reached out for a hug that Sadie reciprocated. Mark was volunteering in his post-Ice life as sous chef Mark Malone. He'd been so busy since the Powered by Plants brick-and-mortar opened that he hadn't been able to go much. But he was terrifically happy. Even Joanie had to admit that as much as she missed seeing him every day, she was thrilled with how he was thriving.

Zee cast a glance at him. "Do you want a lift to work?"

"I have to shower and change. Home first?"

"What am I, your superpowered rideshare?"

Mark kissed their cheek and grinned. "You love it."

Zee's pretend smirk said they totally did.

They gave Sadie a quick squeeze. "Congrats, hon. I can't wait to see your new home."

The words warmed her on the inside. *My new home with Joanie.*

Mark pointed his water bottle at her. "Tell my sister to hurry her ass up. What's she doing?"

"One last sweep to make sure we got everything," Sadie said. They did have to move the truck pretty soon, since their allotted time block was almost up.

Zee looked around to make sure no eyes were on them. They and Mark wrapped their arms around one another.

"Later, skater," Mark said, and they zipped off into the daylight.

Sadie stretched her back with a groan. Moving was such a pain. Why did she do it so much?

Well, *had* done it so much. This move was different in every possible way.

She and Joanie had bought a home—*their* home—together. A townhouse in the Village walking distance to work for her, and minutes of a drive for Joanie. It had the perfect blend of clean lines and coziness thanks to a full remodel that retained the character of the building. One look and they'd known it was meant to be theirs.

The lobby was bustling with midday activity as she reentered the apartment building. Oh, she should check the mailbox one last time.

She went into the alcove. The only mail was an advertisement for a poke place down the street. It wouldn't be convenient after today, so she recycled it. Then she worked the mailbox key off her keychain, her steps slowing toward the main elevator bank.

What about doing mailers for the café? Did they bring in business? Opinions varied among her women's entrepreneur group on marketing strategies that worked. She made a mental note to ask at next week's meetup, since it was at Sadie's Café.

Maybe that was her answer. The coffeehouse hosted so many things now, it was like built-in advertising. With their delicious menu, excellent customer service, food trucks in the front, plus they were a hub for Super Supporters and the queer community and artists and local businesses…

Word of mouth was their biggest asset, and the steady income flowing in was proof she was killing it as a badass business owner.

A guy waiting for the elevators was watching a fashion news video on his phone, sound on for all to hear. Which was normally extremely annoying, only the subject was top-ranked Superhero outfits.

"Number Two on our list is Spark from Vector City," a chipper woman's voice reported. "The redesign is sleek and modern. The equal combination of black and red has a balanced feel, and we can't get enough of that facemask. Some might miss the flowing dark wig, but Spark has said it was decorative and often got in the way. We say this look is *fire*."

Sadie smiled to herself. Joanie had worked really hard with the designer most Superheroes used to have ebony and crimson slashes rising up the suit, almost like flames. Her new facemask was more fitted and curved, giving her better protection and visibility. It also added some flair in the absence of a wig.

Elevator doors opened behind her. She opted to let Video Guy take that one with a mom, a stroller with a baby in it, a fussy toddler, and a huge diaper bag. Most of her friends didn't have kids, and she'd never known how much *stuff* you needed for a baby until Carrie gave birth back in January.

So much stuff. So many diapers. But it was fun to buy her nephew adorable little outfits and noisy toys and make him laugh at family dinners and in video calls. He was super cute.

Carrie was leery about letting Aunt Sadie and Aunt Joan babysit, which was probably a sixty/forty split of Joan's firepower and Sadie's lack of understanding about small humans. Then again, her sister was sus about letting anyone but their parents babysit, so...

At least Joanie was treated as a member of the family. Dad was as excited about the tiny backyard at the new place as Joan was. They'd been drawing up plans for a raised garden that Joan was going to start ASAP. Dad's surprise housewarming gift was a bunch of gardening tools and supplies, only he'd ruined the surprise in his excitement.

Mom was heading over tomorrow to help unpack. Her offer to lend a hand and genuine happiness about the townhouse was sooo appreciated, even if it was because her daughter was moving out of a high-rise and into a residential neighborhood. She was glad Sadie was doing it with a wonderful partner.

The elevator doors to her right opened. Sadie glanced up and met the gaze of a gorgeous woman with freshly cropped dark hair wearing long cargo shorts and an army-green sleeveless tee.

Joanie smiled that lazy smile at her. "Fancy meeting you here."

"Hi." Sadie grinned back and stepped in.

"I was coming to check the mail and see if you guys needed anything."

"Just checked the mail. Zee and Mark are gone. We have to get going."

"Yup."

They rode to the seventh floor for the last time. A pang of wistfulness hit Sadie. "This is our last trip up."

"Yeah." Joanie's beautiful eyes were filled with nostalgia.

The familiar soft bing announced their arrival. Sadie slid an arm through Joan's as they strolled down the hallway. "So many memories here," she said. "This is where we met. Where we fell in love, had our first home together."

"This building is special," Joan said, rubbing Sadie's hand. "It brought us together."

They passed apartment 709, its white door empty.

"My old place," Sadie mused. She'd never met who moved in after her. "I wonder if the vindictive pigeon still terrorizes the balcony."

"Hopefully not."

The door at 714 was also devoid of décor, but that was because it was packed in a truck awaiting a new door.

She didn't like walking in and seeing the apartment empty. It looked desolate. No plants on the balcony, no kitchen gadgets, nothing that made it a home.

"I'll miss this place," Sadie said, getting a little misty.

Joanie was, too. She cleared her throat and settled her hands on Sadie's hips. "I will too, but I can't wait for our house."

"Our house," Sadie repeated. "Our permanent home."

No more moving around, no more hiding. They were putting down roots and creating a safe sanctuary. The happiest, most positive change in Joanie Maloney and Sadie Eagan's lives.

She wrapped her arms around Joan's neck. "And you can plant a big garden. And we can finally adopt a cat—"

"Dog."

"A cat and a dog," Sadie amended with a grin. "Who we'll spoil rotten. And we'll host game nights and Christmas dinner, and snuggle a whole lot."

"*Snuggle* all over the house," Joanie said, waggling her eyebrows.

"Maybe even some morning shower sex."

"Morning shower sex was great."

"Wasn't it?"

"It really was."

"We'll have lots of shower sex, and, and…" Sadie shrugged. "We'll just have the best damn life."

They kissed, Joanie picking her slightly off the floor to Sadie's delight.

Joan's phone jingled on the kitchen island with an incoming text. She grumbled and set Sadie down and went to check it, since she was never really off the clock.

"Jesus, Perry," she said to the device. "You know we're moving today."

Sadie laughed. "You created a monster. You know that, right?"

"I thought he'd get claims completed in a timely manner. I had no idea to him *timely* meant right fucking now." Joan tapped out a reply.

Perry was very thoroughly enjoying his role as Claims Supervisor. Everything about the job had been tailor-made for him. It filled in the gaps to give him something to do when he and Gus weren't hanging out at her place or at the warehouse.

Destine also seemed interested in having them work on returning stolen items. Per liked the idea of bossing even more Superheroes around. It'd be great if the benevolent enterprise caught on.

Elsewhere, Darlene was doing her best to straighten things up in Oceanview. Kelsey had recently been transferred back there with a mountain of required community service hours, which she was happy to do. The guidance she was receiving from the women Superhero network seemed to be helping. She'd also been assigned mandatory therapy sessions to deal with her propensity to threaten to blow stuff up. With Darlene there, the kid was not going to get away with a thing.

Joan had done a few virtual sessions with "the Super shrink." It still wasn't her favorite thing, but she'd acknowledged open communication was vital in all areas of her life. Sadie had noticed Joanie was better at expressing her feelings and needs, which made *her* more open to fully expressing herself.

Dings and swooshes meant an animated text exchange was happening with Perry.

Things had been relatively quiet in Vector City, so damage claims were fewer and further between. Perry had dug into some past denied claims to see if they warranted reconsideration. One of them was for Vector City Coffee.

Amit had been thrilled to get the extra payout.

The Citizens for Human Cities Tour was still a thorn in humanity's side. It'd been retooled as "town halls" in much smaller, much less urban locations. They'd spun what happened in Vector City as proof that cities were unsafe. They "made the choice" not to put their supporters in the harmful path of the superpowered, dodging the fact that *they'd* been the ones to make thousands of regular people sick.

Joanie had attended three of them with Heroes from other cities, taking part in Super Supporters protests and keeping a watchful eye on the reduced but not eliminated threat. She was creating a sort of brain trust with Supers across the country— and Travis up in Yanton—to share information and ideas. Anti-Super sentiment had definitely lessened, while the Super Supporter movement had gained worldwide momentum. It was awesome.

Dale Terwilliger only spoke remotely these days. Not that anyone would have him on as an "expert" anymore. Even the Badger News Network didn't want him to politically analyze.

"Have to move the freakin' truck, Perry," Joan muttered. She swished a text, then a new one dinged. "Yes, we're finally getting the workout stuff out of the warehouse because it's been there too long, Perry."

Sadie giggled. The partially finished basement in their townhouse was going to be set up as a home gym with the old equipment Joanie and Mark didn't want to part with. It'd be nice to have a workout space if Sadie wanted to relieve stress and pump a little iron, so she was on board.

Joan whooshed a text, then shoved her phone in her pocket. "You all set, babe?"

"Yeah." Sadie walked to the open box of cleaning products on the island.

Sitting next to it was the bubble-wrapped bronze Migano horse statuette. Joanie had been waffling on whether she wanted to bring it or not. She'd kept it for years as a memento of her life in villainy.

"Have you made a decision about this?" Sadie asked gently.

Joan set her hand on it. "I don't think I want it anymore. I don't want this reminder." She paused, opened her mouth, closed it. "I don't need this reminder."

"Okay." Sadie gave her a supportive smile. "Then Greta can return it for you?"

"She can." Joan slid her fingers off the bubble wrap. "The guy who owned it was a dick, though."

"Can you donate it to a museum?"

"Maybe. One really far away, like in Italy."

"Why?"

"So he doesn't know about it."

Sadie shot her a knowing look. "Does this have anything to do with revenge?"

"No." Joanie's slow, sneaky grin said *Hell yes, it does.*

She rolled her eyes and dug the keys from her pocket, then set them on the countertop.

Joan did the same with her keys. "It's only a little revenge," she said.

"Okay."

"Like, the barest of revenges."

"Mm-hmm."

"Hardly revenge at all."

Sadie grabbed the box, adjusting her grip for its weight. "You're a very weird Superhero, Spark."

Joanie took the box from her and kissed her cheek. "You've known that from the start."

"True." Sadie could only smile at the woman who was her bright, beautiful future. "I wouldn't have it any other way."

Thank you so very much for hanging out in Vector City. I've loved bringing Sadie and Joan's story to you. This isn't the end, as I will be giving you a short story or two checking in with them to see how everything is going.

All my free bonus stories are for newsletter subscribers only. Be sure to sign up for my monthly author newsletter to get exclusive access at www.kellyfarmerauthor.com.

This superpowered world is a lot of fun to write in. I'll be exploring other cities with new Heroes, Villains and norms. (You may have already met some of them, wink wink.) Keep an eye out for guest appearances by some of the characters you've grown to love.

If you have a few minutes and want to let other readers know about this book, leaving a quick review would be amazing. They really do help authors gain visibility. It's the gift that keeps on giving.

Rock on!
Kelly

ACKNOWLEDGMENTS

As the Superheroes are learning, teamwork makes the dream work. I'm so fortunate to be surrounded by brilliant minds who make my books infinitely stronger.

Big thanks to Nicole Morris-Clark for coming up with the name for this one. I really couldn't think of anything until you suggested *The Brightest Blaze*.

Hugs to Jen Graybeal for your support and enthusiasm for this superpowered series (and my whole author career).

Mackenzie Walton, editor extraordinaire, thank you for always correcting my misuse of *further* and *farther*.

Julie Cassidy, my friend and copyeditor, I'm sorry about never remembering *effect* vs. *affect*. At least I got a handle on my ellipses...or did I?

Steve Buccellato had some great ideas for this book cover to be a progression of the other two in the trilogy. I appreciate all your amazing work and making Superhero headquarters look like the Hall of Justice.

Belated but sincere thanks to Kerry Lockhart for having such cool book covers that I was able to get in touch with Steve to get exactly what I wanted for my own covers.

My eternal thanks to Pamala Knight for beta reading!

The Super Readers have so generously given their time to read an advanced copy of this book. Your awesomeness is as big as Lunk!

Thanks to every reader, reviewer, blogger, Bookstagrammer, BookToker, etcetera-er who takes the time to read and review all the books you enjoy.

Much love to all the wonderful independent bookstores that support independent authors!

Huge thanks to these real-life superheroes who answered the call for the Northern Illinois Food Bank virtual food drive. Together, we raised $550.00 for neighbors in need. Food is a basic human right. Thank you for lending a hand!

Kayla Bhadra

Deborah Gruchalski

Mary Morris

Terry Newton

Christine Palmer

Kathleen Prichard

Patty Teigen

Marnie Warner

Two Anonymous Donors—You're awesome, too!

I knew from the start that the norms would be the bad guys in the final book of the trilogy. (Humans always end up being the real villains.) What came about was more "Art imitating life" than I'd expected. Take out "superpowered people" and replace it with any number of marginalized communities currently under attack, and the ignorant and hateful words still apply.

I felt icky writing the Citizens for Human Power, so my apologies if you felt the same reading those scenes. I hope you're happy Sadie punched one of them.

Keep fighting the good fight, friends. Love will always win.

ALSO BY KELLY FARMER

Vector City Supers:

Secret Spark (Book 1)

Fanning the Flames (Book 2)

The Out on the Ice Series:

Out on the Ice (Book 1)

Unexpected Goals (Book 2)

Calling the Shots (Book 3)

It's a Fabulous Life

ABOUT THE AUTHOR

Kelly Farmer (she/her) has been writing romance novels since junior high. While the stories have changed, one theme remains the same: everyone deserves to have a happy ending. She is the bestselling author of queer contemporary romances with snarky humor and lots of heart.

When not writing, she enjoys being outside in nature, quoting from eighties movies, listening to all kinds of music, and petting every dog she comes in contact with. All of these show up in her books. Kelly lives in the Chicago area, where she swears every winter is her last one there.

To connect with Kelly, talk about current TV binges, and subscribe to her newsletter for access to free bonus stories, head over to:

www.kellyfarmerauthor.com